FORCE

OF

JUSTICE

Also by J.J. Miller

Brad Madison series:
DIVINE JUSTICE
GAME OF JUSTICE

Cadence Elliott series:
I SWEAR TO TELL

Email: jj@jjmillerbooks.com
Facebook: @jjmillerbooks
Blog|Website: jjmillerbooks.com

ISBN-13: 978-10-89786-01-6

FORCE

OF

JUSTICE

(Brad Madison Legal Thriller, Book 1)

J.J. MILLER

CHAPTER 1

I entered the Hollywood Hills mansion in a slipstream of perfume, trailing two A-list babes wrapped in tight, shimmering gowns. As we made our way down a low-lit hallway, Justin Timberlake's 'Can't Stop the Feeling' pulsed through the air, and the murmur of the party drew closer. The corridor opened up to a large living area where two hundred people mingled, each quietly assured there was nowhere on Earth better to be.

A tall blond man in a tux stretched his arms out wide to embrace both women, careful not to spill his glass. As the women turned, I recognized one—Abby Hatfield; a mid-twenties, auburn-haired beauty. She'd starred in a couple of teen movies and then rom-coms before her career stalled just long enough for Hollywood to sense the blood of a has-been. But rumor had it she was about to land a role that would launch her to mega-stardom. She was tipped to get the lead in a new blockbuster franchise courtesy of the party's guest of honor—Patrick Strickland, a film producer so hot right now everyone in Tinseltown wanted to bask in his blaze.

So Abby Hatfield and I had something in common. Mr. Strickland had suggested he wanted to hire me too, but not in such a glamorous role. He told me he needed a criminal lawyer. He said he'd explain the details—and the money on offer—at the party. Countering the feeling of being out of place in something that resembled an Oscars after-party was the fact that I had business there. A fat retainer was just what the doctor, landlord and hip-pocket ordered.

The house was even better than it looked online. And the photos I saw were incredible. I couldn't help but check it out after I'd received Strickland's call. That was a surreal moment. There I was, stewing over bills, when my secretary Megan buzzed me. I watched her face through the glass—a textbook blend of shock and delight—as she spoke slowly and clearly into her headset, saying the one and only Patrick Strickland was on the line.

It took me a little while to believe I was not being pranked, but I played it cool as Strickland explained himself.

"I think I'm going to need a lawyer," he said.

"Mr. Strickland, entertainment is not really my field, I'm not sure..."

"Not that kind of lawyer—I support an army of those leeches. You can hardly crack an egg in this business without fear of being sued for copyright. Entertainment lawyers I've got plenty of. I need a criminal lawyer."

"Okay, but why me?"

"I followed the Lindy Coleman case. Damn shame what happened to that poor girl, but I was impressed by how you exposed the guy who did it."

The Coleman case ended about eight months ago. A young man, my client, was charged with her murder, but I got him off. Generally speaking, that's why defense attorneys are hated by cops and the public alike—to them, we fight to keep scum on the streets. They don't consider the injustice prevention part of my job—well, I guess not until they see an innocent man being spared the chair or life in prison. For a while after that case, the media had me as a white knight. For once I got a ton of publicity—the good kind. Business had picked up but so had expenses. That's where having Strickland as a client could help.

"What can I do for you?" I asked.

"For now, all I want to say is I have a problem. I don't like where it's headed, and I want to be prepared if things go sideways."

"Fair enough. When can I learn more?"

"Saturday."

"Saturday?"

"Night. At my place. You own a tux?"

"No."

"Well, rent one. Come by at eight. I'll make sure your name is on the door."

As soon as I hung up, Megan was in my office, bursting to hear what the hell Patrick Strickland was doing calling Brad Madison. When I told her, she began rattling off names of the glitterati I'd be rubbing shoulders with. I couldn't say I didn't feel a slight tingle at the thought.

I soon saw online that Strickland's mansion was a landmark of LA architecture—one of those rare monuments to both taste and money. Worth about $10 million, its impressive mix of glass and steel made it look futuristic yet homey. At night, all aglow and jutting out from the hillside, it looked like some kind of space station. From inside, the house had LA at its feet—a sweeping view visible from all angles, including an infinity pool that the house was wrapped around.

Such a commanding residence seemed only fitting for a man poised to conquer not just Hollywood and LA but the entire entertainment world. Even I knew that Strickland had secured the film rights for the *Sister Planet* book series—a sci-fi story about humans fleeing the catastrophic effects of climate change by migrating to an undamaged Earth-like planet only to find it's an alien ruse to colonize Earth. The buzz was that *Sister Planet* could dwarf *Harry Potter*, *Hunger Games* and *Twilight* put together. Add in the companion video-game series, and the franchise was looming as a juggernaut worth billions.

A waiter with a drinks tray slid by, and I grabbed a flute of champagne. Taking a sip, I ran my eyes over the room, the glass hiding my smirk of disbelief. Drop a bomb on this place and there'd be no Hollywood. There was a weird feeling of seeing so many familiar faces but not knowing a soul.

I made my way through the crowd to the massive windows and took in the view of the city. It was spectacular. Downtown appeared at once distant and close. You were enticed to reach out and grab it. Only from a distance and at night can Los Angeles look like a jewel, when you're blind to the depravity, violence and hardship that runs through those pretty lights and street lines like putrid water.

I could make out where my office was—a modest but modern space on the second floor of Two California Plaza. We didn't take up much of that floor—just Megan out front and me in my rather large fish tank. A montage of my typical clients ran through my mind— lowlifes, liars, drug dealers, gangsters and cowards. None of them innocent, but many, I was able to prove, not guilty.

I wondered about Patrick Strickland. Was there some kind of sordid backstory to his success? I didn't get to wonder long. A woman's voice interrupted my train of thought.

"Pretty from a distance, isn't she?"

I turned to see a stunning woman taking me in with striking green eyes and a gently engaging smile. Her face was framed by jewelry that cost more than my house, probably half my street. Her age was hard to pick, but I'd have guessed about fifty. Yet she oozed a vivacious charm that could win men half her age.

"You read my mind."

"How are you finding the showbiz crowd?" She rolled her eyes as she said the word showbiz, like it was something way too familiar and drearily self-absorbed.

"What's the giveaway? Is it the rented tux or my distinct lack of magnetism?"

"Oh, don't underestimate yourself. Most people here are either highly insecure, rampant ego maniacs or both. And that includes the lawyers. You sit somewhere comfortably in between. But you're not like most lawyers I know."

"What kind are they?"

"The ones who'd kill you for nibbling their play lunch."

"Well, they needn't be concerned. I don't even know why I'm here."

"I do. And you'd be good for Patrick, Mr. Madison."

I must have given a faint look of surprise that she knew my name.

"There's very little I don't know about Patrick's business. He needs all the trustworthy people he can get. I'm Vivien."

The penny dropped as she spoke her name. Vivien Strickland— Patrick's wife. I don't know why I didn't recognize her straight away. But the photos I'd seen online did not do her justice. I'd read that she married Patrick three years ago, and for each of them it was third time lucky.

"I don't see Patrick anywhere."

"He's in his study. Never let it be said he doesn't mix business with pleasure. Even on his birthday."

"I'm surprised he asked me here."

"Think of it as a casting. Patrick will judge you on more than your expert opinion. He wants to see how you handle... all this."

She tilted her head back towards the roomful of guests. Just as she did, the blond-haired man I'd seen earlier came up and spoke briefly into Vivien's ear. Her face went cold for a moment before her gracious smile rebounded.

"I'm sorry, Mr. Madison. You'll have to excuse me. The hostess's curse—we have to spread ourselves dreadfully thin. I look forward to our next chat."

We clinked glasses before she spun around and left with the man at her shoulder, continuing his confidential news.

I turned back to the view, intending to introduce myself around in a moment.

A minute or so later, I saw a man moving with haste along the opposite wing of the house a floor down. Even from a distance, I recognized him at once—it was Buddy Landry, the former child star who now made headlines for all the wrong reasons. The blond guy was trying to catch up to him.

As Landry passed almost directly opposite me, a door opened and out stepped Patrick Strickland. Landry stood in front of him, agitated and mouthing off. Strickland tried to pacify him. He looked over Landry's shoulder and waved Vivien's friend off. He then ushered Landry into the room. As he did he looked up towards the party, checking to see if anyone was watching. Our eyes met for a couple of seconds, but he remained expressionless before turning inside.

At that moment, it seemed like I was a poor boy waiting to run a rich man's errand.

Little did I know, within a few days, the mighty Patrick Strickland would be charged with murder, and I'd be on the biggest case of my life.

CHAPTER 2

I made my way to the bar for a whisky. The barman poured out a generous shot of Ardbeg with a small shard of ice.

"Make that two, barkeep," came a playful voice in a put-on cowgirl twang.

I spun around to see none other than Abby Hatfield smiling playfully at me.

She took her glass, raised it to the barman and saluted him with a wink.

"Olé to a fine Islay," she said, referencing the Scottish island from which Ardbeg hails, before taking a sip.

"So you know your scotch."

"I'm no connoisseur, but I know a little. Sometimes that was all there was to scrounge out of daddy's liquor cabinet."

"What, no Bollinger? My heart bleeds."

"I know. But you push through, you know, and acquire a taste. Eventually."

"But not before puking after downing half a bottle. I've been there."

"Is that meant to be wise?" Her true accent, straight-up Californian, was showing now.

"Hardly. I've forgotten every bit of wisdom I got from alcohol."

She laughed. It was a slightly husky laugh, filled with warm vitality. No wonder she could light up a screen. There was something both natural and exceptional about her. She could have been on a back porch somewhere sipping iced tea, yet here she was in one of those dresses that put a capital V in "cleavage," presenting a broad arrow of frontal flesh that left little to the imagination.

She caught me looking.

I tried to come up with something funny. "Sorry, I was just thinking thank God I changed my mind about what to wear tonight. I've got a little dress just like that."

She laughed again.

"But it looks way better on you," I said. "As much as I hate to admit it."

Abby curtsied, playing along. "Why thank you. But the drag thing's been done—the *South Park* guys beat you to it."

I loved the story of Matt Stone and Trey Parker attending the 2000 Academy Awards in drag and on acid.

"Of course. That's a hard act to follow. Anyway, I'm Brad."

I put out my hand. She shook it lightly but applied a firm grip.

"Abby. Now I'm sure I've seen you somewhere, but I don't think you're an actor."

"Why not?"

"Because nothing about you looks rehearsed. An actor's worst performance can often be playing themselves. Every expression delivered perfectly but with an almost imperceptible lack of sincerity."

"My God, are you telling me Hollywood is fake?"

A lovely smile lit up her face. "You did not hear it from me, good sir."

"I thought there was a nice camaraderie kind of vibe going on here."

"Yes, and no. Mostly no."

"Okay, give me an example."

14

Abby leapt at the challenge. She bit her lip, scanned the room then looked straight at me.

"Two o'clock. Bald guy. Beard. Tinted glasses. Skin the color of Fanta."

"Got it. Sun lamp guy. Man, that's not a tan, that's a barbecue."

"You know who that is?"

I shrugged. "No idea."

"Danny Shapiro. Second biggest producer in Hollywood. Second biggest producer in this house, more to the point. See that easy smile and snappy banter he's got going? Well, tell me how happy you'd be in his shoes. In the late '90s he almost got his hands on *Lord of the Rings*—he was planning a two-film adaptation—but the rights holder opted for a New Zealander no one had heard of."

"Peter Jackson."

"Yeah, well everyone knows him now."

"And the word is he came within a bee's nipple of getting the book option of *Sister Planet*. But at the last minute, the writer signed it over to Pat Strickland."

"Ouch."

"You don't have to cry for Shapiro. He's done mighty well for himself. Truth be known, though, he's no fan of our good host. I dare say he'd rather this little shindig was Strickland's wake, not his birthday."

"So he hates Strickland?"

"Hate's a strong word, but the rivalry between those two runs strong and deep. They go way back. Rose through the ranks at the same time. Both built outstanding resumes of feature films, both won Oscars and both came to wield big sticks around Tinseltown. But right now Strickland's the undisputed king. There's a whole stratosphere between them."

"So you're saying while Shapiro here puts on a nice front and will sing 'Happy Birthday' with gusto as the candles get blown out, he's nursing a gutful of bridesmaid's bile?"

"Exactamundo."

"Well, I'll give him credit. That's quite an act he's got going on. And you're saying I'd suck at that?"

"That's my guess."

"Hell, I suppose I should be flattered."

"Consider yourself flattered."

Suddenly, Abby gave me a quizzical look.

"Ah, I've got it now. You're that attorney who put Lindy Coleman's murderer in jail."

"You knew Lindy?"

"No, but her story cut close to the bone with me. She reminded me of when I was starting out, trying to make a name for myself but just attracting a growing list of sleazebags who hated me because I wouldn't jump into bed with them."

"Isn't that the devil's pact? The more creeps and paparazzi you have after you, the more you've made it?"

"You don't need success to get swamped by creeps in this industry. Sometimes you get more when you fail."

I was suddenly reminded of Abby's stalled career. I raised my glass.

"To your continued success, then. And a swift kick in the balls to the creeps."

She smiled and met my toast.

Over Abby's shoulder I could see Vivien's man Friday, if that's what he was, approaching with a much more pleasant look on his face. He stopped at Abby's shoulder, lowered his head and kissed her on the neck.

"My God, I could eat you up."

He looked at me and extended his hand.

"Sorry I didn't introduce myself earlier. Freddie Baxter."

He was British. That surprised me for some reason. He was tall—a good six-four—with slicked back hair and impeccably groomed stubble. I guessed he was about 33. Straight-backed and sharp-eyed, I'd bet he was ex-military.

"Brad Madison. Everything under control?"

Baxter looked at me like it was impudent of me to ask.

"If you mean is the party going swimmingly, then yes, old boy, everything is under control. But give it time. The night is young. You should see this crowd loosen up."

There was a brief uncomfortable pause. I heard a faint beep.

"Ah, that's me," said Baxter, reaching into his inside coat pocket to check his phone. "Mr. Strickland says he'll see you now, Brad. You'll find him in the study. Downstairs..."

"I know where it is."

"Good then."

I turned to Abby.

"Break a leg, as they say."

"Keep jailing those creeps, law man."

I laughed.

"I'll do my best."

I nodded at Baxter and left. On the way downstairs, I pondered how it was that women who could have any guy they wanted ended up with jerks.

But perhaps I had Baxter all wrong.

***

I knocked on Strickland's door and entered. I had to stop myself from saying, "Wow." With its bookshelves, modern leather lounges and presidential desk, this was not so much a room as a carefully crafted statement of wealth and power. A massive floor-to-ceiling window framed LA as though it was a masterpiece Strickland had snapped up at Christie's.

"Bradley," Strickland said, turning from the window and walking towards me. I must have stopped in my tracks as I took in the room. "Please, come in."

We shook hands. Strickland gripped hard but not with dominant strength. It always amused me how often short men make a contest out of a handshake. From his effort I could tell his trainer put him through some reasonably testing work but nothing exceptional.

He was a fairly healthy looking 58-year-old, but his paunch betrayed a fondness for the luxuries within his reach. The black of both his hair and beard had given over mostly to a dignified gray. And it was a good head of hair, kept long enough to be slicked back like a mane. His face had a rugged character, a manly appeal I imagined women could find more compelling than beauty.

Everything about Strickland was well groomed—the tux, the Rolex Cellini, the monogrammed silver cuff links, the cummerbund. I gave credit where it was due—he wouldn't appear at all diminished beside his tall, glamorous wife.

He walked over to the liquor cabinet and took up a tumbler.

"What can I get you to drink?"

"I'm good, thank you."

The champagne and whisky were enough to loosen me up without dampening my wits.

"Not even another wee Ardbeg?"

My throat went dry. I gave a small cough. *How did he know that? Had he been watching me?*

Strickland was looking at me with an amiable, chit-chat grin, his eyes reading me with entitled scrutiny.

"You know, Abby is not as—how should I put it—down-home as she seems. She's got boundless natural charm, most certainly, but she's as ruthless as they come."

He was watching for a reaction as he spoke.

"And?"

"And you'll need a lot more in your armory than a law degree and justice as a cause."

I was about to let Strickland in on the fact that I have a wife.

"I know, I know. Of course you're not interested in Abby. You're a married man. At least, a separated man. And I do wish you luck getting Claire back."

How does he know all this? How does he know Claire and I have separated and that I'm trying to patch things up? What else does he know? Does he know about my service record? My occasional bouts of PTSD that resulted in Claire booting me out for her own safety and that of our daughter, Bella?

Right then and there I didn't care how he knew, as much as I wanted to cross the room and rearrange his arrogant face.

"Do you always spy on your guests?" I was still trying to work out how he had kept tabs on me. Hidden cameras, I supposed. *But was Abby wired? Was she in on it? And Vivien. Her too?*

I suddenly felt like I'd stepped into *The Truman Show*, and I didn't like it. It was all I could do to cap my anger.

"I look at it as homework," he said.

"Call it what you like, Strickland, but I didn't come here to be some Peeping Tom's plaything."

"No, you came for the money."

"That's right. But all of a sudden your money has a stench to it."

"Come now, Bradley. Don't be offended. You need to know that I don't enter business relationships lightly. I do my due diligence on any prospective partner, just as you would for your own clients, I'd assume. I'd bet there's much you already know about me."

"You're not my client yet."

"But if I am to be, I need to know precisely who I'm dealing with. In this business, a breach of trust or an outright betrayal can cost me millions—I'd be a fool not to make use of all I have at my disposal to guard against that. I could have hired you purely on your track record in court, and I'm sure that would have been a safe bet. But I have learned so much more about you, Bradley, and that gives me a more three-dimensional appreciation of who you are and what you're about. In time, I'm sure you will know me even more intimately."

My blood came off its boiling point, my breathing slowed.

"Get to the point, Strickland. What do you want?"

He poured a double nip from a crystal decanter into the tumbler. He did the same with another. With a teaspoon he added a dash of water into each. He walked over to me and handed me one.

"Please, Bradley. Join me, won't you? It's a crime, surely, to drink 32-year-old Laphroaig alone."

I took the glass. At about $1,500 a bottle, it was an offer too good to refuse.

He motioned for us to sit, and we settled on opposite lounges. I took a sip. It was pure nectar of the gods. If this was Strickland's peace pipe, I was happy to smoke it.

"That incident you witnessed earlier—do you know who that was?"

"Buddy Landry. A very pissed off Buddy Landry."

"Yes, well, Buddy and I go back a long way. I gave him his big break, but he has since squandered it chasing every vice known to man. If you've followed the gossip press, you'll know he's been a drug addict for years. But now it's ice that's gotten a hold of him, and he's more volatile, more unsound and more a danger to himself than ever."

Was that disgust on Strickland's face or pain? I wondered how Landry could get into this party, let alone know where Strickland was and march up to confront him.

"Are you two close?"

Strickland's chin sank to his chest, and he took another sip.

"It would be too much to say he was like a son to me, but for a time I was a father figure of sorts. Years ago, before I met Vivien, he lived in my old house in the Hills. There was a cabana out back that he moved into."

Strickland explained that ever since he discovered Landry and made him the biggest child star in Hollywood, he had felt a degree of responsibility for the boy. With his parents living on the other side of the country, Strickland became Buddy's unofficial guardian, albeit one with very little authority. By the age of fifteen, there was no telling Buddy Landry what to do. Strickland skimmed over a good many years to get to the here and now.

"Bradley, Buddy is the reason you're here. He is trying to blackmail me. I'd rather spare you all the sordid details for the moment, but I've tried reasoning with Buddy to no avail. What I am prepared to tell you is that if he goes through with his threat, I stand to lose everything—my business, my reputation and even my liberty."

"So you could go to jail for what he's accusing you of?"

"If the police are inclined to indulge in his delusions, yes."

"And you don't want to wait until any charges are laid before getting yourself an attorney."

"Precisely. As I said, I do my homework, and I want to have the best legal brains at my side ready to go rather than wait and see."

I watched Strickland swirl the contents of his glass.

"Mr. Strickland—"

"Please. It's Pat."

"Pat, you've just demonstrated to me the reach of your power—that you have at your disposal the means and the wherewithal to get what you want. I'm surprised this is your approach to getting Landry off your back."

"You mean, why don't I just have him killed?"

"I make no assumptions about what you are prepared to do. But I'm sitting across from one of the most powerful men in Hollywood telling me the rabid claims of a drug addict could bring his entire world crashing down, and your response is to go get a lawyer you saw on TV? Yes, I find that odd to the point of absurd. I've shared pricey liquor with drug lords and gangsters who'd unleash hell to defend their empires. They wouldn't think twice about surgically removing a pain in the ass with a bullet. They'd pull the trigger themselves. So why would you remain so restrained when you're at your most vulnerable?"

"I'm not a gangster, Bradley. I'm a movie producer. The only time I pay to have someone bumped off is if it's in the script. Believe me, I will be using everything I can to try and pacify Landry, but I'll not be resorting to the kind of extreme measures your gangster friends favor."

"They are not my friends. They were clients."

"Which brings us to the matter of whether you and I can come to an acceptable agreement."

I gestured for him to continue.

"As I said, I don't want to be caught napping if and when the shit hits the fan. So, I'm offering to pay you a generous retainer to act as my counsel in waiting, so to speak."

"How much?" I said and took a sip.

"Forty thousand a month."

I almost choked on my scotch. To say I wanted the money was putting it mildly. I'd been doing okay, but I had a five-year plan to get enough savings together to get out of the game, at least in LA. I saw myself settling back in Boise with Claire and Bella. This could be our ticket out. The fact that it was coming from Patrick Strickland mattered not the slightest. I'd be broke if I refused money from people I disliked.

"And if the shit does hit the fan?"

"Well, that depends on the scale of the mess. But I can tell you this—that's when the real money starts. And if it's a shitstorm that hits, well let's just say you could earn enough to make future work a mere option."

Strickland emptied his glass and stood up. I did the same.

"So Bradley. Are we in business?"

He offered me his hand. I took it.

"Yes, Pat. And to lock it in, I'm going to need that first installment now."

He smiled and moved to his desk, pulled a pen from inside his jacket and wrote out a check.

Approaching me again, he folded the paper and slipped it into my breast pocket.

"I'm sure this will get us off on the right foot, if we're not already," he said, patting my shoulder. "I'll set up an automatic monthly payment. My secretary will be in touch to sort out the details."

He opened the door for me.

"Now, I must get back to my party."

We made our way upstairs in silence. Upon seeing him, three party guests moved in to lavish Strickland with what appeared to be genuine fondness. I lost the feeling that I could tell what was fake or sincere anymore, at least in this place.

"Will you stay for cake?" Strickland asked with a charming smile.

"I don't think so, Pat. I'll leave you to it. Happy birthday."

I cut through the crowd and made for the door.

When I got behind the wheel of my car, I put the interior light on, unfolded the check and read it.

Eighty-thousand dollars.

In the space of a couple of hours, I'd made just about as much as I cleared in a year. For that check and a few more like it, I couldn't be happier working for that asshole.

CHAPTER 3

I was treating my investigator Jack Briggs to lunch at an upscale chop house when my phone rang.

"Shit, it's Jared Cohen from *Counterspin*."

As I went to tap the touch screen, Jack's face contorted as if to say, "You're actually going to answer that?!"

Counterspin was a celebrity gossip website specializing in stories about rich and famous people coming unstuck and ending up in court—stories that brought those Hollywood high fliers down to earth and took some shine off all that tinsel. The site came out of nowhere a few years ago when they broke Mel Gibson's DUI rant against Jews. They then got various other scoops that went viral worldwide, like announcing Prince's death just minutes after he drew his last breath.

In no time, *Counterspin* was getting more hits than the *National Inquirer* and five other top gossip peddlers put together. Everyone wondered how they were able to get their stories so soon and be so sure-footed about publishing. The answer to that was a credo LA has come to own—money talks.

Counterspin basically operated as an ATM for snitches. Through pay-for-dirt offers its operators built up a vast network of stool pigeons, each willing to see their own sister shamed for an easy fifty. LA was now infested with their informants—cops, hotel staff, waiters, Uber drivers, first responders, you name it. They even had freelance hustlers out there greasing palms to get any *Counterspin*-worthy photo or tidbit.

You could not dine, ride a limo, fly in, fly out, get a parking ticket, see a movie or get a damn shaving cut in LA without someone tipping them off. Daily, they were flooded with tips, tapes, mea culpas and arrests—each paid according to how big the story was deemed to be. They were so effective at turning incidental events into clickbait that attention-starved celebrities had started to get in on the act, having their PR foofoos inform *Counterspin* about when they were about to walk their dog or go get a tan.

Jared Cohen had been a *Counterspin* reporter since day one, and I'd dealt with him a few times on the Lindy Coleman case.

As I put the phone to my ear, Jack couldn't help himself: "Tell him to go screw himself and post the clip online."

Jack had no time for celebrity sleaze reporters, so *Counterspin* occupied the lowest rung on his scum ladder. If he was at all impressed by their ability to get good dirt fast—people said *Counterspin* was worse than the FBI, a backhanded compliment if ever there was one—he never let it show. Jack prided himself too much on his investigative talents to see them used for mere tabloid fodder. He found the work something of a calling which, to his relief and gratitude, had filled the large void left by a promising career in football that had been cruelly cut short. He was a star quarterback at college before his throwing arm was snapped at the joint. He may not have gone on to rival Tom Brady's NFL record, but from what I've heard he would have come close. And, with Jack's own all-American good looks, Brady would not have been the only footballer to turn Gisele Bundchen's head.

If Jack harbored an ounce of sourness over not fulfilling his boyhood NFL dream, I never saw it. He was one of Brady's greatest fans. And he had gone on to do extremely well for himself. Armed with a deep knowledge of IT, Jack took to trading in tech stocks and got in early on Apple, Amazon and Netflix. He certainly didn't need to work for me to pay the bills.

There was something else he found gratifying about investigative work—he enjoyed applying his intellect to help the cause of justice. He would not help me defend a client he knew was guilty, but he'd stop at nothing to help clear the name of the innocent.

Jack hated the idea that he and *Counterspin* were more or less in the same line of work. As far as I could tell, the objection was a profoundly moral one.

"Slow day is it, Jared? Not sure how I can help, but I'm having lunch right now at Hugo's then off to get a blow job from a street whore, if you're interested."

"Very funny, Brad. But I'm actually working on something that does concern you."

"What's that?"

"I hear Pat Strickland is in a bit of trouble and that he's lawyering up."

"So why are you calling me?"

"Well, I'm told you were at Strickland's party last weekend. Is that right?"

"Yes, I was there. But so were a lot of people."

"But not everyone had a one-on-one with Strickland in his study right after he was accosted by Buddy Landry."

There you go. There was hardly anyone who didn't know to call *Counterspin*. Such first-hand info gave them the confidence they were onto something. In the Lindy Coleman case, I'd quickly decided it was futile to try and stop them. The best I could do was make sure what they had was right. Because once their story broke, it would be carried by every other news service and gossip site worldwide.

"Well, I have nothing to offer on Buddy Landry, but I did meet with Patrick, that's true."

"And what was the nature of that meeting?"

"Jared, you've been around long enough to know about attorney-client privilege, so there is nothing I can tell you about what we discussed."

"But are you repping him?"

27

"Is there a criminal charge against Mr. Strickland, Jared?"

"Not that I'm aware of. But that doesn't mean there isn't one. Maybe we just haven't gotten it yet. But we will."

"I don't doubt that. Mr. Strickland hasn't called upon me to help him out on any criminal matter. But if that changes, I don't expect I'll have to give you the heads up."

Cohen chuckled.

"No, but I'm always happy to hear from you."

"Wish I could say the same about you."

"Talk soon," he said and hung up.

I put my phone away. Jack was looking at me slack-jawed in mock contempt for giving Cohen the time of day.

"Look at you, dancing with the devil. You should be slicing his nuts off."

I smiled and took up my glass of red—a shiraz from Australia's Barossa Valley.

"Don't think I wouldn't like to. But you know the saying about keeping your enemies closer than your friends? I never really subscribed to that until *Counterspin*. It's better to play their game and have some buy-in, otherwise you'll just end up an onlooker watching your own car crash."

A waiter brought two rib eyes to the table. It wasn't common for Jack and me to do lunch, but I'd just banked eighty grand and I wanted to spread the love a little. He'd been critical to my success and always billed me at a discounted rate. What better way to say thanks than a ninety-dollar steak and a couple of bottles of quality red? Plus, he'd had a few days to vet Landry, and I was eager to learn what he'd unearthed. Jack's so good at snooping, he's *Counterspin* material. Not that I'd ever say that to his face.

The restaurant was one of those lamplit plush leathered joints. A bar shelf full of gleaming colored glass on one side and big sunlit windows skirted by dark heavy curtains on the other. The layout was a mix of tables and booths, but it was only half full. The ambiance of the place was relaxed but smart. There was an air of confidence about the meat and the wine list on offer—this was not a place where a waiter might stumble over the source of a wine or the life story of the cow whose meat you were eyeing. And Hugo's meat was the best. The grill infused the dining area with the Chanel No 5 of char smoke.

"So who am I dealing with here?"

"Well, I can tell you right now Buddy Landry has a few options when it comes to pulling Strickland's levers."

"I want to hear all of them."

Jack started with some background. Landry was a talented child actor from the boondocks who had the right look at the right time. His big break came when Strickland spotted him in a TV ad and called him to LA for an audition. Landry aced it, landing the starring role in *One For The Road*, a comedy about two aging robbers who are on the run and inadvertently end up with a kid as a hostage. While they're trying to figure out how to leverage ransom money off the kid's parents, the kid makes their lives hell and eventually gets them busted. The movie was huge, and Landry, who had just turned twelve, became a household name worldwide. By the age of fifteen, he'd done six movies, all tailor made to showcase him and exploit his popularity. But then youth condemned him. He landed in that dreaded Hollywood dead space where being young was worse than being old, and the offers dried up. By sixteen, the most successful child actor since Shirley Temple had reached his expiration date. That's when about the only press he could get was substance abuse rumors.

Jack paused to take a bite of his steak. He was chewing on more than his food.

"You know, here's a kid who needs, more than anything, someone to take care of him, but as far as I can tell he was pretty much left to his own devices."

29

"What about his parents?"

"You mean foster parents. The kid's father died when he was three. Car crash in Phoenix."

"Where was the mother?"

"Not sure, but she wasn't alive or around to raise the boy. The father's uncle and aunt stepped in to take care of him. Wilfred and Layla Landry—a devout Christian couple. They raised Buddy on a pig farm outside Fairmont, North Carolina."

"That's a long way from Hollywood."

"Yeah, but he got there quick. Within six months of shooting a cereal ad, Strickland had him in LA. The rest, as they say, is history."

"So what could Landry have on Strickland?"

"Well, that's the sixty-four-thousand-dollar question, and there are many possible answers."

"Like what?"

"You ever heard of Jerry Newman?"

"Yeah. He manages child actors, but the rumor is he likes to not only find them parts but fondle their parts."

"Right. Well, guess who he managed?"

"Landry?"

"Yup. And guess who delivered Landry to Newman?"

"Strickland. So Landry could have something on him from that period of his life."

I remembered how Landry looked at the party. Good looking but with the harrowed features of a hard drug addict—sunken cheeks and a manic look in his eyes. Itching to pull some trigger.

"At the time, Landry was one of several boys billeted to Newman. Word is, there were parties at his mansion. Pool parties. No women, just men and boys. From what I can gather, some very big

30

Hollywood names attended these parties—men who carried a lot of clout or who had tight connections to it. Agents, producers, directors, publicists. All there getting naked with pretty young boys in the tub. And they pumped booze and party drugs into these kids. They never stood a chance among these vampires. These men held these boys' careers in their hands. Instead of being mentors, they choose to exert their power, charm and influence to fulfill their own sick desires."

"So you're young and want to be rich and famous. And your parents want you to be rich and famous. And so they unwittingly feed you to sharks."

"Great way to get through puberty, hey?"

"Was Strickland at these parties?"

"That's not clear yet."

"So Landry could be claiming he was part of a pedophile ring?"

"Or worse."

"What could be worse than that?"

"Try murder."

"Murder?"

Jack nodded. "You ever heard of Emilio Peralta?"

I shook my head, so Jack filled me in.

"Peralta was another kid Newman managed. He and Landry were friends, but he struggled to make it, career wise. He spent over a year in LA trying to get a break but finally decided to call it quits. So one day he calls his parents to tell them he's getting on a Greyhound, and then he just disappears."

"And where does Strickland fit into this?"

"Strickland dropped Peralta off at the bus terminal. He was the last person to see him alive."

"But Peralta could have just run off. Who says he was murdered?"

Jack pulled out his phone and flipped away at the screen to find something he wanted to show me. When he had it, he handed the phone over. On the screen was a cheap-looking web page.

"What's this?"

"It's a website dedicated to the memory of Emilio Peralta."

"Who's behind it? Some fan?"

"Don't know yet, but check that link at the bottom."

The link text read: "Who killed Emilio Peralta?"

"Now while that story there names no names, it points the finger at a certain suspect."

I looked up from the phone to address Jack.

"So reading between the lines?"

"Reading between the lines: someone is convinced Patrick Strickland killed Emilio Peralta and got away with it."

CHAPTER 4

My intercom buzzer sounded.

"Mr. Madison. Your car's ready, sir."

"I'll be right down."

I was all packed and ready to go. I grabbed my overnight bag and headed out. Parked on the street outside my apartment block was my baby—a 2011 Kona Blue Mustang GT. My heart still skipped a beat at the sight of it. Even more so now—the guys from the mobile detailing team were just giving it a final look over, polishing away the last smudges.

One of them held the keys out to me then withdrew his hand as I raised mine.

"I think I really should take it for a test drive before we hand it back, sir. A long drive."

I laughed.

"Nice try. But I'm late for a date."

I'd been looking forward to this day for two months. I'd convinced Claire we should take Bella out to a dude ranch for a weekend. Sure, a lovely idea for a married couple with a pony-mad five-year-old daughter. Admittedly, a unicorn ranch would be Bella's dream come true, but a regular ranch with hay-eating horses would still thrill her to bits. The thing was, although Claire and I were still married, we'd been separated for just over a year.

I was eager to tell Claire I was working for Patrick Strickland. I couldn't wait to see the look on her face. But nagging away in the back of my mind was a conversation I needed to raise while we were away. The type of conversation that could kill the mood entirely. It followed on from my lunch with Jack about Strickland getting intel on me.

"You need to get more Ed Snowden about your comms," Jack said.

"I thought our opsec was good—not military grade good but decent enough."

"The encrypted comms you and I use should be extended to Claire."

The moment he said it, I knew he was right. My contact with Claire was vulnerable. But I dreaded the thought of even raising it with her:

"Claire, you need to download this Wickr Me app and use it whenever you want to contact me. It's encrypted. No one can hack it."

"Why would anyone want to read the messages we send to each other?"

"I'm not saying anyone wants to, but my new client, you know, has dug up a lot of personal stuff about me with ease, so it's best our conversations not be a weak spot."

"Weak spot? What is this? They're spying on you? On us?"

"No, well, it's unlikely, but I think it's better we don't take that chance."

"Who the hell's your client? The head of the NSA?"

"No, err, a movie producer."

Yes, I could see that playing out brilliantly. A fine way to reassure Claire we should get the family unit back under the one roof. The very thing that got me kicked out in the first place was that she got jack of me bringing my "work" home.

After I returned from my second and final tour of Afghanistan, I had the occasional PTSD episode. But these weren't just cold sweats.

34

More like me getting Claire in a choke hold or me hitting the floor and scrounging around for a gun to kill an enemy that existed only in my head.

I'll never forget the way Bella stood looking at me one night after my screaming woke her—terrified and confused—and if ever I doubted Claire had reason to kick me out, I only had to remember that image of my little girl. It was burned into my brain.

But, like I said, that was a year back. Now my head was screwed on better. The work seemed to help, my career was on the up again, a bit of weed here and there allowed me to detach my mind from the demons, and so I just wanted us to be a family again.

The lynchpin of my five-year plan—to stash away enough money to leave LA and move back to Idaho—was doing it as a reunited family. Claire and I had been getting on well and had been out on the odd date. We kept it strictly platonic until one night a few weeks back we got rolling drunk and slept together. I'd sneaked out before daylight so Bella did not see me and start asking again if I was coming back home. She'd stopped that months ago and appeared to accept our separation with cheerful resilience, but whenever Claire and I were together, Bella's mood lifted to a higher plane of contentment, as though this was how things should be.

But there was no chance Claire and I would be rolling in the hay on this country weekend. She had agreed to the trip on two strict conditions: separate beds and not getting Bella's hopes up.

I walked around the Mustang, admiring the boys' handiwork. She looked just as good as when I first laid eyes on her at the dealer's lot. I opened the driver's door and poked my head in. Everything was pristine, clean and gleaming.

"You've done a beautiful job."

I pulled out my wallet and handed over my credit card. The guy tapped his iPad with the card and returned it. I handed him an extra twenty for good measure.

"Thank you, sir."

I dropped the bag in the back seat and got behind the wheel. At the turn of the key, the V8 came to life with a throaty roar. I sat there for a second, enjoying the rumbling that would touch the sweet spot of any motorhead's soul.

I picked up Claire and Bella from Venice, and then we headed north. It was mid-morning Friday, and we had about a two-hour drive to the outskirts of Bakersfield. It was one of those clear blue days made for happy-ever-after stories. Every now and then I'd catch sight of Bella in the rear-view mirror. It thrilled me to see her sitting back there with a carefree smile on that beautiful face. She was looking more and more like her mother. I reached back to give her leg a playful squeeze and she broke into a laugh. Whenever I turned to Claire, even she looked relaxed. Hell, we were the snapshot of the perfect family unit.

About half an hour into the drive, Claire's phone started pinging with a string of messages. By the way she was glued to the device, it was clear news was afoot.

"Oh, my God," she said. It sounded like good news.

"What's going on?"

"Just a minute," she said excitedly as she typed out a message.

Once she'd sent it, she turned to me. I knew she was beaming even before I took my eyes off the road to see. It was like she was holding a winning lottery ticket.

"I can't believe it!"

"What?"

"Kim Kardashian just posted a photo on Instagram wearing my earrings!"

"Wow."

"Oh, my God. She's got about a hundred million followers. The site's getting swamped. In about twenty seconds I'm going to be out of stock. I mean, I'll have plenty more come Monday, but this is huge. I can't believe it."

"That's awesome, Claire."

Just before she kicked me out, Claire followed through with her long-held desire to design her own jewelry. The pieces were delicate—mere slivers of gold and silver that, in various ways, held a feature stone. Her trademark was black pearls. She had a website made, got some professional product shots done and began looking for celebrities to market her items. Before Bella was born, she was in hot demand as a stylist, but she stepped away to devote all her time to motherhood. Once Bella was two, she resumed part-time work as a stylist but then began to think seriously about launching her own design business. Two years later she was ready to set sail.

Through her connections she'd gotten some exposure in fashion mags. She was happy—things were moving fast. But this was different. An endorsement from none other than Kim Kardashian was a monumental kicker. My wife was becoming a millionaire, and I wasn't at all surprised. She's always been the kind of person money sticks to. Never hurts to have a cash magnet in a marriage—and that had never looked like it was going to be me. That's why I was eager to tell her about Strickland.

I suddenly felt somewhat diminished. Here I was behind the wheel of my fifty-grand sports car splashing out on a dude ranch weekend while Claire was riding a booster rocket into the financial stratosphere. In that moment I thought, *Claire has absolutely no need for me.* It was automatic, a defense reflex, a deep impulse to convert every event into being all about me. In that split second, the way I'd been framing my hope of us getting back together changed completely. If Claire was self-reliant, then she could happily cut every string connecting us—mortgage, school fees, alimony. I guess I'd find out soon enough if that was all Claire needed from me anymore.

As this thought bubble hung in my mind for a few seconds, I just kept turning to smile at Claire.

"What's going on? Tell me about it."

"I just need to make one call, okay?"

Claire was radiant in a way I'd not seen for a long time. Her dark hair was pulled back into a ponytail, one of her own earrings dangled from her perfectly lickable ear, her flawless skin dusted with just a hint of make-up and those full lips that I can, at any moment in time, envision descending towards my loins.

When she finished the call, she turned to me.

"Bradley," she said, all affection stripped from her voice—she could have been calling my turn in a dental waiting room. A sure way to douse that fire in my pants. "I'm not going to be able to stay two nights at the ranch. I need to get back to LA."

"Oh, mom!" cried Bella.

Claire spun around.

"Honey, this is super important for mommy's work. We can stay at the ranch tonight and we'll go horse riding tomorrow, but we need to head home after that."

She turned to me.

"Sorry, Brad."

"No, of course. You've got to deal with it."

This fricking sucks, was what I was thinking, even though I couldn't help but be proud of Claire. Bella thought so too.

"But you said we were going away for the whole weekend," she said.

"Yes, I know sweetheart, but this is an emergency."

I felt I needed to back Claire up.

"Sweetheart, we're going to have an awesome day today and tomorrow. We're going to rustle us a whole herd of cattle, sit around a campfire, toast some marshmallows, breathe some clean country air and have a heap of fun. And if you're up for it, we can do it again soon."

I looked at Claire who was smiling in agreement.

"And next time mom's paying," I said.

*****

We had an enjoyable dinner together. Then, after Bella skipped off to bed, Claire and I shared a bottle of red on the deck of our cabin. I got to tell her about Strickland, but her ears really pricked up when I mentioned the party. She wanted me to describe it in detail. So I rattled off a few names before mentioning the fact that I had a very nice chat with Abby Hatfield.

Some innate reflex flipped in Claire's mind. It was like she wanted the thought of me talking to Abby Hatfield to have no effect on her whatsoever. But it did. And I could see she went almost imperceptibly off kilter as her mind zipped through a range of unsettling scenarios—Abby and I getting on well, getting on famously, drinking the night away, her introducing me to famous friends, Abby and I hooking up, Abby and me at the Oscars—before dismissing them outright. She put on a I'm-happy-for-you smile.

"Abby Hatfield? Really? What's she like?"

"Very nice indeed. Really down to earth."

You can never hate someone famous who's down to earth, but I suspected Claire might be able to find a way.

"And?"

"And a real hoot. I didn't get to talk to her for long. I got summoned by Strickland. But you two would get on like a house on fire."

I don't know why I made such a ludicrous assertion. Men have no idea whether any two women will like each other. Claire just gave me that playful inquisitor look.

"Exactly how well did you get on?"

"What do you care?"

She looked at me like she might just blame the wine and jump me, but her cooler head told her to stay put and go to bed, alone.

"I care plenty, Brad. I always will."

There was a long pause. Claire could see I was working up something to say. When I finally spoke, it wasn't with the utmost confidence I'd envisaged having when I'd played the scene in my mind earlier.

"You know, I've been doing great. I haven't had an episode for months. Works really chugging along nicely. I'm really feeling like my old self."

"Good for you."

"It could be good for us. This Strickland gig could be a real game-changer money wise. Which reminds me, we need to talk..."

I suddenly felt it was apt to raise the issue of encrypting our messages. But Claire cut me off.

"You know, Bradley, I've been giving it a lot of thought. I mean, about us."

"So have I. And I haven't changed my mind. I still want to make this work again."

She took my hand.

"Brad, honey. That's the thing. I can't. I can't do it again. I can't do it anymore. I love you, but I have to be really honest here—my heart is telling me to stay on this current path. For the first time since I was a teenager, I have my independence, and I'm enjoying it. Not because I'm not with you, but because more than ever I've got faith in myself and what I can do. You know, the way the business is going... I'm growing something that I created from scratch, something that I'm really proud of, and I want to give it my all."

She put her glass down and leaned in towards me.

"I used to think Bella would be traumatized by us splitting up, but she's not. She misses you when you're not around, don't get me wrong, but all things considered she's coping fine. She will always adore you, she will always need you, Brad, and I will never do anything to stand between you and her. But I'm on a different path now. I don't want to turn back; I want to follow it."

As she spoke I went off on my own train of thought. No getting back together; no settling back in Boise. Claire wedded to LA more than ever. That meant Bella would be too. That meant I also had to stay. There was no way I'd be moving away from my daughter.

By the time Claire had finished talking, I'd accepted we were done. I felt a bit dislocated but relieved. There was a sense that at last the great cloud of uncertainty had cleared. I could stop hoping, stop conjuring up stupid dreams and making them my goals. I could now resolve to just get on with my life.

Come morning, I was sad but content to let go and move on. I sat on the deck and looked out past the horse corral to the mountains beyond, the peaks still capped in snow. The clean air was tinged with the smell of pasture, hay and manure. It felt good to be in the country again. I could hear Claire and Bella inside the cabin getting ready to come out and join me for breakfast.

"Daddy!"

Bella flew out the door and gave me a big hug then sat herself on my lap.

"When are we going riding?"

"Just a little while after breakfast, angel. So eat up."

The staff had delivered our breakfast order to the deck. Bella lifted a plate cover to reveal a stack of blueberry pancakes.

"Looks like that's yours, sweetheart."

She leapt off my lap, took her seat and began getting everything just so before she tackled her meal—repositioning her cutlery and cup of juice, taking a sip, then picking up the small jug of maple syrup and pouring it onto the stack.

Claire came out after making a few calls. Later, the three of us walked around the ranch and admired the horses. Bella picked out her favorite—a stunning looking palomino named Buttershine. Once she was in the saddle, it was impossible for her to be happier. I made a point of sidling up to her on the trail to tell her we would be doing this again real soon. That was a promise. The smile on her face will stay with me forever.

On the way home, the comedown of it all ending too soon hit Bella hard. Claire, feeling guilty for making us leave early, tried to cheer her up.

"Come on, sweetheart. When we get back what do you say we go get pizza and a big scoop of salted caramel gelato?"

"At that place we went to with Tom?"

The change in Claire was so marked I could sense it even with my eyes on the road. I stole a glance at her.

She was ruffled, scrambling to think. I was having no such trouble: *Who the hell was Tom?*

I gave Claire the raised eyebrow. *Some douche has been out with my wife and daughter?*

My blood hit boiling point, but the vibe in the car was ice cold. In the rear-view mirror, I saw Bella had realized she'd unwittingly put her mother in a spot.

"Yes, Claire. Is that the place you and Tom like so much?"

She eventually found words and tried unsuccessfully to sound light of spirit.

"Yes. Da Angelo's. It's new. It's wonderful."

"Oh, I bet it is."

I held my tongue. It seemed Claire had not been entirely straight with me. What was all that wonderful self-affirmation crap springing forth from her newfound independence? Apparently, that was not entirely true or at the very least highly inaccurate. She'd managed to

42

leave out a pretty big chunk of the story, a chunk who went by the name of Tom.

I barely spoke for the rest of the trip. Claire tried now and then to make small talk, but I didn't oblige. I just wanted her out of the car. My feelings were no longer something to share with her. When we pulled up in Venice, I got out and carried their bags to the door, gave Bella a big hug and told her I'd see her next week. She ran inside.

"Brad," Claire started. "It's early days. I'm not even sure what it is with Tom."

"Yet you take Bella along on a date with him?"

"That was weeks ago. And it wasn't a date. We were just friends back then."

"Look, I don't care what you do or who you see. But I care about how it affects Bella. You think it's okay to be flirting with another man while she still has hopes of me coming back?"

"Don't you dare question my judgment as a mother!"

There it was—I'd committed that mortal sin.

"Right, you've got it all perfectly under control. And I'm sure you've got Bella's best interests at heart."

With those words Claire's fury spiked.

"I'm not the one who gives her nightmares!" she shouted.

Suddenly, it was like the whole world went silent. There it was. The cold, hard truth. My fatal flaw as a father. In spite of all my love for Bella, I was some kind of monster. A Jekyll-and-Hyde dad. She may have only witnessed me in my vivid battle hallucinations two or three times, but it was enough to imprint in her the need to balance love and fear towards me. The thought that Bella was scared of me lacerated me. And Claire knew that.

All the fight left me.

"You should get the paperwork to court and send me the documents."

43

Claire took a deep breath and gave me a slow, sad nod.

I turned for my car.

That was it. We were getting divorced.

CHAPTER 5

Two days later it was Monday morning, but it wasn't going to be the usual start to my working week. As I pressed the second-floor button in the elevator at about ten to nine, I heard muffled shouting. As I rode upwards the noise faded, but when the doors opened onto my floor, the yelling hit with full force, and I knew in an instant it was coming from my office. I sprang out of the elevator.

"I have to see him! Where is he?!"

As I approached, I could hear Megan trying in vain to calm down the guy who was yelling. I pushed open the glass entry door and found myself face to face with Buddy Landry.

It was a surreal moment. On the one hand, I couldn't help but harbor a vague thrill at having one of the most famous people in the world drop in to see me. On the other, it was clear I was not in his good books.

"Madison, you piece of shit. Do you know who you're defending? Do you?!"

He was in agitation overload—sweaty, breathing hard and frantic-eyed. He looked like he hadn't slept in weeks.

"Mr. Landry, you're clearly upset. If you've got a problem, I'm happy to hear you out, but I need you to lower your voice."

He paused for a moment before resuming with the volume dialed down.

"Strickland. You're defending Patrick Strickland."

Damn *Counterspin*. A few days earlier, Cohen had gone ahead and written his story and dropped my name in it. It was standard gossip peddling—star-studded party, Strickland-Landry confrontation followed by "secret" meeting with attorney Brad Madison. Add a couple of quotes from an "unnamed source" and the gist of the story was that Strickland was expecting some sort of trouble from Landry and I was the cavalry.

I'd called Strickland after I'd read the article, saying I needed to know more in case things developed quicker than he anticipated. He wouldn't budge. He wanted to keep me at arm's length. I thought it was bad judgment on his part, but I knew arguing was pointless.

"You can't always believe what you read, Buddy. You of all people should know that."

I kept talking for a short while, staying polite and calm, trying to coax his intensity down.

"Now if you want to talk, let's talk. We can go into my office."

I was standing square to Landry, almost a foot taller and ready to show him the door with or without his consent. Thankfully, there was a scrap of good judgment left in that frazzled brain. He took a deep breath.

"Okay, let's talk."

He lifted a gentle hand at Megan.

"Sorry, ma'am. Didn't mean to scare you."

"That's okay, Mr. Landry. Can I get you some water?"

"Please," he said, looking at the floor.

We walked into my office, and I beckoned Landry to sit. But even after he did, he could not remain still, his body in constant need of adjustment. It was odd to look at him and see the boyish features still there despite their mannish form—he was sadly ageless. But his face had that haunted complexion of an addict, with the skin beneath his eyes in permanent shadow. He had the LA rock star look down pat—dark hair slicked back, goatee, hoop earring on the left side, eyebrow stud and multiple necklaces hanging outside his black t-shirt. He pulled out a soft pack of Lucky Strikes.

"You can't smoke in here," I said.

He froze for a second, looking at me like I was the fun police, then pocketed his smokes. Megan entered with the water.

"Thank you, ma'am."

"You're welcome, Mr. Landry."

As she turned his eyes followed, checking out her ass. Megan was used to turning heads. She had a petite, fit figure and showed it off with style. Not that she was putting it out there to catch some stranger's eye. She was engaged to her high school sweetheart, and once the vows were done, I knew children would soon follow.

The thought of losing her saddened me. She was a bright light of sweet but savvy femininity that would be hard to replace. I may have been the boss, but it was her office and she ran it as neat and ordered as a Swiss watch.

I didn't want Landry there. I didn't want him anywhere near Megan, for that matter. Looking at him, I didn't expect any moment of calm to last.

"Now Buddy, why don't you tell me what this is about?"

"Do you know what Patrick Strickland is?"

"Yes, he's a successful movie producer. And he's somebody you're not particularly happy with."

"I said do you know what he is—what kind of a man he is."

"I've only met the man once, Buddy. At the party, just like the article said. Which is what led you here, I take it."

"That's right. But I know Patrick Strickland very well, and if you only knew—"

"Buddy, sorry to interrupt but there's a reason everyone hates defense attorneys—we stand up for the kind of people society despises. Now I've told you already I'm not defending Strickland on any charge. But if I was, it would not be conditional on his character."

The hate returned to Landry's face.

"So you're little more than a whore."

I was just about done with wearing my peacekeeper hat.

"If you think that's the kind of conversation I'll allow in my office, think again. If you've got something important to say, then say it. Given your state of distress, I thought I'd offer you the chance to talk. I didn't give you carte blanche to insult me. Tell me: Why are you here?"

"Okay," Landry said as he stood and dug a hand into his jeans pocket. He then slammed a thumb drive down on my desk.

"I just wanted to let you know who you're getting into bed with. He's an evil predatory son of a bitch who should be in prison instead of living the life of a king in his castle on the hill. They all are."

"You'll need to explain this to me. What do you mean 'they all are'? Who?"

"Strickland. Shapiro. Newman. Finlay. Webster. Do you know what they did to us? What they are still getting away with?!"

The manic fury was back, his restless body unclear about what to do with all its pent-up rage. It seemed to take all Landry's rational will to stop himself from trashing my office or coming at me. He sucked in a deep breath, pointed at the USB stick and addressed me through gritted teeth.

"You're the whore of a monster. I hope you can live with that."

I stood up, ready to wring his neck.

"You best be going."

Over Landry's shoulder, I saw Jack Briggs through the glass watching us and speaking with Megan. Landry turned around to follow my gaze. I didn't need Jack's help, but it only takes one look for any fool to know Jack's not a man you want to cross. Landry turned back to me with venom.

"I hope you rot in hell."

He shoved the door open, marched past Megan with a glance and made for the elevator. Through the glass I could see him punching the down button furiously. I walked out to see him go. He took a step towards me.

"What a joke you are. You kid yourself about fighting for justice. You're just as corrupt as those you defend. A dead soul chained to the devil!"

A chime rang and the elevator door opened. Landry disappeared, but his presence lingered. His words didn't hurt me as such—hell, I've heard a lot worse over the years—but they triggered an old conflict. You know, the one about your current self versus the shining man you long ago envisioned you'd become? The eager notion that in the years ahead you'd become a finer person? That you'd be fighting a noble cause? Helping those less fortunate? Earning the respect and admiration of your peers? In short, a modern-day knight. Yet I had found that reaching even modest success entailed deep compromises. I'd learned personal ethics and professional ones are not the same, that the perfect defense lawyer is nothing but the chimera of a naive imagination.

Landry was right. I just didn't need him to tell me that. I turned to Jack.

"Somehow I don't think that's the last I'll see of Buddy Landry."

"I'm not so sure," said Jack.

"Looks to me like he's going to have a hard time staying alive."

I turned back to my office.

"Let's see what he brought me."

***

The memory stick contained just one video file. It was a couple of minutes long and opened inside a car. The camera was shooting

49

through a window at night as the car pulled into a driveway. Rain streamed down the glass as the car slowed to a halt. A group of men could be seen standing next to the driveway, sheltered from the elements. The camera shuffled to a low-profile position a short distance from the window. Obviously, the shooter was filming covertly. In the frame were faces of men more interested in their banter than the car. Most were tough to identify, but one was instantly recognizable—Danny Shapiro. With hair on his head. The footage must be at least ten years old. I hit pause on another face.

"That looks like Jerry Newman," Jack said.

I paused the video on a third face that barely came into shot.

"Gabe Finlay," I said. I'm not exactly a film buff, but you didn't have to be to know Finlay was a big budget director. He'd gotten a lot of good press for last year's remake of *The Blob*.

There was a younger man among them. Barely 20 years old. Clearly a gym nut—he was dressed in, what else, a muscle shirt.

"That's Julian Dobson," said Jack.

I gave him a blank stare.

"He was a moderately successful kid actor who saw the future of entertainment in the late nineties. He started a production company making TV shows solely for online streaming. With the dot-com boom taking off, he got swamped in money. He managed to ride out the crash and stick around long enough for better timing. Now he runs a video streaming company that produces Netflix content. Shit that's a cross between soap operas and reality TV."

"What, like *The Hills*?"

"Yeah, but edgier. The millennials love it."

Whoever was shooting the footage stuffed the camera inside their windbreaker but left it rolling. As the car door opened, the men greeted the new arrival.

"Emilio! Good to see you. You're right on time. Come on. Get over here and out of that rain. We're just heading in."

"What's the bet that that's Emilio Peralta?" I said.

A hand reached in and stopped the recording. The next scene was inside a large living area. Again, whoever shot the footage was doing so on the sly. From the interior you could see a poolside party going on outside—voices, laughter, a champagne cork popping—but the cameraman veered away from the glass sliding doors down a hall to a nearby bedroom and into a large en suite.

There was the sound of the door being closed and locked. The cameraman's hand reached out as the lens was directed at a mirrored cabinet. It pulled open a door and picked out a bottle of pills and turned the label to the camera.

"Vicodin," whispered a young man's voice before replacing the bottle. The hand grabbed a small clear bag of pills.

"Quaaludes."

Then another bottle.

"Rohypnol."

And another bag of pills.

"Ecstasy."

And another bag, this one containing white powder.

"And, of course, plenty of coke."

Suddenly, there was the muffled sound of a man's voice calling out.

"Emilio? Emilio, where are you?"

The footage scrambled and went dark as the camera was stashed back inside the shooter's jacket.

"Emilio!" The voice was closer, hide-and-seek playful but with a paternal edge. "Are you in there?"

The man was in the bedroom, up against the door.

"What is it, Jerry?! I'm on the john!"

"I hope you're not treating yourself to my goody bags. They're not for little boys to be playing with all by themselves."

I wanted to vomit. You could hear Peralta was breathless, but he tried to collect himself.

"Give me a minute. I'll be out in a minute."

"Don't be long, pet. The party's kicking up a gear, and there's someone very important here you're going to want to meet."

"I know. You told me already."

At the touch of irritation in Emilio's response, Newman's tone turned sharp.

"Make it snappy. You don't keep the big man waiting."

There was a rustling sound as Emilio reached into his jacket and turned the camera off.

I hit pause.

"Who's the 'big man'?" I was thinking out loud.

"Sounds like Newman has set this kid up with a john," Jack snarled. "It's messed up. This shit is starting to look a whole lot like slavery."

I hit play again. The next scene was back in the living area, which opened out to the swimming pool. There was a teenage boy passed out on the sofa. The camera lowered to a coffee table strewn with empty glasses of champagne and cocktails. The sliding door was open, and across the way in the dark you could see people in the spa bath. It was too dark to recognize anyone.

From further inside the house, you could hear footsteps approach. The camera was hastily stashed way again.

"Emilio," said Newman, now right next to him. "I got you a drink. Why don't you come join us in the spa?"

"Sure. Sure. I'll just go get changed."

"Uh, uh, ah! You know the rule—it's past ten—no clothes in the spa."

"Yeah, of course."

The camera was taken out again, revealing a butt naked Jerry Newman strolling out towards the spa. The frame went to black, then a few seconds later another clip started. The blurry footage showed a teenage boy dressed in just a pair of shorts and a clothed man enter the house from the pool area. The man had an arm around the teen's shoulder and ushered him through the lounge area. Before they disappeared into an adjacent hall, the cameraman finally managed to get the focus properly trained on his subject.

"That's Peralta," said Jack.

My blood ran cold. There was no mistaking the identity of the man with him—it was Patrick Strickland leading the unsteady boy away. The clip ended soon after.

I sat back in my chair. Jack went around to take the seat in front of my desk.

"You know what I'm thinking, don't you?" he said.

"Yep."

"It looks like the 'big man' is your client."

I dipped my head into my hands. This looked really bad. Jack had filled me in on the Emilio Peralta story at the steakhouse. Peralta was another young actor in Jerry Newman's stable. His profile was never anything like Landry's. His was more the typical Hollywood hard graft story. Jack had taken it upon himself to fly up to Reno to talk with Peralta's parents. He left unimpressed. As much as he wanted to feel sympathy for a couple whose only child had disappeared off the face of the earth, he could rouse none. He said the Peraltas were Exhibit A in bad middle-class parenting. They were so objectionable, he said, that what they pined for most was not their only son but the opportunity they'd lost with his death.

Mr. Peralta owned a Subway franchise, and his wife liked playing tennis and quoting Tony Robbins. These two had been desperate to convert their son's good looks and talent into cash. The way they saw it, their sole offspring was a leg-up to the comfortable life they'd convinced themselves they deserved. They were only too happy for Jerry Newman to take Emilio under his wing. He'd waxed lyrical about Emilio, spoke of a promising career, of how it hinged on getting just the right part at the right time—planets-aligned kind of stuff—and how engineering such celestial providence was Newman's special talent. He could steer the kid through the vast maze of Hollywood's talent filtering system.

They said they genuinely thought they were doing the right thing. They trusted Newman to be Emilio's guardian, adviser and mentor, allowing their boy to lodge at Newman's house for months at a time. But barely two years later, he was on a one-way Greyhound back to Reno. Well, he was supposed to be. It was well known that Strickland had dropped the kid off at the East 7th Street terminal. But Emilio has never been seen or heard from since. He was listed as a missing person for weeks before police began looking closer at the case. But after questioning Strickland, Newman and a few others in LA, the case went cold. The cops always believed Peralta was a runaway and were happy to leave it at that. They pictured the boy having a vagabond adventure riding the rails and leaving his self-centered parents far behind. Can't blame the police for that, said Jack. Anyone who'd met the parents might draw the same conclusion—the kid quite possibly never wanted to go back home again.

But in Hollywood the rumors swirled that Emilio Peralta had been murdered. And since it was Strickland who saw him last, the Chinese whispers had him as the killer.

Why? Because, so the theory goes, Peralta was trying to expose a pedophile ring of which Strickland was a member. Given what I'd just seen on the clips Landry had given to me, I could understand that theory.

"We have to find out what happened to this Peralta kid," I said to Jack.

"Sure thing... as much as promising to solve a mystery can be a sure thing."

I picked up the phone. Jack raised his eyebrows.

"Who you calling?"

"Strickland. I've had it with his coy bullshit."

It did occur to me that Landry wanted me to react this way—to rethink whether or not I should represent Strickland. He probably thought if I had a decent bone in my body I'd cut ties with Strickland immediately. And in a sense I was ready to do just that. What I'd just seen portrayed the story of a young man being ruthlessly exploited. But the truth was there was no evidence Strickland had done anything wrong. To see him at a party where men were preying on boys made my skin crawl. But was he in on their sordid behavior? What was his relationship with Peralta?

It was time for Strickland to cut the crap and give me the whole story. And if he wasn't up to doing that, he could find himself another lawyer.

CHAPTER 6

I didn't get to speak to Strickland for three days. His secretary had replied politely to the voice messages I left, saying he'd made a dash visit to Cannes on *Sister Planet* business. He'd be back in 48 hours, she assured me. True to her word, he did return my call in the given time frame. As fate would have it, it was the day Buddy Landry was found dead.

At about six-thirty Thursday morning, my phone pinged with a breaking news alert from *Counterspin*. As soon as I glanced at the words, it was like I almost knew they were coming: 'Troubled actor Buddy Landry murdered'.

I tapped through to the story. It said police were called to Landry's apartment after residents complained of a foul smell coming from within. Exactly when Landry died was yet to be determined. Police investigators were on the scene and treating the case as suspicious. While the police had not released details about how Landry might have died, *Counterspin* reported he had suffered brutal head injuries.

I scanned other news outlets, but none had anything to add. In fact, none were yet prepared to report it as a murder. *Counterspin* was way ahead of the pack again. It would be their story that would spread to millions of people around the world taking the clickbait or watching a new flash.

I got up, hit the gym and then made my way downtown. I was locked in traffic on Wilshire when Strickland rang.

"Bradley, I need to see you immediately," he said when I answered. No hello. No mention of the fact that he had not bothered to return my calls.

"Is this about Landry?"

"You've heard then."

"Well, I know he's dead."

"I've dreaded this day would come for years, Bradley. I was very fond of Buddy, but he was his own worst enemy."

There was a sadness in Strickland's voice that made me half believe him.

"Yeah, well, looks like he's not your problem anymore. Someone did you a favor and went and killed your blackmailer."

"You surely don't think I had anything to do with this?!"

"I don't know what to make of it, Patrick. I don't know what you're capable of."

"Bradley, I know I've kept you in the dark up until now, but that's about to change. Please, come to the lot and I'll tell you everything you want to know."

"Okay. Where are you?"

"Castlight Studios. Security will tell you where to find me."

As soon as I hung up, I called Jack and told him to get down to Landry's place. Jack would have no trouble finding out where it was. Thirty minutes later I was at the studio gate being directed to Strickland's office.

The Castlight lot was like a suburb of LA all on its own. I passed by aircraft hangar-sized buildings, then a street that looked like 1920s New York before wheeling the car into a space out front of a row of bungalows. I got out, looking for number 673. The exteriors of each cottage were identical—small, neat patch of lawn, two palm trees, a white picket fence and a rose bed.

As I entered, a woman's voice greeted me from behind a desk to the right.

"Good morning, Mr. Madison."

The woman stood up and came towards me smiling like I'd made her day. She was fortyish and on the plain side of pretty, but there was an air of happy confidence that made her instantly magnetic. A light blue dress hugged her frame, and around her waist was one of those pencil-thin belts that neither holds anything up nor in. With her dark hair in a bun, red lipstick and white teeth, she was like one of those seasoned and polished flight attendants from back in the day that every man would strive to slyly get a good look at, front and back.

"I trust it wasn't too hard to find us."

"Not at all. I took the New York route."

"Well, aren't you the local?" She put out her hand. "Hannah Maybury, Mr. Strickland's executive assistant. Please, follow me."

She turned for the corridor leading into the house, her high heels hammering the dark polished floorboards. She walked like she was giving a deportment class at finishing school, making that tip-toeing high-wire act seem as natural as walking barefoot on the beach. Her left arm was slightly cocked at the elbow, her wrist kept limp in an unconscious statement of poise.

We passed through a sitting room fitted with two plush sofas and a huge aquarium that took up a quarter of one wall. At the next door to the left she stopped and gestured for me to enter. I turned into the room to find Strickland standing a few feet inside, putting on a big smile to greet me.

"Good to see you, Bradley. Can we get you some coffee? There's a damned good barista round the corner."

"Great. I'll have a macchiato."

Set in front of Strickland's desk was a black leather sofa on one side and two matching arm chairs opposite it. In between was a coffee table littered with various copies of *GQ*, *Vanity Fair* and *Variety*. No doubt, Strickland was on the cover of at least one of them. Hannah left and Strickland motioned for me to take one of the two chairs. He took the other.

The office walls were crammed with large framed posters and photos. There were stills from the sets of Strickland's movies—him with this famous movie star and that famous director. Him with an eye drilled into a camera's viewfinder. Him holding an Oscar.

On the wall opposite me, all the pictures were centered around one huge color print—*One For The Road*. There was Buddy Landry looking cute, cocky and clever, sandwiched between two bumbling old cons. Strickland saw I'd noticed it.

"That's where it all began," he said.

"That much I know, Patrick. But it's time we got deeper than Wikipedia. I've been calling you for days."

"Yes, I know. I'm sorry."

"Landry came to see me."

Strickland's expression went dead flat.

"When?"

"Monday morning. He came to my office. Mad as a hatter, but he abused me for dealing with you. And he left me something."

"The video?"

"Yes. There's a lot I need to know from you, Patrick. But explaining what you were doing at that party and what you were doing with that half-naked kid would be a good place to start."

I didn't want to state that my representing him was on the line. If I thought he was bullshitting me in any way, I was going to drop him.

"I know what it looks like, Bradley. But I swear—I went to get Emilio out of there."

"How so?"

"First, let me go back a bit further. You know, when I set Buddy up with Newman, that was just the done thing. He was a good agent. He was dedicated to the kids he took on. He got results. He was

59

charming, smart and thorough. There was no one else doing anything like that at the time—specializing in young actors. He was seen as a pioneer. He got a lot of kudos for that. No one, and I mean no one, ever suspected he had ulterior motives."

"That his books were filled with young boys wasn't a giveaway?"

"It just wasn't the way we looked at it. At first, that is."

"When did that change? I mean, for you. When did the penny drop?"

"It was when Buddy was unhappy and wanted to get a place on his own."

"Move out of Newman's house?"

"Yeah. I knew he was upset. I thought it was girl problems or that he didn't like the house rules. He was rich enough to buy his own place, but he was barely fifteen. Still, he was determined to move out, so I suggested he move into the cabin. And he did."

"But he said nothing about Newman?"

"Nothing. To this day, I don't know if Newman did anything to him, but those kids were hugely dependent on that guy. Get him offside and your career's over."

"But you say you went to help Peralta. So you knew something was going on."

"This was a while after Buddy had moved into my place. Emilio was hanging around there a lot. I didn't know him very well, but he was a good kid going downhill fast. His spirit was gone. And it was about this time that the rumors were building about Newman. That he was demanding, you know, rent off his kids. And in hindsight, Emilio was the perfect victim. He was all dreams and no career, so he lived on the promises Newman made to him. But there was a price."

"Sexual favors?"

"Yes, there's that. And perhaps worse."

"What do you mean?"

"Look, I never really bought into it, but there was a rumor that some kind of club existed where boys like Emilio were pimped out. Then over the years you'd hear stuff that was real out there, sinister shit."

"Like what?"

"Like a few Hollywood power brokers, including Newman supposedly, forming something called the Titan Club, a highly secretive group who preyed on street kids. Got off on abusing them and filming it all."

"You didn't believe it?"

"No more than I'd believe the Illuminati is currently plotting to overthrow Washington. To my mind, it was pure conspiracy theory."

"Explain to me why you were at that party."

Hannah entered with the coffees. She set them down and left, returning a few moments later with a jug of chilled water and two glasses. Strickland waited until she had left.

"I wanted to get him away from Newman."

"That's not what it sounded like, and it's not what it looked like. Newman was talking like you were coming to enjoy yourself with Peralta."

"Yes, well that's how he explained it."

"How about you explain it."

"I'd seen Emilio at the cabin. He'd stay occasionally, hanging out with Buddy. And I was worried about him. And I thought about when Buddy wanted to leave Newman's. He said nothing to me about why he wanted to leave, but I started to think it might have been on account of Newman's behavior. And I guessed that might have been the root of Emilio's problems too. So I decided to step in."

"How?"

"I rang Newman one night, asking where Emilio was and saying I wanted him for an audition first thing next morning. He stalled, saying there was a little party on and Emilio had had a little too much champagne. Newman started making out like Emilio had helped himself while the adults weren't looking. Then he started insisting it was his job to get Emilio to the audition. I wasn't going to take no for an answer. I told Newman I was coming over to get the kid. I said I was going to make damn sure he made that casting."

"So you get to the house?"

"I get to the house. Newman met me and took me to see Emilio. He was out by the pool, lying on a sun lounge. He was wasted."

"Who else was there?"

"Shapiro and others were in the spa. And I caught a glimpse of Julian Dobson, who was inside playing a video game."

"No other boys?"

"No. But it was a bit weird."

"In what way?"

"Well, they—Shapiro, Finlay and the others—were all friendly. Kind of too friendly. Asking if I wanted to stay for a drink, get in the tub and all that. But it was like they were putting it on for my sake. I mean, they wanted it to appear like it was just a bunch of guys winding down, but I could just tell they were waiting for me to leave. Whatever I was seeing was what they wanted me to see, know what I mean?"

"I think I understand."

"But Emilio was not just drunk. He was totally out of it. And he was wearing these shorts that looked kind of awkwardly pulled up. I thought right then that he hadn't dressed himself. I managed to wake him up and get him on his feet. And I escorted him out of there."

"Then what?"

"He slept it off at my place. And when he woke up I tried to get him to tell me what was going on. But he told me nothing. He just got angry and said he wanted to leave Hollywood and go home. So we went and got his things from Newman's, and I drove him out to the bus station and put him on a Greyhound."

Strickland's account seemed a reasonable match to what I'd seen on the video. The way he told it, he didn't know for sure whether the boys had been drugged. And he would not have known that any of the men present were hitting on the boys. The one thing that didn't fit was Newman telling Peralta: "Make it snappy. You don't keep the big man waiting."

"Patrick, the way Newman speaks to Emilio, it's like they're expecting you at the party and that you, you know, are expecting Emilio to be served to you."

Strickland bowed his head and shook it. He then massaged his forehead before taking a deep breath and addressing me again.

"I simply don't know how to explain that. That wasn't the nature of my visit, I swear. I wanted to help Emilio. I didn't go there to... you know. It makes me sick to think Buddy believed I'd do such a thing."

"Well, he was obviously convinced that was the case."

Strickland's desk phone started ringing. He stood up to get it. Just after he put the receiver to his ear he looked at me.

"Send him in."

He put the phone back in its cradle.

"Detective Wolfe's here."

✳✳✳

Hannah appeared in the doorway and swung her arm like a game show hostess for her guest to enter. A smile-less man wearing a suit jacket and jeans appeared. He was about five ten in height, but width wise he almost filled the door frame.

"Good morning, detective," said Strickland, stepping towards him.

I'd never laid eyes on Elliott Wolfe, but from what I'd heard he was tenacious and whip-smart. Precisely the man you don't want on your tail. He nodded curtly as he entered the room before taking Strickland's hand. His jacket fell open to reveal an LAPD badge and gun. He turned to me.

"Detective Wolfe. This is my attorney, Brad Madison."

Wolfe dropped his hand but otherwise didn't move. I nodded his way. He did the same, slowly enough for it to be barely worth the point. He had a rugged presence that suggested he didn't need a gun to take anyone into custody. And that's how he looked at me—like he wanted to cuff me—but I guessed that was the kind of impression he enjoyed making.

You could say Wolfe and I were bound not to see eye to eye, considering my job is in some respects to make his harder. I don't stand for anyone being punished beyond what can be convincingly proved. And, like most cops, he no doubt viewed me as a grub who kept crooks out of the slammer, propping up cocktail bars with dirty money.

"So what's going on?" I asked like I didn't know.

"I'm investigating the murder of Buddy Landry."

"Yes, but how does that concern my client?"

Wolfe took in a slow breath and ran his eyes around the room. His gaze rested on the *One For The Road* print. He stepped up close to it and read the credits.

"You and Buddy Landry go back a long way, I take it, Mr. Strickland."

"That was the first movie we did together. It changed both our lives."

"For better or worse?"

"A bit of both, it would be fair to say, but everything considered, better by a long shot."

Wolfe raised an eyebrow.

"I wonder if Landry felt that way."

Strickland gestured for us all to sit. Wolfe took one of the armchairs. I felt I was going to enjoy watching Wolfe's stoic act, so I took the sofa across from him. Strickland stepped around and sat next to me. He spread his hands out.

"Detective, what can I do for you?"

Wolfe pulled out a small pad, flipped through it to find a blank page, then held his pen poised.

"Let's start with your relationship with Buddy Landry. Tell me about it."

Strickland went into some detail, explaining how he'd discovered Landry and how they were once rather close. He said he took the boy under his wing when his acting career took off. He told Wolfe about how Landry wanted to escape from Newman's house and that he offered Landry the cottage. But he wasn't a guardian: Landry came and went as he pleased.

Up until he wanted out of Newman's place, Landry appeared to be having the time of his life. He was building a stellar career and had the world at his feet. There was no hint of a problem. Then suddenly Strickland felt Landry was kind of troubled. His attempts to communicate with the boy went nowhere. The one time Landry did open up, he lashed out and said he hated Strickland. Soon after, he vacated the cottage, and Strickland did not see him for years. Then word got out that Strickland had landed *Sister Planet*, and Landry came pleading for a role.

"He thought my movie was the answer to all his problems."

"What do you mean?"

"He believed a role in *Sister Planet* would resurrect his career. You get a lot of that in Hollywood. I can't tell you the desperate lengths actors will go to to get a part. They'd ship their mother off to a whorehouse to get a prized role."

"And Landry was that kind of desperate?"

"Yes. He saw the project as a second chance. It would motivate him to stay clean or to dry out, or both. It would give him the money to rebuild his life."

"And you turned him down?"

"I had no choice. He was a mess. A dangerous mess. Highly unstable and volatile. He didn't have a clear thought in his head. I told him he needed to somehow focus just on getting himself better."

"How did he take it when you turned him down?"

Strickland looked at me. So far there'd been no need for me to weigh in or interject, but Strickland was clearly in two minds about how much to share about the blackmail. I nodded. Strickland turned to Wolfe.

"He didn't take it well. In fact, he began to threaten me."

If Wolfe was intrigued he didn't let it show.

"What kind of threats?"

Strickland weighed his thoughts.

"The kind of threats that come from a drug-addled lunatic—they were of utterly zero consequence."

Wolfe looked up from his pad and rested his right hand on the arm of his chair.

"Mr. Strickland. What about you? Did you ever threaten Mr. Landry?"

Strickland gave a wry chuckle.

"That's pretty funny. The only thing I ever threatened that kid with was common sense. But I struck out on that front."

Wolfe flipped through his notes.

"So you never sent him a text three days ago, saying... let me get this right... 'Stop this madness or I will destroy you'? Or 'Keep this up and you're dead'?"

Strickland sat back in his chair. I cut in. I had no idea where this could go. If I was going to be any use to Strickland, he needed to open up to me.

"Detective Wolfe, do you mind if I have a word with my client in private? Just a few minutes."

Wolfe shook his head and gave me a look every cop gives you when you wedge yourself into their affairs. The look you'd give a parking officer you'd caught writing you a ticket when you're two minutes over. I walked Wolfe to the door and shut it behind him.

"Patrick, old Columbo here is zeroing in, yet I'm still in the dark about your movements the day Buddy was killed. You need to bring me up to speed right now, you understand?"

Strickland nodded. He said before he caught his flight to Europe, he went to see Landry. He was angry. He felt Landry was being more than a nuisance; he was being vindictive. He took Landry's threats to go public with horrible stories of abuse and murder as being a calculated bid to catch Strickland at his most vulnerable. He could not understand why Landry had turned so spiteful towards him, and he treated the claims about him interfering with boys and killing Emilio Peralta as ludicrous. Yes, he did send those threatening texts, but he drove to Landry's in the hope of trying to convince him he was wrong.

As for the conversation he had with Landry that day, it was a roller coaster ride. Hostile to begin with, it morphed into a heartfelt exchange. He said, mentally, Landry was not completely haywire. He was quite sober, if a little on edge. Strickland told him he never understood why he turned on him so fiercely. He knew he hadn't been there for him when it mattered, but Strickland reminded Landry that he'd shut Strickland out. He told Landry the claim that he was a member of the Titan Club or was into young boys was a flat out lie. He told Landry how devastating it was to have someone whom he loved like a son think him so vile. He was immensely relieved to find Landry accepting his word and apologizing.

With everything seemingly on an amicable footing, Strickland said he told Landry he was just a call away. He urged Landry to get help and vowed to support him in any sober or sincere effort he made to get his career on track after rehab. Hell, maybe there could be a role for him on *Sister Planet II*, *III* or *IV*.

But then Landry suddenly turned like a switch had been flipped inside his brain. It was as though everything they'd just talked about never happened and a new false but vivid reality had taken residence in Landry's head. He started shouting and repeating the accusations that Strickland was a monster and a murderer. Strickland began to genuinely fear for his life. He backed away from Landry and stormed out the door, returned to his car, where he sat, shaking.

On his way home, he had called Vivien to tell her what happened. He said she didn't say much but was not very sympathetic. That was understandable, since Vivien knew more than anyone how much was riding on *Sister Planet*. She said a blackmailing scandal of this sort could scuttle the whole deal. She said maybe spending a couple of days in Europe would do Strickland good—help clear his mind. And who knows, she said, maybe Landry will get distracted by some other manic obsession and just disappear.

"Okay, I get it. Now promise me I'm not going to hear any more surprises when Wolfe comes back through that door?"

"No," he said with a kind of teenage indignation. "Get him back in."

I opened the door and stuck my head out. Wolfe was past me in a second.

"I won't take up too much more of your time, Mr. Strickland," he said.

Strickland and I took our seats, but Wolfe sat himself on the arm of the chair and folded his arms. He checked his pad again and then looked down at Strickland. You could tell he was reading every slight body movement, every barely perceptible eyelid flinch, nostril flare, head turn and lip shift.

"So you did threaten to kill Mr. Landry?"

"It was not as bad as it sounds. I was angry, and he was being a pain in the ass."

"I deal with a lot of pains in the ass, Mr. Strickland, but I don't threaten to kill them. What exactly was this madness you referred to in that text?"

"He said I was involved in some disturbing matters, and that's all I'm prepared to say about it right now."

"I think you should reconsider. If you've got nothing to hide, that is."

Strickland looked at me, and I nodded. He then divulged to Wolfe everything he'd just told me.

When Strickland was done, Wolfe put his pad and pen away and clasped his hands together in his lap.

"Just a couple more questions, Mr. Strickland. Do you own a firearm?"

"Yes I do. A Colt 45 pistol. It was a gift from Gus Burbank, a five-star general and a good friend of mine."

"You must have some interesting friends," he said, slightly dismissively. "Where do you keep it?"

"At my house—in my office desk drawer. Why are you asking about a gun, Detective? Buddy wasn't shot."

Wolfe let the silence hang for a while.

"We think Mr. Landry was clubbed to death with the butt of a pistol. By the look of his wounds, it would have been something very much like a Colt 45. Would you mind if I send some officers around to inspect your gun, Mr. Strickland?"

I jumped in.

"You'll need a warrant."

"I have one."

"Detective, is my client a suspect?"

Wolfe kept his eyes on Strickland even as he addressed me.

"Our investigation is still young, Mr. Madison. It's early days. There's still a lot to figure out. But my hunch is Landry was killed by someone he knew."

"Why's that?" Strickland asked.

"It just doesn't look like there was anything worth stealing, for one. The place was a dump. So robbery's out."

"What about drugs? Who's to say he didn't owe the wrong person too much money?" Strickland asked.

I looked at Strickland, trying to tell him silently to zip it.

"Yes, there may be other theories to consider, but right now I'm particularly curious about your relationship with Landry."

"Is that so?"

"We found some paperwork in Mr. Landry's apartment. I'm not at liberty to go into any kind of detail right now because we haven't pored through it all yet. But I can tell you it appears Mr. Landry was making his own investigation and that you, Mr. Strickland, were one of the key subjects of it."

Strickland waved his hand impatiently.

"Are we done? Can I get back to work? It seems I'm not the only person who immerses themselves in fiction. But at least I can distinguish it from the real world."

Wolfe got to his feet.

"We're done for now. Oh, but there is one last thing."

"What's that?"

Wolfe fished a plastic bag out from his inside coat pocket. "A swab. Do you mind?"

Strickland gave a shrug of resignation—another layer of dignity had been stripped from him. He opened his mouth. Wolfe spoke as he swabbed and bagged the sample.

"Mr. Strickland, I need to ask you to not leave LA. Is that clear?"

"Crystal," said Strickland, his jaw tight and his mind seemingly full of many words he was fighting to hold back.

CHAPTER 7

Landry was cremated in a discreet ceremony only his parents attended. His memorial service, held at the Hollywood Forever Cemetery two days later, was a circus. A media pack a hundred strong set up camp around the Santa Monica Boulevard entrance.

When I pulled in, TV reporters were already doing live crosses. I could guess what they were saying. It was now common knowledge, thanks mostly to *Counterspin*, that Landry had been beaten to death, that his head had been caved in with a blunt object (only *Counterspin* specified a pistol), that police believed Landry knew his killer, and that Patrick Strickland was a person of interest.

The media was in overdrive over Landry. Depending on which so-called source you listened to, Landry was either clean and on the verge of a major comeback or a death-riding addict in need of a tough-love intervention. Either way, there was a lot of mileage in the story. He hadn't been this hot in years.

Almost every mourner at the ceremony was a celebrity—rock stars, movie stars, sport stars and even a TV chef. I was there at Strickland's request. He said he wanted me there "just in case." I guess he suspected Wolfe might try to make a grandstand arrest and wanted backup.

Trying to find Strickland, I made my way through the crowd, passing a string of somber chest bumps, hugs and head shaking. It was then I saw the first person I thought looked genuinely grief stricken: Abby Hatfield.

"Hey, whisky man."

Abby was wearing a sleeveless black dress with her hair pinned up. She was dabbing her eyes with a folded handkerchief.

"I'm sorry. You and Buddy were close, I take it."

Abby put the handkerchief back into a small handbag.

"Years ago we were. We kind of lost touch, but suddenly it feels like only yesterday when we had our little crew."

I was surprised Abby was standing by herself. Or rather I was surprised Freddie Baxter wasn't latched onto her.

"Did Patrick ask you to come?" she asked.

"He's got me on a string at the moment."

The mourners began to move to their seats. Abby put her hand on my forearm.

"You be careful."

I was bemused by such an unexpected remark, but she looked dead serious.

"What do you mean?"

She kept her voice low. Her bearing changed. An angry fire had risen within her, and it drove every word.

"Buddy was murdered. They killed him in cold blood. It wasn't about a drug debt or a burglary gone wrong. It was about show business. He was making trouble for some very powerful people, and they silenced him."

"Are you saying Patrick killed him?"

She paused, weighing not only what she should say but how much.

"Hollywood's a ruthless kingdom. When you get to the top, maybe it's easy to convince yourself you can do whatever you want. Even get away with murder. Maybe it was Patrick, maybe not. He's not the only one who would have wanted Buddy dead."

Abby paused for a second.

"Just watch yourself."

She turned to go. I grabbed her hand lightly.

"I need to know more. Can we meet for a drink?"

I winced at how that sounded. She half smiled.

"Trying to pick me up at a funeral? How classy."

"No, I'm just—"

"This isn't *Wedding Crashers*, you do realize?"

It took me a second to understand her reference. And when I did I shuddered to think she'd liken me to the desperate pick-up artist played by Will Ferrell.

"Abby, I'm sorry. It just sounds like you have something to say, and I want to hear it. I think I need to hear it."

Abby glanced around then unclipped her handbag discreetly, took out a card and pressed it into my hand before turning away to find a seat.

I loitered at the back row of chairs set out in the open air. Looking down the aisle, I saw the memorial to Landry at the front—a big TV screen displaying a series of photos of him. Just a few days ago he was in my office, slandering Strickland. And now here he was, the latest in a long line of tragic Hollywood lives—those who had it all only to tailspin spectacularly into ruin.

I felt sorry for Landry and wondered about who else but Strickland might have wanted him dead.

Suddenly, I felt a firm hand on my shoulder.

"Glad you could make it, Bradley."

I spun around to see Strickland. But it was a Patrick Strickland I'd never seen before. He was visibly upset—eyes red and glistening with tears, voice quiet. There was a warmth to his presence that took me aback. Gone was the defiant emperor of Hollywood, and in its place was an ordinary man humbled and conflicted by his proximity to the death of a loved one.

I must have looked puzzled.

"I loved that kid," he said to explain the tears. He then stuck out his chin and looked ahead with stoic purpose.

"Let's get a seat."

✳✳✳

The service was a series of moving tributes delivered by Landry's former co-stars and friends. I sensed Strickland would have liked to say a few words, but as a suspect that would have been tactless. Other mourners showed Strickland empathy and respect, but there was a veiled wariness in their manner. He seemed to bristle at the fakery and the unspoken social confines in which the taint of suspicion held him.

During the speeches he nodded with every tribute, and every now and then he'd have to catch his breath and brace his body to fight back tears. I suspected he would have liked to stand up and offer his own heartfelt eulogy. It was clearly hard for him to remain silent.

Once the formalities were done, Strickland made his way up to an older couple standing by an urn containing Landry's ashes. I watched him shake their hands and keep hold of the man's palm in a prolonged grip. I assumed this was Wilfred and Layla Landry—Buddy's foster parents. They looked the picture of good, honest folk whose hearts had been crushed.

As Layla wiped tears from her eyes, Vivien walked by right in front of me. She wore a broad black hat and sunglasses and didn't give me a sideways glance.

"Hello, Vivien."

She stopped abruptly, like her name was the last thing she expected to hear.

"Bradley. I didn't see you there."

Given her distracted state, I wouldn't have been surprised if Vivien had just left it at that and kept on walking. But she stopped and quickly found her social verve. We talked about how moving the service was and rehashed some of the more surprising and humorous anecdotes from the speeches. But while some speakers acknowledged Landry's battle with addiction, no one referenced the abuse he claimed to have suffered. Before and during the service, I'd watched Newman, Shapiro, Finlay and Webster. All four were somber decorum personified—quiet exchanges, sober nods, empathetic pats. If Landry's accusations were true, how could these men have the gall to even be here? Once again, like at Strickland's party, I felt I'd entered an alien world where pretense was an artform.

"You know, Vivien," I said before looking over towards Newman. "How Jerry Newman can feel comfortable showing his face around here is beyond me."

Vivien barely paused.

"What do you mean? Why wouldn't he be here? Buddy owed his career to Jerry."

Her tone jolted me. She didn't give her words a second thought.

"What do I mean? The guy accused of raping Buddy Landry turns up to his funeral and behaves like he's lost his beloved son? You're okay with that?"

Vivien locked eyes on me without blinking.

"Jerry did everything for that boy. I don't think many people appreciate how hard Jerry worked to build Buddy his fortune. But he frittered it away and ended up with barely a dime in his pocket. And he died trying to discredit all the men who made his success possible. As much as I was fond of Buddy, he was too weak—too weak to cope with fame and too weak to show due gratitude."

I could not believe my ears. Vivien could barely contain her contempt for Landry.

"To be honest, Vivien, I'm stunned you could be an apologist for child abuse."

"Oh, for God's sake, Bradley. I didn't pick you as a bleeding heart—but I guess it's no surprise. You're a newcomer to the game. Well, let me set you straight—getting taken advantage of is the price everyone pays to get ahead in this business. It's practically a rite of passage. Give the men what they want and you get your name up in lights and the lifestyle you dreamed of. The life you craved. The life you'd kill for."

"Who are you speaking for exactly? Are we talking about you now?"

Vivien pouted as a mild reprimand. It seemed I was too naive.

"Too much is made of this, Bradley. Personally, I think everyone would be better off if they just shut up about it and got on with their lives."

I didn't know which decade Vivien thought we were living in. Her disdain was perverse, like something a conceited survivor might reserve for those too weak to endure. I wondered what she herself had consented to to get ahead.

"So the old casting couch routine is just the way of the world?"

"It is in this world, honey. People talk about 'sleeping your way to the top' like it's a progression of slutty acts that you allow to happen. They have no idea. You don't always get to choose who screws you. Maybe women can deal with it better than men. They're stronger that way."

"But these are kids entrusted to men who hold their future in their hands, who have ultimate power over them. And they abuse them, pimp them out and get them hooked on drugs. And that's okay?"

Vivien straightened her back.

"You make it sound so despicable, so tragic, so evil. Dear God, the suffering is so overplayed, the whining so feeble. But the truth is anyone, no matter how old they are, has a choice. They can leave any time they want. They just have to pick up the phone and call mommy."

"Did you ever call mommy?"

I took a punt, but it seemed obvious Vivien was a victim herself.

"Some mothers don't want to hear that kind of nonsense."

At that moment, Abby approached, extending her arms out to embrace Vivien.

"Dreadful, isn't it, darling?" said Vivien as the pair hugged. "Such a stupid damned waste."

Suddenly, I became aware of stirring voices behind me. I turned to see Elliott Wolfe flanked by three uniformed cops stepping determinedly through the crowd. His gaze was fixed ahead on someone over my shoulder, and I didn't have to guess who. I moved quickly to get to Strickland's side. As I did, I saw the expression on his face change as he watched Wolfe approach. It was like he was resigned to his fate yet felt disappointed Wolfe would exploit the moment so cheaply.

"Patrick Strickland, you are under arrest for the murder of Buddy Landry."

I'd seen this coming, but I didn't think Wolfe would be desperate enough to opt for the Hollywood production arrest.

Two other factors besides motive and proximity had compounded Strickland's suspicion. First, the DNA test had returned positive—it was all over Landry's body. Second, the gun Strickland said was in his desk drawer wasn't there when the cops looked. The only reasonable explanation he could offer Detective Wolfe was that someone might have stolen it during his birthday party. Given those developments, I knew Strickland's arrest was not a matter of if, but when.

I did what I could to dissuade him, but Wolfe insisted on cuffing Strickland out in the open. I took my jacket off and draped it over

Strickland's wrists, but it was a thin disguise. They led Strickland away, and he exited the cemetery in the back of a prowler. With lights flashing, the car moved slowly through the gauntlet of cameras before heading downtown on Santa Monica Boulevard.

I trusted Strickland was smart enough to take the advice I'd given him earlier.

"The first rule if you get arrested?" I told him. "Shut the fuck up. The cops won't be done building their case, so do not give them anything to add to the file.

"The second rule? Keep your mouth shut. The instant you open your mouth you'll be testifying against yourself. That friendly cell mate they put you with? Odds are he's an informant.

"But you could be in there for days. Months if they refuse you bail. So, if and when you absolutely have to open your mouth, stick to three topics and nothing else: sports, food and America's Got Talent."

When I told him this, Strickland nodded his head sternly. But he wasn't going to let me be the only one handing out orders.

"Madison," he said, pinning me with a steely glare. "If it does come to pass that I'm charged for this thing, I expect you to start showing me you're worth what I'm paying you. Now I may get out on bail, I may not, but either way my business and this whole *Sister Planet* project is going to come under immense pressure.

"I reckon I can hold it together for a few weeks tops. After that, no matter how innocent I am, I'm ruined. So here's the deal. If and when they cuff me, I'll be doubling your monthly rate. And I'll be offering you a bonus. The first million I have to put up for bail will be yours plus five percent of anything over."

I nodded my head. But I stemmed the urge to ask if he knew what he was offering. Of course he did. If the judge, like most, followed the bail schedule to a T, he would set bail at one million dollars. But if he thought that wasn't enough to curb Strickland's temptation to flee, he might set an amount no rich man could afford to lose. In some cases bail has hit thirty million.

"Are you sure you want to do that?"

He sat back in his chair.

"Yes. On one condition."

"What's that?"

"That you don't let this go to trial."

He paused like he knew he didn't have to say what he was about to say.

"You've got to find Buddy's killer."

CHAPTER 8

It was the kind of LA spring day you can pretty much bank on—cloudless and mild. Perfect for a little girl's birthday party. The day before, after Landry's funeral, I'd called Claire to break the ice. For the sake of Bella's party, I wanted to put our differences aside. There were a whole lot of issues we needed to run through on the divorce—like the terms of my access to Bella—but they could wait a while. Claire welcomed the truce and gave me a list of things to do. Just like old times.

I arrived at Claire's house in the morning and got to work setting things up in the yard—a bouncy castle, balloons and streamers. Claire and I stuck to party talk with Bella chiming in every second breath. My beautiful little girl was about to turn six. She'd grown so quickly, her sprouting limbs already making her tall for her age. Gone were the days when she was small enough to lie stretched out in my lap as we watched *Paw Patrol.*

When the castle was fully inflated, I called out to Bella and we christened it together. I then took a seat on the back steps while Bella ran inside to get changed into her party dress. I felt Claire's fingers touch my shoulder.

"She idolizes you," she said. "I'll never do anything to diminish that. You know that, right?"

I nodded as she sat down beside me. "Thanks. I only hope I won't do anything more to diminish that."

I could never shake from my head how I've scared Bella in the past with my PTSD crazes, and I dreaded it happening again.

"Brad, I'm sorry for what I said the other day. Look, she may not understand exactly what you go through now, but she will someday. Just be sure to never shut her out."

I nodded. We sat in silence for a few moments.

"How's the case going?" she asked.

I told her about the deal with Strickland. A million bucks if I absolved him of guilt before the trial started.

"Wow," she said. "That's some carrot. Not to mention the kudos involved for you. The papers can't seem to get enough of the case."

"And you? How's business?"

"Insane. But good insane."

She took a deep breath and turned to me.

"Please don't think too much about Tom, and please try not to hate me. The truth is he and I are not an item. I don't want a serious relationship right now. That's what I've had all my adult life. I've always relied on someone else—you. But now I'm in a position that I didn't really choose for myself. I was compelled to make choices I never ever thought I'd have to make. I'm still really hurting, I'm still really sad and I'm trying to sort all my emotions out, but going back is not the answer. I think we've had our time, Brad. We both need to embrace the change."

Through my own sadness, a sense of calm came over me. It was the relief of letting go of a whole bunch of hopeful stuff that had persisted in my head for so long—feeling it was my right, my duty, my calling to reclaim my family and my wife. I saw these now as illusions I'd held for my own sake. My feelings for Claire hadn't suddenly evaporated. But I sensed I could be pleased for her to be happy without me.

Mind you, this was the very dawn of acceptance. If some dude had walked up right then, put his arm around Claire, kissed her long and looked at me all chummy like we're all cool with this moving on shit, I'd have caved his teeth in.

I turned to Claire.

"It's good to see you doing so well. I'm happy for you. I really am."

We hugged it out. Then I stood up and went to hang the piñata.

✱✱✱

By one o'clock I was on my way to Landry's apartment in Canyon Drive, Hollywood. I'd arranged to meet Jack there to see if we could drum up any info from the neighbors. I parked straight across the street and scoped the place. It was a two-level Spanish building—white adobe walls, arches and curved terracotta tiles that looked straight out of a spaghetti western.

I crossed the street to begin looking for number four. I saw Jack pull up and waited.

"The kid earns fifteen gazillion and ends up here," said Jack by way of hello.

"At least he had something left to show for it."

"That's it there."

Jack was pointing at the upper level street-front apartment. A single flight of stairs led up to the front door from a small courtyard. I walked down the street a little and saw another flight led down from a rear door to the car park area. From the back street, I could see there were about twenty units in the complex.

"Let's get started."

We walked back around to the front entrance and split up—Jack door-knocking from one end of the ground level, me from the other. The first two residents I tried weren't in. On the next knock, a hunched but sharp-eyed man in his 70s appeared, dressed in a coffee-stained t-shirt and boxer shorts. The warm air that floated out from his apartment smelled of overripe fruit and dirty laundry.

The man was wary at first, but after I introduced and explained myself he got chatty, saying he never heard anything unusual because he was hard of hearing and kept the TV up loud.

"What I can tell you is I saw a fella on those stairs that Monday afternoon," he was pointing at the flight leading up to Landry's door.

"You sure it was then?"

"Yep, it was the day I missed half of *Ellen* looking for Black Jack— that's my damned cat."

"What'd the guy look like?"

"Short, kind of stocky. Maybe sixty."

"Have you spoken to anyone else about this?"

"You're the third person to come by asking about that kid. The first was a cop, the other was a reporter. And the only people I have less time for than cops is reporters."

"So you didn't tell them anything."

"I'm never rude, young man. As much as I'd like to tell them to go jump in the lake, I err towards my better nature. I just kept telling them I'm half deaf and don't get out much. They got bored and left."

I thanked him and left him alone.

After we'd finished Landry's block, we had only gleaned a couple more scraps of info. We then started on the apartment block behind. Five levels of ten apartments each. Half the residents weren't there and the rest had nothing solid to contribute. About forty minutes later we regrouped on the back street.

"I'll come back again tonight and call on the ones who weren't in," said Jack.

Just then a Latino man in his thirties approached us from the block we'd just left.

"You the guys asking questions about the murder?"

His tone was tough. It was hard to tell if he wanted to fight or talk.

"That's right," I said.

I told him I was defending the accused and introduced Jack.

"The name's Carlos. I saw a car pull up here that afternoon, right where you're standing."

"What sort of car?"

"Real nice. It was a big coupe. White. Not sure of the make—could have been a Jag or something foreign and fancy like that. All bright and shiny like it was straight outta the lot. But it was a beast. It freakin roared when it took off. Man, that thing was the beauty *and* the beast."

"Did you see who was driving?" I asked.

"A guy got out and walked up Canyon Drive towards the corner. About half an hour later he was back."

"Was there anything suspicious about his behavior? Like, was he in a hurry to leave?"

"Not that I could tell. No, he just kinda strolled back and got in like he'd been visiting his aunty."

"He wasn't looking around to see if anyone was watching?"

"No. It wasn't like that."

"You didn't catch the plates?"

The man shook his head and pointed up to his apartment.

"Not from that angle."

I thanked him and got his number in case we needed to reach him again. Carlos returned to his block, and we began to walk back to our cars.

As we reached the sidewalk, Jack stopped and tapped my arm. He was looking up toward Landry's place. A couple was standing on the sidewalk looking up at Landry's apartment. The woman was holding a bunch of flowers. It was Wilfred and Layla Landry.

We approached slowly. The two of them appeared to be in prayer. They crossed their chests, and then Layla set the flowers down at the foot of the steps. She then took a handkerchief from her sleeve and dabbed her nose and eyes.

Jack and I kept a respectful distance. Wilfred put his arm around Layla's shoulder and pulled her closer. They stood there for a minute or so and then turned to leave.

They seemed more resigned than surprised to find someone watching them. Little wonder, given the media frenzy they'd been subjected to since arriving in LA to bury their famous son. Perhaps the only surprise was that neither Jack nor I had a camera pointed at them.

"Mr. and Mrs. Landry, I'm terribly sorry for your loss. I'm Brad Madison. I'm defending Patrick Strickland, who, as I'm sure you know, has been charged with Buddy's murder."

They both remained silent and wary. Then Wilfred spoke.

"If you don't mind, we'd rather be left alone."

He looked at me as though by common decency I would stand aside and let them be. I just couldn't.

"I completely understand, Mr. Landry. But while you may think I'm defending Buddy's killer, my mission is to find out the truth. Because Patrick Strickland is not responsible for this crime, and I need to find out who is."

Wilfred nodded.

"I don't believe Mr. Strickland did this. He did so much for Buddy. He had a real soft spot for the boy."

"Then would you mind if I asked you a few questions?"

Wilfred looked at his watch.

"We need to be heading to the airport, son. We're going home."

I offered to drive them to the airport but they said they had a hire car.

"Of course. Look, it won't take long, I promise. Can I buy you a coffee?"

The grief-weary couple relented. There was a Denny's nearby, and we took a booth looking out onto Sunset. Wilfred and Layla sat opposite Jack and me. With cups of coffee to sip on, they were a little more at ease.

"We used to take Buddy to the Denny's in Lumberton as a treat," said Layla. "He could just about eat his height in pancakes."

Once we got chatting they began telling us how they'd never been able to have children despite being desperate for a family. They put the disappointment behind them for many years. But then, when they were in their early fifties, their nephew Jake Hayes was killed in a car crash. They'd only come to know Jake two years before when he contacted them out of the blue. He told them he'd become a dad and that they were his only remaining family. Over regular phone calls they got to know and grow fond of Jake. They exchanged photos but never met until Jake said he was planning to visit with three-year-old Buddy. They never made it. Jake was killed in a car crash the day before they were supposed to leave. But he had prepared a will which requested that in the event of his death he wanted Wilfred and Layla Landry, if they were willing, to take custody of his son, whose legal name was Aaron. The will explained the boy's mother had disappeared and made no attempt to make contact for two years. Jake wanted his son to have a loving home.

The God-fearing Landrys didn't think twice. They moved quickly to apply for custody. The family court's efforts to find the birth mother came to nothing, and the Landrys were granted legal custody. They continued to call the boy Buddy as a tribute to his father, who never referred to him as Aaron. Jake had explained that Buddy was more apt because that's how he saw the young boy in every way—his lifelong pal.

They told us about Buddy's love of acting and of bringing him to LA. How thrilled and proud they were. But big problems followed, like how to manage both the farm and Buddy's skyrocketing acting career. Initially, both had accompanied Buddy to Los Angeles, and the three of them stayed in the Oakwood Apartments in Burbank, which was full of starry-eyed kids and aspiring actors. But with the frequency and length of LA's demands, they settled on Layla accompanying Buddy while Wilfred stayed at home to run the farm.

They met Jerry Newman, who seemed such a gentle, likable man that they were happy, on Mr. Strickland's recommendation, to hire him as Buddy's manager. But Wilfred's heart problems began soon after. Then all of a sudden Buddy was a household name around the world and about the biggest star in Hollywood. They could not make hide nor hair of the multitude of deals that came Buddy's way and were grateful to Mr. Newman for handling the business side of things. He was able to explain everything very simply and clearly, and the money was pouring in—more than they knew what to do with. Still, because of Wilfred's illness, Layla could not leave him alone, so they took Jerry up on his offer to accommodate Buddy and look after him. They effectively entrusted him with the role of guardian.

Wilfred shook his head.

"We made a big mistake. We were overwhelmed by the whole process. Buddy was like this child emperor who had Hollywood literally bowing down before him."

"It was utter madness," Layla said. "But in a wonderful, surreal kind of way; like winning the lottery."

"We didn't know anything about the dangers lurking beneath the surface," said Wilfred. "We're not fools, but we were too trusting of all those nice smiles, flattery and big promises. We only really began to see the dark side after it was too late."

"What do you mean, Wilfred?"

Wilfred bowed his head and swallowed hard. He looked up again with tear-filled eyes.

"After a while Buddy would call us to say he did not want to live at Jerry's anymore. He wouldn't say why. But he didn't sound like himself. I don't know if he was taking drugs at that stage, but sometimes his speech would be slurred. Occasionally, he'd be in tears saying he just wanted to come home. Then when he did come back, he seemed to hate the farm.

"So it ended up he had to live in Los Angeles full time because there was one movie after another and all the related commitments that went with it.

"We sought Mr. Strickland's help, and he said there was a cottage on his property Buddy could use and we gave it our blessing."

Wilfred said Buddy seemed happy with the move but, though they didn't know it at the time, his life had already started to go off the rails. Then, just after he'd turned sixteen, Buddy took the Landrys to court to get full legal control over his income. They were shocked by the move but could no longer engage the boy in conversation. They were forced to hand over millions they had banked for his future, and they didn't see another cent.

Once the financial matters were settled, they didn't hear from Buddy for years. They were heartbroken and blamed themselves but prayed every night that Buddy would call with the will to repair their relationship.

"That never happened, unfortunately," said Wilfred.

"Did Buddy ever explain why he didn't want to live with Jerry anymore?"

This question seemed to be more than the Landrys could bear. Their faces filled with such remorse they were literally lost for words. After almost a minute, it was Layla who spoke.

"We are just humble farm folk, but we got an education in things we never wanted to know. Terrible things. We didn't know just how evil people could be. We know now what they did to Buddy—and by they I mean Jerry Newman and his friends—and it cuts deep down to our very souls to think we're responsible for that. God forgive us, we were deceived by dazzling lights and flattery, and we fooled ourselves into thinking what we were doing was in Buddy's best interests. But we fed our boy to wolves. It is only by clinging to the good Lord's strength that I can even draw breath."

"We should have just kept him on the farm. He was happy there," Wilfred said. He checked his watch.

"We must go, dear. Mr. Madison, I'm not sure we've been much use to you, but we believe Mr. Strickland is innocent. We wish you luck."

We walked them to their car and saw them off. It was good to know they were leaving. They were too damn good for this city.

CHAPTER 9

The day of Strickland's arraignment, I ran into assistant DA Lawrence Lewis outside a cafe round the corner from my office. It was like running into a cover of *GQ* magazine. He's one impressively groomed dude—tall, lean, handsome and snow-white teeth.

But that only scrapes the surface of his magnificence. Lewis had brains to burn and enough drive to arm a revolution. One of Stanford Law's finest exports, Lewis liked playing jazz piano, wearing three-piece suits and wowing jurors with silver-tongued sermons. His career was so full of promise you could imagine him one day making Obama look like an underachiever.

The puritan streak in him was strong. Whatever was in that grande cup he was holding, I bet it wasn't anything as crude as coffee. More like some kind of Himalayan tea infusion primed with a shot of goji berry shavings or quinoa seed oil. His idea of winding down was a three-hour kick-boxing workout. I'd seen him go at it in the gym. And he could be as devastating in court as he was on the heavy bag. With sound and fury, he could make even the most circumstantial of evidence seem damning. So all up, Lewis was the kind of guy I loved to beat.

We stopped and talked briefly. Lewis knew I'd be applying for bail, and I knew he'd be strenuously opposing it. Typically, I wouldn't hold much hope of getting bail for a client charged with murder. But Strickland wasn't the usual suspect. Had no criminal pedigree whatsoever. And there would be no case for Lewis to argue, unlike other clients I've had, that his bail funds would be sourced from criminal activity.

When I said something to that effect, Lewis smiled and confidently predicted that, regardless, Strickland's bail would be denied. So I took the opportunity to remind him of Phil Spector, the famous music producer who was alone in his Alhambra mansion with an actress he'd picked up from the House of Blues when the woman was then fatally shot in the mouth. Spector walked out with a gun and said to his driver, "I think I've killed someone." A couple of days later, he was out on one million dollars' bail. The way I saw it, if I couldn't get Strickland out on bail, I should give the game away.

Still, I hadn't made any promises to Strickland. Luckily for him, the judge was Meredith Gleeson, a very smart, fair operator who wouldn't be swayed by the baying media, political pressure from her higher ups or Lawrence Lewis's artful character assassination.

When the hearing came, we pleaded not guilty to first degree murder and requested bail. Lewis stood up and declared Strickland was a cold-blooded killer, a vengeful man inclined to do everything in his power to ensure his new multi-million-dollar movie project would not be derailed by scandal. The police, Lewis told Judge Gleeson, had a strong case against him. He had made dire threats, witnesses placed him at the scene at the estimated time of Landry's death, his DNA was found on the body and while the murder weapon had not yet been found it was very much like Mr. Strickland's, which just happened to have mysteriously gone missing around the time of the murder.

Lewis also went as far as to argue witnesses in Strickland's upcoming trial would have reason to fear for their safety with him at large. Then there was the fact that Strickland had the money and means to make himself disappear. During Lewis's quite gripping three-minute monologue, I wondered what it might be like for Strickland to sit there and listen to some eloquent stranger portray you so convincingly as a menace to society.

Of course, I argued the public had no reason to fear Strickland. I also made it patently clear it made no sense for Strickland to flee. His future was tied to his work. He had every reason to stay and prove his innocence because everything now depended on it. Strickland's liberty, wealth and standing all hung on his ability to clear his name. His reputation had already taken a massive hit since being charged, but he was an innocent man thrown into the most testing circumstances. I said we were resolved to prove his innocence and the judge could have every faith Strickland would dutifully meet all bail obligations.

"I'm granting Mr. Strickland bail," Judge Gleeson said before fixing an eye on me. "But I don't think one million dollars is sufficient to keep a man of Mr. Strickland's worth attentive to the seriousness of the offense with which he has been charged. Bail is set at five million dollars."

"Thank you, Your Honor," I said.

We'd had contingencies for paying up to ten million, so it was some relief for the figure to be half that. It was a small victory but an important one. Strickland looked relieved and thanked me.

"So now, as the deal stands, you stand to make $1.2 million if you get these charges dropped."

I was packing my briefcase.

"I won't pretend that that didn't occur to me. But we've got work to do."

"Come back to the studio."

Outside the court, Strickland walked up to a car. But this was not just any old car; it was a gleaming white Rolls Royce Wraith. Costing about three-hundred grand, this was a motorhead's wet dream: a phenomenally powerful 6.6-liter, twin-turbo V12 engine that could zip its plush leather-and-walnut cabin around at speeds of up to 160 miles an hour.

As Strickland stood there, the door opened of its own accord and he stepped in. I bent down to see who was driving. I found Freddie Baxter looking straight back at me. He ignored my greeting nod, and once Strickland was in he wasted no time getting out of there, flooring the beast to life.

***

We were seated at an outside table out the back of Strickland's bungalow. Ms. Maybury had gotten the lot's catering service to bring us lunch and called us outside when it was all laid out.

"You're not one of these people who hate seafood, are you?" Strickland asked, dipping a shrimp into cocktail sauce.

It appeared Hannah had simply ordered what she knew Strickland would like and doubled it. Not that I was complaining. I assured him a meal of fresh oysters, shrimp and lobster was fine with me.

"Good. I've got no time for people who say they hate seafood. Appetite's like a handshake. It reveals character. I don't mind if you're into all that paleo, gluten-free baloney, but refusing seafood is the sign of a closed mind and timid character."

Strickland poured out two glasses of Riesling and put the bottle back on ice. Then his phone rang. He looked at the screen like he was in half a mind to let it go to voicemail.

"I need to take this. Excuse me."

He took a sip, tapped the phone and walked back inside to his office. Five minutes later he returned looking grim. And angry.

"Gutless piece of shit," he said, putting his phone down on the table and picking up his glass.

"That was Conrad Stone, head of Castlight."

"What did he have to say?"

"Take a look."

Strickland pointed at his phone. I picked it up and saw a *Counterspin* article displayed. It was headlined, 'Is murder-accused Strickland about to get shunted by Castlight chief?' According to a source, Jared Cohen wrote, Stone was uncomfortable having Strickland on the lot. The source said he or she had it on good

94

authority that *Sister Planet* would be put on ice, Strickland would be sacked and he and his production company would be evicted. It also suggested, citing the source again, that Danny Shapiro was being approached to take the reins of *Sister Planet*.

When I was done reading, I handed the phone to Strickland.

"So what did Stone say to you just now?"

"He said the article was a pack of lies. That he was going to 'sue those *Counterspin* bastards out of business.' He was saying, 'We're sticking with you, Pat. We know you're innocent, Pat.' And all that BS. But then comes the clincher. He said it might be in everyone's best interests if we park *Sister Planet* till all this blows over."

"And that's not a good idea?"

"Hell, no. That's exactly the way they can take it off me."

He stood there thinking for a second before speaking again.

"Stone's a lying son-of-a-bitch. If it's a choice between his word and that of that piece-of-shit article, then I'd take the article. It just rings true. God help me, I'd burn the whole project to cinders rather than see Shapiro get credit for it. He's circling me like a vulture."

I could see the pain it caused him to only briefly contemplate Shapiro getting hold of his baby. He picked up an oyster, tilted his head back to swallow it and dropped the shell back on the plate. He grabbed a napkin to wipe his mouth and hands.

"I need to get to work. The only way I can hang on to *Sister Planet* is if the cast sticks with me."

"I assume contracts are signed already?"

"That's the problem. Last week I had a queue of Hollywood's biggest names wanting to sign—George Carrick, Tommy de Franco, Kurt Whitelock, Susanne Casey, Judy Barton... hell, you name it— but all the schedule details need to be ironed out before we put ink to paper."

Each of those names could command more than ten million a movie. The budget for *Sister Planet* must be phenomenal. Strickland was deep in strategy mode.

"I need to focus on George. If I can lock him in, the rest will fall into place. And there's no way George will flake on me. He'd still be a frickin' pizza delivery boy if it weren't for me and he knows it."

He looked at the lobster like he'd forgotten it was there.

"Now that's just too good to go to waste."

He piled some onto a small plate and made to leave.

"Patrick. Before you do anything else, we need to discuss your case."

He stopped in his tracks but still looked unconvinced about my choice of priorities. Having switched into movie producer mode, it was like he'd forgotten he was facing life in prison.

"Okay. Yes, of course."

He returned to the table and took a seat. It was strange to see him amenable to someone else telling him what to do.

"What do you want to know?"

"Who would want to set you up for murder, for starters."

"Who would want to frame me? How long have you got?"

He put his elbows on the table and took a bite of lobster. He shook his head as he chewed, then sipped his wine and gave me a rueful smile.

"I couldn't even walk two yards in this lot without bumping into someone who wanted to see me fall."

"I thought you ruled this place. I thought people were glued to you. If what little I saw at your party was any indication, you're revered by half of Hollywood."

"Bullshit. Oh yes, they showered me with affection. It was beautiful. But it wasn't loyalty and it wasn't love. That's just the raw currency of Hollywood—the promise of fame, or the promise of more of it. Yes, when you've got something like *Sister Planet*, every actor in this town would line up for days just to feed me grapes.

"You've got no idea of the desperation that drives success in this place. Yes, the whole movie-making thing is a creative blast but beneath all that talent—genius even—is junkyard-dog tenacity and craven insecurity. Early success, that initial joy you get when you first make it in this industry, is a relief. We savor that with the required humility, but then holding onto success becomes obsessive—despite our better selves, we all end up junkies for fame and fortune."

Strickland picked up a fork and prodded at his plate. It was the most honest and reflective I'd seen him. A little sad even.

"Patrick, if I'm going to find the real killer, I need alternative suspects."

The fire snapped straight back into him.

"Well, that article's a good start. Danny Shapiro."

Strickland ran me through their competitive relationship, much of which I'd heard from Abby.

"You could call it a rivalry, but I honestly don't see it that way."

"But you snatched the *Sister Planet* movie rights from under his nose, as I understand it."

He raised an eyebrow.

"Now who told you that?"

"Does it matter?"

"Of course. Abby."

"If it's true, then I'd say you and Shapiro are fierce rivals."

"He fell asleep at the wheel negotiating the film rights with the author, Gordon Banks. And thanks to Vivien I was able to swoop in and sign Banks up."

"Vivien?"

"Yes, she and Banks were friends in some past life, and when I mentioned the book to her one night she told me they were old friends. So we both took him out to lunch. I gave him the grand vision of wild success, but it was Vivien who really sealed the deal. Banks was putty in her hands."

"But now Shapiro is maneuvering to take control?"

"I'd bet my house on it. It would be the ultimate win-win for him—he becomes King Hollywood while I'm rotting in jail. But I'll always have an ace up my sleeve."

"What's that?"

"The book option. It's mine. They can't make *Sister Planet* without me."

CHAPTER 10

I cut the Mustang ignition in the basement car park and texted Abby to tell her I'd arrived.

"Tenth floor. Meet you in the lobby," came the reply.

I got out of the car and followed a sign to the elevator. Inside, next to the tenth-floor button, was a brass plate with "Chelsea House" engraved in capital letters.

Chelsea House was a members-only club that had been around for five years or so in West Hollywood. In that time it had built quite a name for itself. It was famous not just for who it let in but who it refused. The club courted creative types as opposed to just anyone with money, power and/or fame. It was a place where a scriptwriter could hang out to type or talk away the day without having to order anything more than a glass of water. For an establishment to apply a discerning eye that excluded some powerbrokers was Hollywood heresy, but it worked. Everyone who was anyone wanted to be accepted as a member. And if news got out that some brash bigwig's membership application had been declined, it was reported with barely concealed glee.

One thing above all else gave the club its true cred: discretion. Taking photos inside was banned, which meant it was a paparazzi-free zone, and there were no autograph hunters. Breach anyone's privacy and your membership was canceled—it didn't matter how many Oscars or Emmys or Grammys you had to your name.

The other thing I knew about the place was it didn't like suits. That meant not just the outfits themselves but the professionals whose occupation demanded they wear them. So Wall Street brokers and, hell, workaday defense attorneys like me, were not considered member material. I approached feeling like a gatecrasher.

The elevator doors opened and Abby greeted me with a smile. She looked me up and down and seemed impressed by my appearance. I put it down to the tailored sports coat. We walked towards the bar, stopping for her to sign me in to the satisfaction of the doorman.

"Let's grab a drink, shall we?"

"Great," I said. "Something tells me it's beer o'clock. Or will ordering a beer get me kicked out?"

"No, that's fine, so long as you're not after Bud or Coors. It's all craft brew."

"I can live with that."

We entered a bar that some interior designer must have pocketed a fortune for putting together. The eclectic array of seats, lamps, lounge chairs and tables, polished timber floor and wood-paneled bar all came together with a warm, nostalgic effect. It was a perfect blend of modern and vintage. The vibe was mellow, classy and very cool. And quiet. It just felt discreet. We sat in two wingback chairs with a low table between us.

"This is quite something," I said. "I understand they're pretty fussy about who they let into this place."

"That's why I asked you to meet me here."

"No snitches, right?"

"You'd be amazed. This place is like a vault. Everyone here knows to keep their mouths shut about what they see."

"Really? This is *Counterspin* proof? I find that hard to believe."

"If anyone—staff or members—gets sprung for leaking something they saw here to the media, they're out. And no one wants to lose their access to this place. Believe me. It's a safe house."

A waiter came to our table. I ordered a pale ale, Abby an Aperol spritz. Neither of us spoke for a few seconds. Then I felt the need to break the silence.

"So, do you feel comfortable enough to continue the conversation we had at the service?"

She smiled but only just. She seemed nervous.

"Easy, tiger. We only just got here."

I regretted coming across as impatient. She had intimated that Shapiro and others posed an imminent threat to me, and I wanted to know why. That's why I'd called her. And that's exactly why we were here. But I was happy to put that conversation on ice. I had to lighten the mood.

"Sorry, it's not every day you have a date with a movie star."

"Is that what you think this is?"

"No, but you never know. Play your cards right and it could be."

She laughed.

"Aren't you married?"

It hadn't occurred to me to take off my wedding ring.

"Yes, but it's now official," I grinned wryly. "We're getting divorced."

I took a sip of beer before continuing.

"I enjoyed talking with you at Patrick's party."

"I did too."

"But your friend Baxter didn't seem to like me much."

"He doesn't like anyone much."

"Well, he seems to like you a lot. Like, breakfast-lunch-and-dinner a lot. And he seemed to want to run me out of town just for talking to you."

She toyed with her straw.

"Freddie and I are just friends."

"Is he that possessive with all his friends? Struck me as an odd piece of work. Or maybe that's his British charm."

"Yes, he is eccentric but also very sweet."

"He's very tight with the Stricklands. What is he, their butler?"

Abby gave me a look of mild admonishment.

"No. Freddie's a man of many talents, and he's made himself indispensable to the Stricklands. The word is he was a hunting guide for Patrick in Africa. They were on foot somewhere when a male lion sprang out from the scrub and charged at Patrick. Freddie shot it as it lunged, and it dropped dead at Patrick's feet. They got to know each other and became friends. He used to be in the SAS, you know. He told Patrick a few stories, and Patrick was so impressed he thought he could make a movie out of them. So, naturally, Freddie came to LA."

If only I had a dollar for every soldier I'd met who thought his war stories should be on the big screen.

"So now he's a scriptwriter?"

"Among other things, I guess. He still lives in South Africa but spends a few months in LA doing stunt work and developing his script. He's got his own place but spends a lot of time with the Stricklands."

"He and Vivien seem to get on very well."

I said this in a light-hearted way, a bit of saucy innuendo. But it fell flat on Abby. She was getting bored. She leaned forward.

"Enough of Freddie. I'm going to go powder my nose. Order me another one of these, will you? And while I'm gone, think of something better to talk about."

I watched her go. A minute after she disappeared around the corner, I saw someone I recognized appear at the entrance to the bar. It was Danny Shapiro. He had company—another man—and they paused briefly to look the bar over before moving on.

My curiosity got the better of me. I got to my feet and followed them to a large dining area and watched as they were escorted to a table. Shapiro's companion was in his late forties, weedy build, about five-six. He wore round glasses and had his long black hair pulled back in a ponytail. I had no idea who he was, but I wanted to find out. I took out my phone, switched on the camera, started recording video and pretended to take a call. I then walked past the pair's table, angled the phone towards them as I passed, stopped briefly before moving on.

On my way back to the bar I sent the video to Jack.

"Who's this with Shapiro?" I wrote.

I caught a waiter near our table and placed my order. I'd just sat down when Abby returned. I decided to keep my questions to one topic and one topic only: Abby Hatfield.

What I already knew was that she had moved to Hollywood as a teenager, having convinced her parents to back her dreams by presenting them with a video. It was a series of her playing different roles—all making a case for her to pursue her acting career. In it she played her drama teacher, school principal, a fictitious agent, and then various impersonations: Jodie Foster, Meryl Streep, Julia Roberts and a hilarious Quentin Tarantino. The common thread was that young Abby Hatfield had the talent, brains, drive, resilience and maturity—not to mention looks—to forge a successful acting career. All up, it was the soundest of logic for her parents to allow her to make the move. There was no reason why she could not continue her education by home-schooling, try out for roles and, hopefully, get cast all at once. And she convinced her parents that starting young did not have to be a story of early burn-out and exploitation. Her parents were sold, and she and her mom moved to LA. Straight away, Abby took a job at Staples to help out with the money. After eighteen months and too many rejections to count, she got her first role: a small part in a feature film. More roles followed over the years, then at seventeen she was given the starring role in another teen comedy lauded by both box office and critics. That's when she really got noticed.

But now, in her mid-twenties, her star, while not exactly falling, was no longer on the rise. A lead role in *Sister Planet* would certainly fix that.

Abby opened up to me on the vagaries of fame and fortune. It could be wonderfully exciting at times, but creatively it was a high-wire act. The script you and your agent loved could turn out to be a stinker of a film. So long as there was another offer on the horizon, there was always the opportunity to put the crap movie behind you. After a while her voice trailed off and she stared out towards the window.

"I can't believe Buddy's gone."

"When did you two meet?"

I was glad to see she didn't mind me asking. She said they'd met on the set of her second movie, in which she played Landry's younger sister. They got on really well, and while nothing happened initially, they later dated for a short time when Landry was at his peak. It did her profile wonders to be linked to him romantically, but they were still kids.

It was a wild ride but mostly in an innocent way. They had private areas of clubs set up pretty much just for them, a bunch of rich and famous teens who could party unsupervised and dance all night. Abby said while she did not drink, Buddy did, and he began dabbling in pot and ecstasy. Her mom saw danger in their relationship and gave Abby an ultimatum—stop seeing Landry or we pack up and go home. Abby had the sense to call it off and knuckle down. If Landry was the poster boy for how to grow up wrong in Hollywood, Abby was the role model for how to survive. But they stayed in touch, and that was how she eventually met Strickland, through Landry.

"I'd go over and hang at Buddy's house, the one Patrick let him use. I hoped Patrick would be the one to help Buddy get his life together."

"Did Buddy ever talk about being abused?"

"No, never. But I guess it was probably something he never wanted to admit to."

Abby was getting upset.

"Abby, at the funeral you said there were others who might want Landry dead. Who do you mean?"

"Well, there's that loathsome snake Newman. For God knows how long, he's been preying on young boys and just gets away with it. You know, he plays the kind-hearted friend, the well-connected facilitator, but he's the goddamn devil. And to this day, he's the top child actor manager in town. Parents are beating a path to his door, and producers and directors all use him without giving it a second thought."

"As horrible as that is, the question I need to focus on is would he be capable of murdering Buddy?"

"Who knows? But with Buddy running around making a lot of noise, threatening his virtual monopoly of the child actor trade, maybe he figured he had to."

"At the funeral you were angry. Who else besides Strickland could be a suspect? I need names, Abby."

She paused to think, which was weird, because at the cemetery she looked like she could reel off a list of names. Maybe she'd thought better of sharing her suspicions. That made me wonder—if she was putting Newman's name forward, who was she protecting?

Landry had mentioned two others: Gabe Finlay and Randall Webster. Both men, Jack told me, were said to like young boys, and both were linked to the mysterious, but quite possibly fictitious, Titan Club.

"What about Finlay and Webster?"

Abby shook her head like she wasn't buying it.

"No idea. The thing you've got to remember when names get flung around is everyone in this town has something to gain from someone else's downfall. You know the word schadenfreude? Kind of quaint how the Germans actually saw fit to create a word to describe that warm little glow you feel in your heart when someone else falls flat on their face. Schadenfreude. I think it's a beautiful word. It may have been invented in Europe but Hollywood owns it now. It's ours, baby."

She was stalling.

"But there's no one else? You seemed to have some concrete ideas about who the murderer could be. You actually told me to be careful. Who should I be careful of, Abby?"

Abby's discomfort was obvious.

"Well, I had a lot of strange ideas floating around in my head that day, and I was angry and wanted someone to blame."

She leaned closer towards me and lowered her voice.

"But the more I think about it, the more I think it's possible Patrick did it."

I put my drink down and leaned back in my chair. There was a conspicuous lack of conviction in her voice. She was lying. And that surprised me. And it gave me second thoughts as to why she had agreed to meet me.

"What's going on, Abby? You suggested to me there were a few people you suspected."

"There were but—"

"Well, can we start with them instead of my client?"

"I really don't want to go there."

"You mean you don't want to go there anymore."

I moved in closer and kept my voice down.

106

"What about Shapiro?"

Her eyes pinched ever so slightly.

"Bingo. I'm going to assume that's the name at the top of your list."

"You know what they say about assumptions, don't you? I never said I suspected Danny."

"Oh, Danny, is it? And just how well do you know Danny?"

"Everyone knows Danny."

I was getting tired of her evasiveness.

"Abby, what the hell's going on? Do I have to remind you that Strickland is looking at spending the rest of his life in prison for a murder he did not commit?"

"You don't know that for sure, though. Do you?"

I paused. She was right. All I had now was Strickland's word for it. And to be honest, I wasn't utterly convinced. The way he had played me, I just never felt absolutely certain he was on the level. And maybe the prospect of me walking away with a cool million dollars plus change had blinded me to the possibility that he was guilty. But in his favor was the fact that there were too many gray areas. And I couldn't discard the thought that there were other people who had just as much to gain from Landry's death as Strickland did.

"No, I don't know that, but I also know that you're not being straight with me. I want to know more about Shapiro. Is he the reason you told me to be careful?"

Abby lowered her eyes. She took a nervous sip.

My phone buzzed. It was a message from Jack: "It's Gordon Banks. *Sister Planet* author."

Shapiro was making a play for the book rights. Strickland seemed to think he could never be dispossessed of them. Maybe he was wrong.

"Is something wrong?" Abby asked. She'd caught me staring mid-distance.

"Abby, you know why I started asking about Shapiro?"

"No, why?"

"Because he's here. When you went to the restroom, I saw him walk in."

Abby stiffened.

"What?"

"He's right next door having lunch. Maybe you should go ask Danny to come join us for a drink."

Abby looked flustered and more than a little scared. She reached for her handbag.

"This was a mistake. I'm sorry. I don't know what I was thinking."

"I thought you were thinking you wanted justice for your friend Buddy."

Her head seemed to be swimming.

"I do. I do. I just…"

"What?"

"We have to get out of here."

"What are you frightened of?"

"I'm such an idiot."

"What are you talking about?"

"I came here precisely because I knew Shapiro wasn't a member."

"Well, he's here as a guest. He's with Gordon Banks."

Abby paused, not sure of what she should say. But I was getting the impression she was about to confess something she was not proud of. Guilt was written all over her face.

"He approached me."

"Who? Gordon Banks?"

"No, Danny. He's asked me to—"

I saved her the anguish. "Jump ship. I see. He wants to take over *Sister Planet* and secure all the talent Strickland's lined up. Has he signed you up?"

Abby shook her head.

"I'm not disloyal. I'm not sure about Patrick's innocence, but I told Danny the least I could do was wait and see if he clears his name."

"I think that's a wise move."

We made for the elevator.

"Well, Danny didn't."

"Let me guess—he gave you the 'you'll never work in this town again' line?"

The elevator door opened. Abby stepped in and pressed the basement button impatiently. She said nothing.

"You don't know Danny Shapiro or you wouldn't make a joke like that."

"Did he threaten you? Is that what you're saying?"

"Not quite. With *Sister Planet* in limbo, he can't burn his bridges. He still needs to deploy his abundant charm."

We reached the basement.

"But if he gets the movie, he will remember I hesitated, and he will destroy me."

"You're serious?"

She stepped out.

"Do I look like I'm joking?"

I took her arm to slow her down.

"Abby, I need to know more. It's vital for the case. Can we go somewhere else to talk?"

She nodded.

"Sure. My place."

*** ***

The North Elm Drive address Abby gave me was not far from Chelsea House. I took my time to make sure Abby got there first. When I arrived, I buzzed the intercom at the security gate.

"Hey. Go straight ahead. Down the garden path, literally. Then take a left and up the stairs. Number six."

"Okay. I think I got it."

On either side of the cobblestoned path were hanging plants and small water features. It was dead quiet and tranquil. The bustle of the Sunset strip just a few hundred yards away felt like another world.

I turned as instructed and followed the steps up to number six. Abby stepped onto the landing as I climbed.

"Hey. Welcome to chez Hatfield."

"Man, I feel like I'm in Costa Rica. It's so green and light here."

"That's what I love about it."

She shut the door behind me and walked through to the kitchen.

"You want another beer? I was thinking of opening a bottle of red."

"Sounds good to me."

I took a look around. The place was quite small, homey, clean and neat. There was a predominance of Scandinavian style furniture which would have cost a small fortune, but overall there was no real sense of ostentation or wealth. I was a little surprised. It was the kind of place you'd expect a regular twenty-something professional to be living in. I guess I had an expectation that because Abby was a movie star, everything about her lifestyle would be over-the-top impressive. That her place felt like a humble home was a reminder for me to leave my preconceptions at the door.

Abby emerged with two glasses and a bottle. She put them on the coffee table, picked up a remote control to get some music playing and then poured. She handed me a glass. I could see from the label it was French.

"I take it you don't mind a Bordeaux?"

"Not at all."

Abby sat back in her chair. She was at last relaxed.

"Sorry about freaking out a little back there. But Danny—God, he's a piece of work. And I can't really afford to piss him off right now."

"I understand."

"You know, I'd like to think Patrick is innocent but, sorry, I have my doubts. I'm kind of stuck right now. I don't want to abandon Patrick, and I don't want to incur Danny's wrath. He would make my life hell."

"Seriously?"

"You have no idea of the power that man wields. Before Patrick was charged, he was number one, no question. But even if Danny is playing second fiddle, second fiddle in Hollywood gives you God-like power. He does whatever the hell he wants. In every way—who he screws, who he screws over, who he hires and fires, who he bullies and threatens and hassles and, occasionally, charms. This town dances to his tune. And the reason he gets away with it? He makes beautiful films that win people's hearts, that win Academy Awards and that make actors' careers. But they are magnificent films made by unhappy people."

Abby went on to list the people he'd bullied, the women he'd demeaned, the directors he'd belittled, the actors he'd humiliated and the crews he'd sacked. He could charm the pants off actors he wanted to sign but made it his personal mission to destroy them if he was turned down.

This was power that ran deep and wide. If you were blacklisted by Shapiro, no producer would hire you, no director would go to bat for you, no lead actor would let you be cast lest they get fingered themselves. You'd be lucky to even crack an independent film. That's how insular the vast empire of Hollywood could be.

"Hey, I wanted to ask. Were you friends with Emilio Peralta?"

She looked puzzled.

"Yes, we were good friends. Why are you asking?"

I told her about Buddy's visit and the video he gave me. While I had nothing solid yet, it seemed Peralta was trying to gather evidence to expose Jerry Newman, and perhaps others, as a pedophile. But I thought it might go deeper than that. Suppose the Titan Club was real? What if that was what Peralta was trying to expose? And what if Buddy was helping him? And if Shapiro was a member, that would give him reason not only to kill Peralta but Landry as well.

"That may be taking it a bit too far, but from what I know, some of what you are saying is true. Emilio did want to out Newman and his sordid parties. I knew he was trying to get whatever footage he could on them."

"So you guys were close."

"As only kids can be. God, they were special days. It was wonderful. Emilio, Buddy, Julian Dobson and me, we had LA at our feet and were starring together in great movies. In life and in films, we were living our own *Breakfast Club*. But then our careers all took different tangents. Buddy's went down, Emilio's went out, Julian's flatlined and mine..."

"Yours went up."

Abby said that although the friends didn't hang out with each other like they used to, the depth of feeling was still there.

"I miss them terribly. After Emilio disappeared, I felt like I'd lost a brother. He was so warm and generous and kind to me. And funny."

"You said disappeared. I thought he was murdered."

Abby nodded, then took a deep breath and held it in.

"Yeah, I know. I know. But, and this may sound crazy, part of me thinks he's still alive."

"Do you mean that's what you prefer to think? Because he's not alive, is he? I'm sorry if that upsets you, but since I've been on this case that's the way everybody talks about Emilio."

She stayed silent. I pressed on.

"Buddy was convinced Strickland murdered Emilio."

"Well, that's what Buddy thinks."

Abby stood up and walked over to some shelves on the wall opposite. She picked up a framed photo, came back and handed it to me. I looked at the photo. It was Landry, Peralta, Dobson and Abby.

"That's us in Mexico, on vacation."

"It's a lovely photo. Happy times."

Abby leaned towards me. She was so close the smell of her perfume carried the warmth of her skin.

"Here."

She took the frame from me, unlocked the back and removed the print.

"Look at the back."

I flipped the photo around. On the back someone had written a couple of poetic lines relating youth to diamonds.

I looked at Abby.

"Am I missing something? Is there a message here?"

113

She shook her head.

"It's the lyrics of a song. 'Forever Young'. You remember *The OC*? God, I loved that show. The four of us did. We'd watch it together every time we could. And this was a beautiful cover version of an '80s song done just for the show. We felt like it was written for us. Dumb, I know."

I didn't have to struggle to understand that feeling—to have a song that threaded together the hearts of you and your best friends, a song that gave your young lives that exquisite sense of being profoundly unique yet grand and eternal. For me and my buddies, it was 'Dirty Magic' by The Offspring, and I only have to hear the first notes of that song to be transported to those exalted days of blowing a spliff up the chairlift and getting fresh tracks all over Mount Washington.

"So this is an intimate message, right?"

"Right, but you know when I got this? It came in the mail three weeks after Emilio disappeared. Three weeks after Strickland dropped him off at the bus station."

"Where was it sent from?"

"Here in LA."

"And you think he sent it?"

"At first I didn't. There was a note with it that said, 'Emilio would have wanted you to have this'. I didn't know what to make of it, but the cops investigating his disappearance didn't seem too interested. For them the most logical explanation was that Emilio had just split and then maybe taken an ill-fated detour somewhere along the line. Maybe he never left LA. But then about two years later, I got an email."

"What email?"

"Same message, but this time there was a link to the song on YouTube."

"And you think it was from Emilio?"

"I'd like to think so."

"So why wouldn't he just come out and say hi?"

"I don't know. I replied to the sender's email asking if that was Emilio but got nothing at all back. It made me happy in one way—to think that he was alive. That's what I wanted to believe, and I figured he just didn't want to renew any ties to LA. But I thought he might be letting me know he was thinking of me."

"Or else someone was messing with you."

Abby shrugged.

"Yeah, well you do get a lot of that in this place."

"Do me a favor, will you, and forward that email to me. I want to see if I can trace it."

There was silence for a moment, and I looked at her not as a movie star but as a beautiful woman I wanted to get to know more of.

"Can I ask you something?"

"Ooh, this sounds intriguing."

"When I met you, I thought you and Freddie were an item."

Abby gave me the sweetest smile. She said nothing. Leaving me hanging.

"But it seemed to me he didn't like me chatting with you."

Abby laughed. She had one arm resting on the head of the sofa, her fingers touching her hair.

"You mean flirting with me."

"Uh, yes. Well, yes that's exactly what I was doing. But to be fair, I was just trying to keep up. You started it. There I was, you know, happily minding my own business at the bar, ruminating over some very serious matters of law, and then, then you appear."

Slowly I sat upright and leaned in towards her.

"My God, you are breathtaking."

I'd barely finished the words when our lips met. It was that wonderfully surreal moment when all the doubt about whether she was interested in me or not melted away. I did feel we had a connection, but as far as I knew it could have been all in my head. But with Claire and me going our separate ways, I was free to act on my desires. And I fancied Abby the moment I saw her—just like millions of other men around the world. I never thought I'd be having my own *Notting Hill* moment, but here I was.

After a minute or so, she pulled away slightly.

"Well, well, Mr. Madison. Mighty fine looks and a dream to kiss—you are something. I bet you don't get many girls saying no to you."

"But something tells me you're about to."

"I'm really not a jump in the sack on night one kind of gal—but you make a hell of a case for breaking that rule."

I laughed.

"I'd be a lousy attorney if I didn't."

"We're going to have to call it a night, before I change my mind."

"I understand. But I want to see you again. Soon."

"That makes two of us."

We kissed again. And again. I pulled away this time.

"I've got to get out of here."

I pressed my lips against hers once more and felt the soft probe of her tongue. I got to my feet, and as she followed I gave her my hand. When we got to the door our hands dropped. Abby held her arms behind her back and looked at me in a way that made me feel ten feet tall.

"I'll call you," I said.

"That'd be nice."

I walked down the stairs and just about skipped along the path to the security gate. I headed through, reaching for my keys, and heard the gate slam behind me. But that wasn't the only thing I heard.

Footsteps rushed up quickly from behind, and as I turned, something hit me hard under my left ear. There was a severe shot of pain and my sight was blinded momentarily. I felt myself falling towards the ground. I was a sliver away from blacking out but enough synapses remained intact to enable me to fold myself downward, breaking the fall with my knee. Without that dim vestige of thought, I would have hit the deck head first and the concrete might have kissed me into a dead-end coma.

Lying there, right cheek on the sun-warmed pavement, I felt my attacker's boot crash into my ribs. Amid the pain I felt a crack within. Barely conscious, I felt the assailant rifle through my back pockets and unearth my wallet. Unbelievable—I've walked some dodgy streets at dodgy hours in downtown LA and have never been accosted for anything more than a smoke, but the moment I set foot in Beverly Hills, I get pounced.

There was a pause as he counted my money. He'd made about five hundred bucks for himself. He bent down close to my ear. His breath was puffing in my face through a balaclava. I half expected him to thank me.

"You scumbag piece of shit. Keep defending that murdering fucking child molester and you're dead."

My head snapped back as he delivered a boot into my face. I passed out to the sound of his vanishing footsteps.

CHAPTER 11

"What the hell happened to you?!" Assistant district attorney Lawrence Lewis tried his best to look a little concerned, but he was mostly amused. And not troubled enough to get up from his desk. He just sat there looking at me, trying not to laugh.

It had been sixteen hours since I'd hauled myself off the pavement outside Abby's house and driven myself home. I'd stayed there most of the morning. All night, I'd wondered who my attacker could have been. Given the press the case had gotten, it could have been any maniac who decided I was part of the pedophile problem. I simply didn't have a clue who it was.

The man I saw in the mirror looked like he'd lost all five rounds in the octagon. My right cheek was a swollen bruise with a two-inch cut I'd strapped with butterfly plaster. My lip was split and my chest felt as though a fridge had been dropped on it. If I could have delayed seeing Lewis, I would have, but I'd requested discovery, and today was the day. I fully expected him to have a field day at my expense.

"I fell off a ladder," I said. I wasn't about to tell Lewis anything.

"Right. So who'd you land on? Mike Tyson?"

He couldn't help but burst out laughing. It took him a while to collect himself.

"Please, Brad. Grab a seat."

I winced as I sat—the cracked rib was going to take a while to heal. Lewis shook his head.

"See, this is what happens when you decide to be a defense counselor. You devote yourself to keeping scum out of jail and sooner or later it comes back to bite you."

"Spare me the lecture, Lawrence."

Lawrence Lewis was brilliant and righteous. Good qualities for a prosecutor, sure enough, but qualities that left him open to the classic prosecutor's flaw—blind fidelity to his own beliefs. Once wedded to his version of events, he stuck to that story to the exclusion of all others.

I'd been sounded out to join the DA's office a few times over the years. A key aspect that comes with the pitch is the claim of moral high ground. Guys like Lewis see themselves as fighting for everything that's honorable and good about our justice system. They are there to ensure crime does not pay, that offenders get due punishment for their actions. They are the righteous gears of justice society demands with clear conscience.

That's the noble theory, but in reality those gears have been buckled and bent every which way by police and prosecutors to get what they want. When the facts don't stack up, when the evidence doesn't wash, when the weight of their argument is lacking, that's where professional creativity comes into play. With an aim to convince a judge or jury, these guys—sometimes—just can't let truth get in the way of their good story. That's how innocent men and women end up in jail or even the electric chair. And that's why I became a defense attorney and why I will never swap sides. People need protection from the justice system. It can be a cold, cruel and deadly machine if it has you in its sights. But people have a right to a fair trial, and their guilt must be based on burden of proof. That's my job, and I'll defend my role, and my clients, to the hilt.

I could have asked Lewis to send me the files, but I like to conduct the discovery process face to face. It had been two weeks since Strickland was charged, and it was time to see all the evidence the cops had against him. I also brought along the evidence I had gathered to prove Strickland's innocence.

This represented a chance for both of us to show our cards, see where we stood, and maybe agree to not go to trial. For us to reach that point, Lewis would have to accept that Strickland should not be the main suspect, or I'd have to be willing to take a plea deal. I slid a folder towards him.

"I got you something."

He did the same.

"Good to see you're moving up in the world. You're now on the payroll of the richest murderer in the country. I guess congratulations are in order."

Lewis liked to make out that he could not wait to get up on his stage—the courtroom floor—and wow the jury into unanimous conviction. The trial might be months off—and it would never happen if I could help it—but this was where the jousting began. He wiped a speck of dust off his suit sleeve. He lifted his left arm slightly and turned to see if any more specks needed removing. Satisfied there weren't, he clasped his hands together on the table and looked at me with amiable calm.

"What have you got, Brad?"

It really didn't matter what I had. Lewis was already convinced he had a winnable case. I had to try and convince him he was on the wrong track.

"What have I got? Just a rock-solid alibi. A powerful man who cared for the victim, who dealt with his harassment, his blackmail, in a very civilized manner. He sought ways to help Landry, to calm him down. This was a man who cared a lot about the victim. Sure, Landry was a live wire, but Strickland loved him like a son."

"Love can be a killer. You know that."

"Yes, I do. But you and I know that the motive in this murder is fear."

"That's right. Pat Strickland feared his empire would come crashing down if word got out he was a sexual predator."

"Yes, that's true, even if the claim is false. You don't have to be guilty to fear slander. Shit like that sticks forever."

"So we agree Patrick Strickland had a pure motive."

I nodded towards my file.

"Check it out. There were others whose motives were even more pure, because what Landry could expose about them was the truth."

"What are you talking about?"

"Danny Shapiro and Jerry Newman. You know who they are, right?"

Lewis nodded.

"Hollywood heavyweights. Shapiro's a producer, Newman the top child agent in town."

"That's right. Then there's Gabe Finlay and Randall Webster. Two more very influential players in the entertainment world."

I put my hand on the file.

"Check out the video here. They're all in it. Those are the guys you should be investigating. There's still time for you to go after the real perp, Lawrence. Patrick Strickland ain't your man. He's innocent."

"I don't prosecute on a whim, Brad. The evidence I have points to Strickland caving Landry's skull in."

"Lawrence, do you know what Shapiro is doing right now?"

"No. Enlighten me."

"He's making moves on Strickland's film—a project worth billions of dollars."

"Yeah, well maybe that's just business."

"Just business. Try greed. You want to look at pure motive. How much more does Shapiro need? He's got both the fear of exposure, the fear of going to jail, and a Fort Knox pile of gold at the end of the rainbow if he gets hold of Strickland's movie."

Lewis lifted his eyebrows slightly to concede I had an interesting point.

"You're saying Shapiro framed Strickland? Where's the proof?"

I raised my hands in exasperation.

"That's what the cops should be working on, Lawrence!"

"Sorry, you're going to have to do better than that, Brad. Maybe you and I should talk about a plea deal. Because, as opposed to scuttlebutt, I've got actual evidence to stand my case on."

I picked up the folder as he talked, telling me how damning the evidence was against Strickland, how several witnesses saw him at Landry's place the day he was murdered and how he was a volatile man who followed through on an explicit threat to kill in order to protect his career.

"Oh, yeah," he added. "And Strickland's DNA was all over the body."

"Yes, I know. Two dudes hugging it out, for Christ's sake."

Lewis was unmoved.

"Fighting it out, more likely."

I flicked past the witness statements, paused a little at the arrest sheet and checked out the crime scene photos. Then I came to a bunch of printouts contained in a separate clear plastic sleeve.

"That pile of paper you're holding is a ton of pain for your client, Brad."

I opened the sleeve and took the papers out. It was a collection of handwritten notes. Scanning through the pages, I quickly understood what this was—a rather messy attempt by Landry to keep a journal. In the latter pages there were entries about various times Landry had contacted Strickland, about how he was pleading for Strickland to give him a break in *Sister Planet*, about how Strickland refused. This alone sparked a two-page rant. Then I saw two lines marked with a blue highlighter pen. Lewis knew exactly where I was.

"There you go, Brad. What does it say again? 'Pat went mental. He said if I didn't take his offer and disappear, he would blow my brains out. And he meant every word of it.'"

I put the pages back into the sleeve and continued looking through the file.

"People say stuff they don't mean all the time, Lawrence. You reckon a jury can't tell a brain snap from a genuine death threat?"

Lewis just sat there with a wry smile on his face. It was almost like he felt sorry for me.

"Don't let pride stand in the way of cutting a deal here, Brad. I've never seen you bring such a weak case to me."

"You're prosecuting the wrong man."

"So you say. But I'm going to need a lot more than a tickle to remove my teeth from Strickland's ass. You do not have a plausible alternative suspect, and you know it."

With that I got to my feet, slowly. But Lewis's folder was still on the desk. I bent over to pick it up and my rib knifed me like a bitch. I couldn't help but wince.

"I'll get you the proof," I said through gritted teeth.

"Good luck with that, Brad. But listen, don't beat yourself up over it."

He let out a burst of laughter.

"Asshole."

He laughed even harder. I turned for the door.

"Go get 'em, Rocky!"

I could hear him getting worked up to the point of tears as I made my way to the elevator.

Enjoy it while you can, buddy. It's just going to make it all the sweeter to kick your ass in court.

I called Strickland as soon as I left and told him we needed to talk. He invited me up to his home. On the way I took the opportunity to call Abby. She answered not too fast, not too eager.

"Hello there. So no two-day rule?"

I could hear the smile in her voice.

"Hi Abby. No. I just…"

"Some might say you're a bit quick off the draw."

"Abby, I wish this was just a social call."

"What do you mean?"

"After I left your place, someone jumped me and left his footprint on my face."

"What?! My God, are you okay?"

"I'm fine. Just a little sore."

"Oh Brad. I'm so sorry. Jesus. To think there was a mugger lurking in my street. That's crazy. It was broad daylight, too."

"This wasn't a mugging. He knew who I was."

"How do you know?"

"He told me to quit defending Strickland. Called him a pedophile and all that."

"I feel sick. I don't know what to say."

"Abby, do you have security cameras at your place? Any that cover the entrance?"

"I'm sure we do. The system is hooked up to a private security network—you know, they respond if one of our alarms is tripped."

"Right. I'd like my investigator Jack Briggs to get a look at any video from yesterday. Would you mind sending me their details?"

"No problem."

"Thanks. I appreciate it. How are you anyway?"

"Good. Got a meeting with my agent. So, you know, just getting ready. But to tell you the truth, since you called I've started to feel a little, you know, lonely. It's the darndest thing."

I laughed.

"Listen, I'm going to have to lay low for a few days. Can I see you next week?"

"Sure. I can wait. God, how messed up are you?"

"Puffed up face. Cracked rib."

"Jesus."

"I ain't pretty, but I'm okay. Look, I'll call you soon, okay?"

I hated that I had to wait to see Abby again. It was wonderful to feel genuinely thrilled again. I hadn't been this amped about a woman since I first started dating Claire. I didn't want to wait until next week to see Abby. I wanted to drive straight to her house.

"Okay."

"And don't forget to send me that security number."

"Way to go, Brad. You sure know how to kill a moment."

She laughed as she hung up.

***

When I buzzed Strickland's gate, it was not him who answered. It was Vivien.

"Come on in, Bradley."

As I walked into the lounge area, I saw Vivien seated on a sofa.

"Hello Vivien."

Her expression turned to alarm when she saw the state of my face. She sprang off the sofa, nearly dropping her iPad, and shuffled over to me.

It had just hit midday. Sunlight was pouring in, and Vivien Strickland was dressed all in white—cashmere poncho, jeans and heels. She looked like she was expecting *Hello!* magazine to turn up any minute to shoot a six-page spread.

She stopped a foot away from me. Her lipstick was Lolita red, and what a weapon of seduction that mouth was. She crimped those green eyes of hers as she inspected my cheek. Her hand reached up to my face and touched my chin.

"What on Earth happened to you?"

"Seems I pissed someone off."

She lowered her hand and gave me a schoolmistress look.

"I didn't picture you as the type to pick fights, Bradley."

"I didn't. I was hit from behind."

She took a sharp breath in.

"My God. Someone just attacked you? Out of the blue?"

I nodded.

"I think you need stitches, dear. That's a nasty cut."

I don't know why, but Vivien's show of sympathy seemed somewhat vacant. It was like caring was what she thought she ought to feel.

"It's fine, Vivien. I need to see Pat. Is he in the study?"

She nodded.

"Sure. You know the way."

As I walked down the stairs, I looked out to the pool. A man was swimming a lap towards me. He hit the wall and sprang up out of the water in one smooth, athletic motion. It was Baxter. He swept his hair back and bent to grab a towel. The guy sure kept himself in shape. On the left side of his chest was a tattoo of a winged dagger, the insignia of Britain's elite Special Air Service or SAS.

Baxter noticed me as I rounded the corner. We were just a few feet apart with a wall of thick glass dividing us. I couldn't help but think of Abby and how Baxter would feel to know what was happening between us. Despite what she told me, I sensed he wanted her for himself. I nodded a greeting at him and he did the same. He then raised his eyebrows, cocked his fists and swung his right sharply across his eye line. It was a mimed question: Did somebody catch you with a right hook? I shook my head and smiled.

"No," I said, shaking my head. I held up my hand like it was a wall I accidentally ran into and shrugged my shoulders with a grin. He nodded slowly while deploying a "yeah, right" smile.

I kept walking. The door to Pat's office was open. I rapped on it lightly as I entered. The room was surprisingly dim. Translucent blinds were drawn across the massive windows, giving the room light but no glare. Pat was seated at his desk, texting and then holding his phone out at arm's length to better read what he'd typed. He beckoned to me with his left hand.

"Come on in, Brad."

Strickland hit the send button with the same deliberateness you'd use to shove a letter into a post box.

"Take a seat. How did the discovery meeting—Jesus Christ, what happened to you?"

I was so over this by now, but I had no choice but to repeat myself. Strickland listened and was visibly disturbed.

"So the threat stands if you continue to defend me. Are you going to keep defending me?"

"Of course, I am."

I pulled out the files Lawrence had given me.

"Pat, we need to address a few things. The cops are building a very strong case against you. Much stronger than I thought. We have no time to waste if I'm going to find the real killer."

I'd photocopied every page of Landry's scrambled journal and highlighted the sections of interest. Going through them aroused a deep sense of guilt in Strickland, more so than ever.

"I should have done something," he said.

"But you did, didn't you? You rescued Emilio."

"It hurts to think Buddy actually believed I was such a monster. If I had tried harder, maybe that hatred would never have taken root."

I turned to the pages where Landry referred to Julian Dobson—aka "Jules".

"That talentless piece of shit," spat Strickland. "He hung off Buddy like a leech. Spent his money. Stayed in my house. There was no way Buddy was going to knuckle down with that idiot around."

I pointed out that every time there was an entry about "Jules," it was almost always paired with an attack on Strickland.

"Seems the feeling was mutual. Dobson didn't have a kind word to say about you."

"Maybe he was filling Buddy's head with a million reasons to hate me."

"I think you're absolutely right. Look at this."

I pulled out Landry's phone records.

"Now, by your estimation, you were at Landry's around half past three."

I pointed to the bottom of the list.

"Check this out. Landry made his last call at 3:39. So that was either while you were there or just after you left."

"I can tell you right now he wasn't on the phone when I was there. Give me that."

Strickland grabbed the sheet, keyed in the number then hit "dial". His eyebrows rose immediately and he quickly hung up.

"Well, look at that," he said, staring at his phone.

"I'd forgotten I had that douchebag in my contacts."

He angled the screen towards me. A name was displayed at the top: "Julian Dobson".

CHAPTER 12

Another day, another *Counterspin* article on Strickland. His plight was gold to them, and they were mining it for all they were worth. Not that they were alone. America and the world beyond couldn't get enough of the saga about a Hollywood kingpin charged with murdering a faded child actor. But *Counterspin* remained the spearhead, and every reporter assigned to the story kept a close eye on their feed.

Most of the recent articles were either harmless background pieces tracing the rise and fall of Strickland or minor updates on the murder case. But today's story almost had me coughing up my OJ. It had become clear *Counterspin* had sided against Strickland and they were out to fuel his public damnation before his trial even began. They wanted to drive the coffin nails deep and bury the man breathing. This latest story was a pure hatchet job, using a sole unnamed source to infer Strickland was the type of man to abuse and even kill teenage boys.

The source claimed he was an old friend of Landry's and Peralta's. He said both had told him Strickland had bribed them into performing sexual acts with him. He said the boys had no choice. They feared Strickland, and they believed their only chance of staying employable in Hollywood was to do whatever he said and keep their mouths shut. The source said both boys had spoken of Strickland's hot temper and violent behavior. When angry, he had them fearing for their lives. Then the source fired off one final shot: "Emilio always said he feared Strickland might kill him one day, so I'm not surprised he's been charged with Landry's murder."

Who else but Jared Cohen had written this piece of trash. I had a mind to call him and tell him we were going to sue. There was no corroboration from any other source, and Strickland was not given a right of reply. Instead, I opted to file it away for later use, maybe in an appeal.

This kind of slander could prove extremely dangerous to our case. I doubted this would be the last time *Counterspin* leaned on this "trusted" source. I had to find out who this person was. I got on the phone to Jack.

"What's up?"

"Did you read—?"

"Yeah, I'm headed there now."

"Where?"

"*Counterspin*'s office. I figured the best way to find that source is to have Cohen lead me to him."

That's why I loved working with Jack. Once he's on a case, he never goes to sleep on it.

"Right, I'll call you when I'm nearby."

"What do you mean?"

"I'm coming."

"Haven't you got some lawyer books to read? Some papers to file? Some nails to clip? Shoes to shine?"

I laughed. Jack loved ribbing me about being a suit.

"I'm on my way."

"Dude, admit it. You want my job."

"No, Jack. I want to see this weasel for myself. See you soon."

I hung up, looked up *Counterspin*'s office on my phone and within 30 minutes I was tapping the glass on Jack's car, which was parked opposite their building.

"Anything yet?" I asked as I got in.

"No, but check that guy up there on the corner."

I looked to where Jack was pointing. There was a black 1970 Cadillac convertible parked about a hundred yards up ahead on the other side of the street. It was hard to tell from behind, but the guy looked like a try-hard—Ray Ban Wayfarers, short back and sides, well-groomed beard. He was sitting there drinking a Starbucks and blabbing into his phone like a player.

"Who's the hipster?"

Jack lifted the Nikon DLSR camera from his lap. It had a telephoto lens on it a foot long—damned thing looked like it could fire a mortar. He pressed a couple of buttons to bring up an image in the back display and angled the camera to show me. I recognized him immediately.

"Julian Dobson. Pure coincidence he's hanging out around *Counterspin* HQ?"

"Let's wait and see."

Five minutes later I was checking emails on my phone when Jack tapped my shoulder with the back of his hand.

"Check it out. There's your buddy."

Across the street, Jared Cohen was walking towards Dobson. He stopped and took a good look around. I ducked. Jack didn't bother.

"It's cool," he said when the coast was clear. I sat up again and saw Cohen approach Dobson's car with a large envelope in his right hand. He greeted Dobson then leaned over, all nice and chill, and rested his forearms on the passenger-side door.

Jack raised the camera to his eye and fired off a burst of shots. He kept firing, and as he did, Cohen dropped the envelope onto the seat. The pair slapped hands before Cohen straightened up and Dobson drove off. Cohen ambled back up the street looking very pleased with himself.

"Look at that smug bag of shit. I've said it before and I'll say it again, you need to freeze him out. You take his calls, you feed him lines and all the while he's laughing at you."

It wasn't that I disagreed with Jack. I never said I liked Cohen; I just understood how and why he operated the way he did. But I'd be lying if I said I didn't want to cross the street and wipe that smile off his face.

"I hear you, Jack. But I swear, that son-of-a-bitch won't be getting the last laugh. That pleasure is going to be all mine."

I pushed the door open and walked back to my car.

✳✳✳

I was operating a split strategy for Strickland—first and foremost, my aim was to prove my client's innocence by finding Landry's real killer. If I pulled it off, then I'd pocket my $1.2 million and there'd be no trial. But that was a big "if". So in the event that we ended up in court, I needed to be fully prepared.

My aim was to interview every person on the prosecution's witness list, and that's where my two strategies sometimes overlapped. There were two on the list I considered prime suspects— Shapiro and Newman.

I looked forward to meeting Newman with a kind of vengeful zeal. Everything I'd heard about the man I didn't like—a creep who was able to swan around Hollywood unchallenged, untouched and unaccountable for any damage he'd done to God knows how many young men and their families. When I rang to arrange an appointment, I expected him to shun me or find an excuse not to be available. So I was surprised when he not only took the call but appeared to free up his schedule to see me.

Newman ran his business out of Beverly Hills atop a four-story sheet-glass building that rose up from Wilshire Boulevard. A sign 'The Newman Agency' ran across the top exterior. I gave my name at the desk and took a seat. On either side of me were confident, good-looking kids brought here by hopeful parents. They were all buoyed by a contained excitement that they were, possibly, on the threshold of a life-changing experience. This was day one of their dream coming true.

I couldn't help but think of Buddy Landry and how, not so long ago, he had been here with Wilfred and Layla, blissfully unaware of the storm about to hit them and the devastating trail it would leave. I'd arrived ten minutes early and was expecting to wait a good while, but my name was the next called.

"Mr. Newman will see you now," the receptionist said, gesturing to the side. "Just down that way to your right."

I thanked her and did as she directed. Newman was standing at his door, smiling, pleased to see me.

"This way, Mr. Madison."

He was an inoffensive-looking man. Sixty-something, shiny bald top rising from a garland of cropped gray hair. His buttoned short-sleeved shirt was too big for him everywhere but his belly. It was tucked into pleated trousers over comfortable shoes. His handshake was barely firm, in keeping with his gentle, calm and pleasant demeanor. He seemed incapable of upsetting someone, let alone hurting them.

I took a seat and began to introduce myself more fully.

"Oh, I'm well aware of who you are, Mr. Madison, and who you represent. What can I do for you?"

"Mr. Newman, there are a few things I'd like to discuss. First is, you are listed as a prosecution witness."

"Yes, that's right. So while I shan't be rude, there's not a lot we can talk about on that front. I'm sure you understand."

"Well, that's up to you and whatever advice Mr. Lewis has given you. But I can only assume you'll be offering material that is disadvantageous to my client."

"Mr. Lewis did warn me you'd come by. But I don't mind telling you that I've been asked to provide some insights into Mr. Strickland's relationship with Buddy Landry."

"I'd assumed as much. But what I'm most interested in is *your* relationship with Buddy Landry."

Newman shook his head in pity.

"That poor boy. Such a tragic waste. He was very talented, you know. He could have sustained a long and illustrious career if he had listened to me. But as you are no doubt aware, we had a falling out many years ago now, and I haven't seen nor heard from him since. One day, he just up and left without one word of thanks.

"Ingratitude is an idle sin, Mr. Madison, and unfortunately one that is far too common. I took that kid to the top of the world. And what happened when he went to live with Mr. Strickland? His life, career—everything—went to wrack and ruin."

"My understanding is that he left you because you were taking advantage of him."

"And who told you that, Mr. Madison? Patrick Strickland?"

"No. I heard it elsewhere."

"Well, it's interesting what people choose to remember, and forget, because I was like a father to that boy. Without me he couldn't cope. He needed care and direction, and Patrick Strickland did nothing to provide that for him."

"I was told he began going off the rails under your guardianship. I was told you were sexually abusing him."

Newman's pleasant expression never faltered. If he felt the conversation was in unsettling territory, it didn't show.

"So I've heard, Mr. Madison." He let out a big sigh. "You know, it's very easy for people to say these kinds of things. And to be totally honest, this kind of accusation is not uncommon in Hollywood. It's nothing new. If you want to believe what people say about me, Mr. Madison, you need to understand that you may be dealing with very unreliable memories from young people who don't properly understand what is happening."

"I'd say they could understand they were raped very easily. I'd say that would be an experience that would live with them forever with crystal clarity."

"Whoa, you've gone far over my head, Mr. Madison. But you should know that, in this industry, not everyone's forced onto the casting couch."

"No, some are drugged to get on there, aren't they?"

Newman's face twitched into a brief mask of confusion.

"What is that supposed to mean?"

"It means I know Buddy Landry was not only trying to blackmail Strickland. He was out to blackmail you, too. Let me paint a scene. A party at your place. A few of your friends there. Buddy and a few of his friends... Like, say, Emilio Peralta..."

Newman's lower eyelids sagged so that he momentarily looked like a man on the gallows. I continued.

"Lots of alcohol. Lots of drugs. Lots of men who pulled the strings of those boys' careers. How could they say no?"

"What an imagination you have, Mr. Madison."

"But it's not something I've dreamed up, is it, Mr. Newman?"

The gentle charm Newman possessed when I'd walked in had evaporated. Now his eyes were cold and his mouth tightly grim. I realized then that Newman hadn't seen the footage Landry had given to me. It seemed Landry's blackmail hadn't gotten that far.

Now that Newman was off balance, I wanted to push him a little further.

"I happen to know that Buddy Landry was not just blackmailing my client. He was blackmailing you, too."

He stammered out his denial. "That's nonsense. Buddy had no reason to blackmail me."

"Really? You didn't think those young boys would ever grow up and find the voice to defend themselves?"

"You're indulging in fantasies, Mr. Madison. Those boys liked to party. And they liked to make up stories."

"And I suppose the Titan Club is pure fantasy as well?"

Newman coughed up a smug little laugh.

"My word, Mr. Madison, it appears you are quite prepared to believe everything you hear."

"So are you saying you are not a member of the Titan Club, along with Danny Shapiro?"

"I'm not going to indulge in your speculation."

He had relaxed again, supremely confident I was not a threat to him, which made me distrust him all the more. This was not just a lone man lying. This was a deceitful man who felt assured that he was protected by some unseen corrupt force, a deep knowledge that all he had to do was play it cool and other more powerful allies would have his back. Never more than in this moment was I convinced the Titan Club existed.

"Where were you the day Buddy was killed, Mr. Newman?"

"And what date would that be?"

"May nineteen."

He checked his desk diary.

"I was at home. Then went out to attend the Carnaby young music awards and got home around eleven. Why? Do you think I need an alibi, Mr. Madison?"

"I won't be advising you on what you need, Mr. Newman. I'll leave you to get back to business."

"Thank you, Mr. Madison. It's been a pleasure. If you need anything else just call."

"I think I have everything I need for now. I'll see you in court. After our chat today, that's a conversation I'm really looking forward to."

Newman stood and put his hand out hesitantly. It was an act of ingrained politeness that he half-knew was not right. I looked at his hand and left it hanging. As I walked out, I could almost hear his panicked mind ticking over.

***

Entering Otto's restaurant was like walking into a second home. Warmly lit, white-clothed tables, framed scenic photos of Italy hanging on the walls and the welcoming smile of the beautiful Antonella Conti. Ten months ago, I'd helped Antonella's husband Marco beat a spurious assault charge, and since then it seemed they were forever in my debt. Claire would love this place—in fact, I was planning to bring her here as part of my campaign to win her back. We shared a love of Italy and Italian food. We'd spent a couple of weeks there years ago just before I flew out for my first tour in Afghanistan with the marines. Sharing a meal or a coffee in a place like this enlivened our memories of that wonderful trip. But I wasn't here to savor the past. I was here to enjoy the present.

There was an offshoot to the main restaurant, a small cellar room that you could book for more private gatherings. Tonight, it would just be a table for two. It was the perfect place to bring Abby. Antonella showed me to the table.

Abby and I had agreed to arrive separately, and I made sure I got there early. As Antonella unfolded my napkin and laid it in my lap, I looked around the room. It was a feast for the eyes—wall-to-wall racks of wine, the dusty bottles laid on their side and hand-written cards pinned to the racks denoting category, year and origin. It felt like a hidden alcove in Rome. I told Antonella a light red would be good to start.

"Leave it to me," she said before returning with a Tuscan Sangiovese. She poured me a taste, and I made quick work of it and nodded.

"We're in the very best of hands, Antonella. Thank you."

She bowed slightly and left.

I spent ten minutes checking emails before I heard the sound of heels on the tiles. I looked up to see Abby, and the vision of her took my breath away. For an instant I felt self-conscious standing there, as though I had no right to be the man she'd come to see. Her black dress was the kind of sexy that inspires a man to dream. Her hair, worn out so that it fell to her shoulders, jostled as she approached. She looked around the room—eyes wide, face beaming—with joyful awe.

"My God! What is this place?!"

I stood up, kissed her cheek and breathed in her perfume. She seemed unaware of the power of her beauty, or at least its effect on me. She was just so natural, which was really at the heart of her appeal. Her looks were something she obviously took pride in, but they were just the tip of the iceberg of what excited me about her.

She stayed close to look at the wound on my face. The swelling had gone, but some of the bruising remained. Her fingers touched my cheek lightly.

"Goodness me. You still have no idea who did this to you?"

"Afraid not."

The security footage from her townhouse had shown nothing. I was just left thinking it was some kind of vigilante who'd followed me that day. Abby held my chin in her hands and smiled.

"It makes you look rather dangerous, Mr. Madison."

After a moment's pause, we kissed. I wrapped my arms around her. Then she leaned back and looked around the room.

"You approve?" I asked.

"It's insane. I love it. I've never heard of this place."

We moved to our table. Antonella appeared and discreetly placed Abby's napkin and left. I couldn't take my eyes off Abby—the way her lips moved, the confidence in her shoulders, the ease in her body as she rested her forearms on the table, the way her bracelet danced on her wrist as she tucked her hair back, the sweet pink fold of her ear.

"So my plan is to lock you up in here with me till we clear these shelves."

She laughed. "I could think of worse. So long as the food can match this wine."

"The food is the best."

I felt excited and at ease at the same time—that's what this incredible woman did to me. I didn't have to try to be interested, interesting, funny or smart. Our conversation just had a buoyant flow. But as the meal progressed, there was always something pressing in the back of my mind.

After our mains and onto our second bottle of red, I ventured to raise the subject of Dobson.

"Abby, there's something I need to talk to you about. Something work related."

She leaned in towards me.

"I'm all ears."

"It's Dobson. He's taking money from *Counterspin* to feed them dirt on Strickland. It's fake dirt, but it's serving its purpose—to demonize Strickland."

"What's he been saying?"

"You don't know? I thought it was now compulsory reading for everyone in Hollywood. Today they ran a story in which their anonymous source said Pat abused young actors and probably killed Emilio."

"So what makes you so sure he's lying?"

"Because Dobson could have gone to the press about Strickland any time—years ago, even—if he just wanted to see him punished. So why now? No, this is a play. I'm sure of it. He's out to make sure Strickland goes down."

"Why would he do that?"

"Because he's in tight with Shapiro. And if there's one person who wants to see Strickland locked away, it's Danny Shapiro."

To my surprise, Abby wasn't bothered by the conversation. A curious look came over her, like she was hatching a plan.

"I've got an idea."

"Really? Go on."

She leaned in closer.

"What if I go and have a talk with Jules."

I was uneasy.

"That doesn't sound like a good idea."

"Wait. We go back aways. We talked about catching up at the funeral. I could just say I want to touch base and talk about Buddy. Then I could steer the subject onto Emilio and see where it goes. Hopefully, he'll say what he truly believes about Patrick. I'll tape it all on my phone."

I had to admit I liked the idea.

"When did you last see him? Wouldn't he be suspicious?"

"We bump into each other quite a lot. I played myself in one episode of *The Strip*, his Netflix show. We still get on okay."

I didn't need to toss it over for more than a few seconds.

"Okay, but you meet him in a public place where I can be close by, just in case."

"As you wish, Tarzan."

I was relieved. That went better than I'd expected. I thought bringing up Dobson would ruin the mood, but we slipped straight back into an easy rapport. Abby asked about Claire, and I told her about us moving on, finally. I kept it brief, just long enough to mention how thrilled Bella would be to know I knew Abby Hatfield.

When Antonella brought the check, something wasn't right. It was too cheap. Then I realized she had not charged us for the wine—a couple of hundred bucks' worth. I protested, but she insisted there'd be no argument.

"I've had a wonderful time," Abby said holding me with a naughty gaze. Then she reached for her purse.

"So have I."

Her hand pushed across the table and left two keys on a ring with a leather tab.

"Come find me," she said and stood up. She walked out of the room without looking back, knowing that I was taking in every inch of her. I pocketed the keys and took a little time to finish my glass of wine. Then I dropped a wad of bills on the table and left. Antonella was busy with another table, but she turned to me when I was at the door and gave me a smile and the most discreet of nods.

I turned the key in Abby's door and pushed it open. I could not see her and called out to announce myself.

"Just a minute," she called from her bedroom. Then in a few seconds she appeared, barefoot in that black dress. She lifted her arm up and placed her hand on the doorway.

"Can I get you something?"

I walked over to her, took her in my arms and kissed her hungrily. I felt her hands come around my neck. Her leg slid up against my thigh.

I lifted her and backed her into the bedroom. Our hands worked to free ourselves of clothes. I lowered myself to take a breast in my mouth and felt around her back, reaching lower and lower. She moaned lightly as my fingers rounded on her and gasped as they went deeper. I placed her on the bed and traced a line with my tongue past her navel and downward. Her hips rose up against me as I moved. In time I felt her hands behind my head beckon me up. I obliged.

As I straightened, I winced as a sharp pain struck me. The damned rib.

"You okay?"

"Yeah," I said. "My ribs. Just a little stiff."

She reached down for me.

"Just a little?" she giggled.

CHAPTER 13

I had a theory I couldn't shake. If Shapiro had had Landry killed, perhaps with Dobson playing a role, then things were going beautifully for him. Strickland was copping the blame, and through *Counterspin* they were keeping a foot on his throat. If Shapiro was as ruthless as Abby said, he was on track to committing the perfect murder. As for Newman, I hadn't discounted him, but murder didn't appear to be his cup of tea. Yes, he was a sleazebag who was being blackmailed. Yes, he had a lot to lose, but I didn't see him having the balls to have Buddy Landry killed. Maybe I was underestimating Newman, but to me it was clear the man who had the most to gain from Strickland going down for murder was Shapiro. Like Strickland, he had the power and the connections to make any problem disappear. And he was clearly preparing to drive the knife into Strickland when he took the stand.

I could imagine him relishing the impact on his rival if he pulled it off. I mean, how insignificant would Strickland feel settled down to decades in prison if the show just rolled on seamlessly without him? Surely, this was Shapiro's money shot. But as much as I believed my theory, I was getting no closer to proving it.

For his part, Strickland was struggling to hold it together, what with the press reports and the humiliation of having to show up at the police station twice a week to comply with his bail conditions. He was spending most of his time at his studio bungalow. He'd taken to sleeping there, as if his very presence helped ward off the likelihood of his removal. His fate was getting grimmer by the day, and he had someone to blame for that—me.

One morning, he left a message asking me to come see him. He said it was important. When I walked into his bungalow, there were several boxes on the floor in front of the reception desk. Hannah Maybury was busy packing items into a box.

"Good morning, Mr. Madison." From her expression I could tell this was not a happy day.

"Miss Maybury. What's going on?"

"I think it's best you speak with Mr. Strickland. He's in his office. Head on through."

There were more boxes in the corridor. Before I reached the office door, Strickland called out.

"Is that you, Brad?"

I turned in to see Strickland standing beside his desk holding some papers in his hand. He smiled ruefully.

"You know what this is, Brad?" He shook the papers gently.

I shrugged.

"It's a script. We get hundreds of them every year. We can turn maybe a dozen into movies. Most end up in the bin and consigned to some poor writer's hard drive for the rest of his life. But this one— this one was special. I knew it before I'd even turned the first page. It's the original script for *One For The Road.*"

As he spoke, I made my way in and lowered myself into one of the arm chairs. Strickland then pointed the script at the poster on the wall.

"I was having lunch at the Four Seasons when this kid—he was a waiter—walks up to me, says he's written a script and begs me to look at it. Now this sort of thing happens all the time. Some schmuck's been holed up in his room for years thinking he's crafting an Oscar winner, dreaming up his acceptance speech in which he thanks the Academy before indulging in anecdotes about his creative struggle, drive and inspiration. The rapturous applause. The whole yellow brick road. But no one he's allowed himself to confide in about the script could bring themselves to tell him it was shit. Well, that's not a problem I have. The sooner people know the truth, the sooner they can get on with their lives unencumbered by the delusion that Hollywood needs them.

"So this kid comes up, he looks like he's barely started grad school, and tells me he's got a script that's going to make me a lot of money. I tell him I could be rich just by getting a cent for every time I heard that. But he's persistent and confident, and I guess he got me on a good day. He took that risk. I could have had him sacked on the spot. I tell him to pitch it to me in 25 words or less. Jesus, I sometimes think I say that more often than I blink. But anyway, this kid gives me the pitch and I like it. 'Where's the script?' I ask him, and he pulls this out from inside his jacket and hands it to me. He tells me he'd been shopping it around for two years with no luck. I was like, 'When did you write this thing—kindergarten?' With the help of an agent, he'd tried to get it in front of Universal, Paramount, Fox, you name it. None of them gave him the time of day.

"But the kid was right. I took this pile of paper and turned it into almost half a billion dollars. The biggest movie Castlight has ever made by a country mile. The writer—Tanner Woods—is now a millionaire with three blockbusters to his name. He's not even thirty. This script made Castlight what it is today, vaulting it into the big leagues to rub shoulders with Paramount, Fox and Universal. It enabled them to build this entire lot. Conrad Stone has me to thank for being where he is. But how much loyalty do you think that gets me with that SOB?"

I shook my head at his question, not that he was expecting an answer. I had a feeling he was working around to telling me what the hell was going on. Strickland flopped the script onto his desk and came and sat opposite me.

"They're out to destroy me."

"Who's they?"

"A league of cowards. Stone wants me off the lot. He was in here earlier. Had the nerve to say it wasn't his choice alone, it was the board's. But I've become a liability. Having a producer up on a murder charge is not so good for business. Doesn't make for a nice

146

backdrop when you're hitting investors up for a cool million to drop into the next holiday season blockbuster. He told me he held them off as long as he could. Said he was worried about what was going to happen to *Sister Planet*."

"And what is going to happen to *Sister Planet*?"

"What's going to happen?!" he seethed. "That depends on what happens to me, Madison! It's my movie!"

His anger sprang him to his feet, and he began pacing the room.

"No one's making that picture except me! It's my name on the book option—Banks can't get out of that or I'll sue him!"

"Maybe the studio is prepared to wear that cost to make a fresh start. Besides, Stone could reasonably argue the film could not be made with you as producer given your current position and—"

"And what?"

I hesitated but I had to come out with it now. "The possibility that you end up in prison."

"What the hell are you saying, Madison? You're supposed to be on my side."

"I am. I'm just seeing it through their eyes. Giving it to you straight. You said that's how you like to operate."

"Very funny, but while we're on the straight talk, aren't you supposed to be finding the person who actually did kill Landry? Wasn't that the deal?"

"That's certainly part of it. You've put up a hell of a big carrot, and I'm doing everything I can, believe me."

"Maybe a bit of stick is needed."

"Pat, I still have to prepare for a trial that neither of us wants. And if that trial comes to pass, both you and I need to be prepared."

"I thought we'd done all that already."

Over the past few weeks, I'd spent time with Strickland going over his story multiple times. We'd gone out to Landry's apartment together, and he'd walked me through every step of that day what seemed like a hundred times. The text messages, the visit, the reconciliation, the return of Landry's hostility, Strickland's departure, his conversation with Vivien, the return home, Baxter dropping him off at the airport. And every time, Strickland's story was encouraging—the same and with only slight variations.

Occasionally, my questioning would prompt him to remember one new element or another, but to me his story was solid. Although he cooperated, I thought Strickland resented the need to prepare for trial. I guess he felt that he had commissioned me to undertake the simple task of clearing his name and had promised to reward me handsomely for it, but every day that passed without me being able to declare mission accomplished was a failure.

"I know we have to prepare for trial, but what are you doing to prevent a trial in the first place? What are you doing?"

"I've told you what I'm doing. I'm trying to find the real culprit."

"Well, either you're not trying hard enough, or I've overestimated you."

"I can assure you neither of those is true. If you don't like how I'm handling your case, you can fire me at any time."

"Don't tempt me."

"I'm not tempting you, but finding out who killed Buddy is not straightforward."

"Well the police seem to think it is."

"The cops don't want to make it any harder on themselves. They don't want to have to rethink and rework their entire case. Nor does the DA's office. They've got no reason to stray from their belief that you killed Landry. I wish I could tell you otherwise. So I've got to do their work for them. Present a case to them on a platter."

"So who do you think murdered Landry?"

"I don't want to tell you too much at the moment. But I'm on a lead that could prove fruitful."

Strickland looked at me with a deadpan face.

"You know, Vivien says I should get myself another lawyer."

I was shocked.

"Really? Vivien said that? She's always made out to me that I have her fullest confidence, right from the get-go."

"Well, she thinks you're distracted. You seem to be more occupied with getting into fights and chasing tail than finding the real killer."

He looked at me like he didn't have to name names. Somehow both he and Vivien knew I was seeing Abby.

"What I do in my private life is none of your business."

"Really? You're sleeping with one of my principals, for crying out loud. An actress whose loyalty I've been trying to secure and who is balking at giving it to me. So yeah, normally it would be none of my concern where you park your pecker, but in this case you've parked it right in my frickin' garage. How can I be sure that none of what we discuss—our attorney-client privilege—ends up coming out in your latest round of pillow talk and then works its way to the others? I could have a mass boycott on my hands."

"Don't be ridiculous. And don't you dare question my professionalism."

"Jesus Christ, Madison. I invite you into my world, and you get weak at the knees, starry eyed and fall for the first piece of ass with a movie credit. Did you get her autograph before you hopped into bed with her?"

I was stuck for what to say. I couldn't tell him that I was crazy about Abby. I couldn't try to justify the relationship on the fact that we had a strong connection, even though that was true. I couldn't say that my relationship with Abby was beneficial to the case—she provided access and insight into Landry's past and could prove vital to clearing his name. I couldn't say that she was in fact about to help me get a confession from the man I strongly suspected killed Buddy Landry. I knew I was keeping my end of our bargain up.

"Patrick, if you have serious doubts about my work, my commitment, my dedication to ensuring your ongoing freedom, then the ball's in your court. It won't be hard to find someone else to take the case. Now, it's not my job to believe you're innocent, but I do. My job is to stop you from being unjustly convicted, to make it as hard as possible for the state of California and all its might, its weight, its power to put you away for the rest of your life. My job is to be there when some hotshot prosecutor is winning the hearts and minds of twelve good people and to snap them out of it, to bring them back to the fact that the supposed facts do not lead to the foregone conclusion they're being asked to swallow. I've put my all into your case—first to find the real killer and then to defend your innocence to the hilt. You hired me because you believed in my ability. My faith in your case is only getting stronger. I want the real perpetrators brought to justice, and I will do everything in my power to make that happen. If you have lost faith in me, then fine. It's your call."

Strickland had calmed down. He was staring into the half distance, and for a brief moment he looked lost, utterly discouraged.

"Don't stop," he said. "I don't listen to everything Vivien says. Do what you've got to do."

He stood up and looked around the room like he didn't know where to start.

"I've got to get my shit outta here. Starting tomorrow I'll be working out of my house."

What work could he possibly have to do? It looked like a question he had no answer for. His career as he knew it was over.

"You'll be back," I said. Strickland sighed, stood up and dropped the script into a box.

"Yeah, maybe."

CHAPTER 14

I kept my eyes on the road ahead. Two hundred yards up was Dobson's Cadillac running north along the Pacific Coast Highway. Abby had no problem getting her old pal interested in meeting up.

When Abby called, he suggested they head down to Malibu. They could go to Sandbar, the beach restaurant they used to frequent when they were barely sixteen and the staff served them cocktails on the sly. Most of the time they'd be in a star-studded group in which a couple were older than 21, but who needed an ID when you could rock up to a venue and never have to say, "Do you know who I am?!" The doormen were always hip to the in-crowd—the bar owners wanted their custom and were willing to take the risk.

The plan was for Abby to try and get anything from Dobson to indicate he and/or Shapiro had had a hand in Landry's murder. I wasn't expecting an open confession—I just needed a lead. I had to find a big bone to throw Detective Wolfe to at least get him thinking he might be on the wrong trail.

I'd given Abby a transmitter for her to slip inside her silver leather iPhone wallet. It wouldn't draw suspicion if she placed it on the table when she and Dobson were talking. All I had to do was call the transmitter and it would silently come live—I could listen as long as I wanted or just hang up and call again.

I didn't dial in on their conversation on the drive up. I was free with my own thoughts. The get-together with Dobson had taken a while to arrange given Abby's jet-set schedule. But after a couple of weeks, the date was set. Watching Abby's hair in the wind up ahead, I had mixed emotions. Just the thought of her and the nights we'd spent together got my pulse racing, but I had some reservations about asking her to do this.

From what she told me, Dobson was no threat to her. I'd seen him from a distance, and he was a solid unit—about five-eight tall and chesty. He was no stranger to the gym, and I bet he was no stranger to steroids. He liked to show off his guns—surprise, surprise—which were hairless canvases for sleeve tatts. When we talked about the sting, Abby insisted Dobson wouldn't hurt a fly. He was sweet and camp—a gentle gym junkie.

I wasn't convinced. My bet was that that kitten-hearted sweet pea had roid rage potential in him. Part of Abby's motive to do this was to prove me wrong. What she wanted more than anything was to allow me to see the Dobson she knew—a regular teddy bear. But my take was that maybe there was a side to this guy she never saw. And just because he was gay didn't mean he couldn't lose his temper and beat another man to death.

My thoughts turned to my dad. He loved Cadillacs and would have swooned over a 1970 drop-top like Dobson's. It made me think of how fond he was of Claire. There was that beautiful morning when we were out fishing, wading side by side into the steadily flowing Lochsa River. He'd only met Claire a few times at that stage when I'd brought her home for the odd weekend, but he'd really taken a shine to her. I guess he saw, and was pleased to see, how much in love Claire and I were.

"Son, I don't presume to have a whole lot of advice for you when it comes to romance, but I can tell you this—marry your best friend," he said.

"You saying I should propose to Jim Rafferty?"

I couldn't help myself. He laughed.

"You know what I mean."

He then flicked his fly rod back and, with a couple of whips, cast the whistling line 30 yards out. I'll always remember that moment, him standing there aglow in the lively, dappled light. I just felt centered in my world, connected with my dad and happy with my entire lot in life. It was the moment I decided to propose to Claire.

When we got back to LA, I got things in motion. Called her father, who was pleased as punch, bought a ring worth a month's pay and invited Claire to my place for dinner.

She knew something was up the moment she arrived—the candle-lit table set for two, my flat looking unusually tidy and Air's 'Playground Love' coming smoothly out of my shitty CD player.

I didn't waste any time. I was nervous as hell. I told her I'd bought her something. She looked at the boxes of Chinese takeaway.

"What? Eggrolls?"

"No. This."

I bent down on my right knee and presented her with the ring. My God, the look on her face had me worried. She looked mortified. But she was smiling at the same time, at least as far as I could tell, because her hands were clasped in front of her mouth. Was she trying not to say no immediately? Let me down easy? But then her hands fell away, and she was nodding her head, her eyes filled with tears.

"Yes. Yes. Yes."

The relief was immense, but then I was flooded with joy. I stood up, put the ring on her finger and took her in my arms. The food went cold while we made love.

Dad was gutted to learn we were now getting divorced. When I told him, I felt like I'd let him down, allowing my marriage to deteriorate like it had.

Being heartbroken over Claire wasn't going to kill me, but the pain of her loss had become a quiet sorrow I felt occasionally. Like right now. But I thought of Abby and how I loved every moment with her. We hadn't spent a whole lot of time together in recent weeks, given she had flown to South Africa to shoot a fragrance commercial, but we couldn't keep our hands off each other. She rocked my world. I didn't know how long it would last, but I didn't care. I was living for the day, and when Abby was around it was always a very fine day indeed.

I saw Dobson pull off the highway into the Sandbar parking lot. I pulled over short of the club and called the transmitter. I could hear Abby and Dobson chatting as they shut the car doors and walked inside. I hung up and found a parking spot a good distance from Dobson's Caddy. I got out, took a flight of stairs down to the beach and walked a hundred yards north, staying well out of their line of sight.

I sat down in the sand and looked out over the low surf toward the setting sun. An hour later, with the light fading, my phone buzzed in my hand. It was a coded text from Abby to let me know the conversation was getting interesting.

I called the number. The first thing I heard was the sound of a chair being moved. I could hear Dobson sit down and get comfortable. He let out a sigh.

"Man, I love this place," he said. "Don't know why I haven't been here for so long."

"We seemed to have so much time just to hang out back then. I'm just realizing how much I miss those days. It's sad to think what's happened since."

"You're doing okay for yourself, Abby. Buddy, not so much."

"He was such a wonderful, sweet guy. I was hoping things would come good for him again."

"We talked about it a lot—him getting his shit together and staging one of the great comebacks. I really thought it could happen."

"Really?"

"Yeah. Hollywood loves a comeback. Why? You didn't?"

"No, Jules. I mean I wouldn't know, but I thought you guys were hanging out and, you know, partying pretty hard."

"Really? You heard that? From who?"

"Does it matter?"

"It does to me."

"He turned up to Patrick Strickland's party completely messed up, made a scene and was escorted out. After that everybody was talking about him."

"And me?"

"Well, yeah, your name did come up."

"In what sense?"

Dobson seemed to have his nose out of joint.

"Jules, you've sold coke to half the people in that room. You and Buddy had been seen out together, papped together, doing what you've always done. You can't be offended by that kind of reputation—you guys went out of your way to earn it."

Abby's touch of humor eased the tension off.

"Damn right we did. Hey, since we're on the topic, do you fancy a bump?"

"I'm going to say no. I'm not so easily persuaded these days."

"Who the hell in Hollywood says no to coke? It's sacrilegious."

"So I'm a rebel, of sorts."

"Ah, the margaritas," Dobson said.

"Two margaritas," a waitress said, putting them down. "These are on the house."

"That's very kind. Thank you so much."

I could almost hear Abby's charming smile. After a moment, Dobson spoke.

"So, a toast."

"To Buddy."

"To Buddy, one of a kind."

There was a long pause. I heard a glass being set down.

"Jules, what happened to him?"

"I know just as much as you, babe. Patrick Strickland murdered him."

"But I mean before that. There was something not right, deep down. Even when we were dating, I knew he was deeply troubled. But he never confided in me. He just made out like everything was okay when it clearly wasn't."

"You just asked me what happened to him, and I told you."

"But you said Patrick Strickland murdered Buddy."

"Exactly."

"But I'm talking about years ago."

"And the answer's the same. Strickland began killing Buddy years ago."

"What are you talking about? That doesn't make sense."

"He abused him, Abby. Patrick Strickland was abusing Buddy. And he pimped him out. That's when Buddy started to die."

"Are you sure? How do you know? Did Buddy tell you this?"

"Yes. Several times. And that's why Strickland killed him, because Buddy threatened to go public. He finally got up the courage to do it, and he had absolutely nothing to lose."

"I don't believe it. Patrick would never..."

"Oh come on, Abby. Are you really that naive? Or is it because you just don't want to see? Maybe getting that role in Strickland's film is more important to you."

"How dare you. You did nothing to help Buddy. You just sold him more drugs when he could never say no."

"Yeah, like you really cared about him. He never heard from you. It's easy to be his friend now that he's dead."

"You're an asshole, you know that?"

I could hear Abby gathering her things to leave.

"Abby, wait. Calm down. I'm sorry. Look, we're both pretty emotional right now. Being here, remembering the good old days, missing our friend. Please, let's not end the night like this. Come on, sit down. I'm sorry about what I said."

"Me too."

There was silence for a short while as they took a drink, I assumed, and cooled off.

"Jules, I need to know. Did Buddy actually have any proof about Strickland?"

"Yes. Take a look for yourself."

"What is it?"

"It's a photo of Strickland collecting Buddy after Tom Hanson molested him."

Tom Hanson rose to prominence in the 1990s and then remained one of the highest paid actors in Hollywood. But there had never, as far as I knew, been so much as a rumor that he was a pedophile.

"That's Tom, Buddy and Strickland outside Tom's trailer on the set of *Danger Money*."

"And is that you?"

"Yes, that's me. I tagged along too. But look at Buddy. He was the biggest Tom Hanson fan. This guy was his idol. He would have been star-struck just to be within eyesight of Hanson. But look at him—he's shell-shocked. Strickland ran the old, 'Hey, Tom Hanson wants to meet you' routine past Buddy and then delivered him like a mail-order bride."

"Oh, my God," she said.

"And look here. See the watch? That was Hanson's thing. He'd go, 'Hey, are you a G-Shock guy or a Seiko guy? I got a bunch of watches in my trailer. Still in the box. Dealers keep sending them to me. Why don't you come by and take your pick?'"

I heard Abby catch her breath.

"Buddy's just been given a Seiko chronograph. And he looks like his world's just caved in."

Abby started to sob.

"Oh, my God. Poor Buddy."

Another sound followed after which I could barely hear the conversation. Abby must have put the phone in her bag.

"Abby, what are you doing?"

"I just need a moment," she said, sniffling. "I'm going to the ladies'."

A minute later I got a text message from her.

"I'm out. Not helping you anymore. Patrick is a monster."

✳✳✳

Abby ignored my texts and calls the rest of the night. I thought the least she could do if she was going to bail on me was to show me the photo. Next morning, I went to her house. When she finally answered the intercom, I was let in with a fed-up sigh. Wow, how quickly a relationship can nosedive. When she opened the door, she stepped back with folded arms. Her whole manner told me she was already tired of talking.

"Abby, what the hell's going on?"

"I'm done. I'm out. I'm not helping you help Strickland. That's what's going on."

She made for the kitchen and returned holding a glass of juice.

"Okay. But you need to tell me about that photo."

She took a gulp of juice then looked at me with unblinking eyes.

"You heard Jules. You were listening. It's exactly what he said it was."

I motioned for her to elaborate.

"I'd like a bit more detail, Abby. Please. Did you get a copy of it?"

She shook her head.

"So you believe Strickland delivered Buddy into the clutches of a pedophile?" I asked.

She gave me a "do I have to spell it out for you?" stare.

"Did Buddy ever say he got hit on or abused by Hanson?"

"I told you before—he never mentioned anything about abuse to me."

"So how do you know what happened?"

"He told Jules."

"He told him what?"

"That, you know, various people have abused him."

"When did you find that out?"

"On the drive to Malibu."

Damn, I should have listened in instead of daydreaming about Claire.

"Did he say who abused him?"

"Jules said he was saving that for court."

I could just picture it—Dobson spinning his tale about how Strickland was an abuser. The jury would lap it up and yearn to bury Strickland. I'd need a miracle to save him.

"Abby, I need you to do something for me."

"I told you, Brad. I'm not helping you help that man."

"I need you to get a copy of that photo for me."

159

"No way."

"That's it. That's all I'm asking. Tell him you want it just to remind yourself how much to hate Patrick Strickland and how you'll never work for him again. But I need that photo. I'll get to see it anyway, because it's going to end up in court. But that will be too late for me. Please, just get me the photo and I'll leave you the hell alone."

She stood up, walked to the front door and opened it.

"I'll get it. But you need to go."

She had the slightest hint of uncertainty about her. Like her head wasn't clear about her decisions.

"And you and me?"

Her expression flat-lined. Then she smiled.

"Brad, right now everything's a mess. I'm angry as hell about a lot of men I used to look up to. And then there's you. And right now, I don't know whether to fuck you or forget you, but I want you out of here before..."

I stood in front of her. I could feel her breath. I wanted to kiss her more than ever.

"Before what?"

"Before I start hating you. Now get out."

"One last thing. Did Julian tell you who took the photo?"

"He said it was Emilio. It's all making sense. Emilio Peralta was trying to build evidence against Strickland, and Strickland must have caught on to it. That's when he decided to kill him."

"You don't know that."

"Got a better theory?"

"Yeah, but you're not going to want to hear it."

"You got that right. Out!"

***

On the way to the office, Strickland called. He'd just received a call from Gordon Banks' lawyer to officially notify him that if he was convicted, the book option deal would be null and void. Strickland sounded like a broken man.

"Where are you at, Bradley. Where's the killer?"

I told him I was still working on it, but as enthusiastic as I tried to sound, he wasn't buying it.

"Face it. The case is going to trial."

He was right. The set date was just a week away now. And for the first time I half considered us sounding out a plea. But I knew Strickland would never go for it.

"You're right. But we're ready, Patrick. We're going to get you the justice you deserve in court."

"That's what my enemies would be saying."

"You're innocent, Patrick. And I will prove it. Trust me."

"We're beyond that now, Bradley. I'm kind of stuck with you now."

He let out a wry chuckle and hung up.

I believed everything I said, yet I felt momentarily dazed. It was the feeling of kissing a million bucks goodbye.

CHAPTER 15

If you believed what you read in the press, the trial of Patrick Strickland was a foregone conclusion. Over the past six months there had been hundreds of Patrick Strickland stories. *Counterspin* led the way. They leaned on Dobson, their "industry insider," for more and more dirt, and he delivered. It was character assassination by a thousand quotes. And now the hack corps looked at the trial as an endless buffet, salivating at the prospect of gorging themselves on tales of sex, drugs, depravity, lies, skullduggery, greed, power and deceit. A harsh light was about to be shone on the dark side of Hollywood, and they had a front row seat.

Strickland was furious at how he was being portrayed, but he'd become reclusive, just about only leaving his house to do his bail drop-ins. He read everything written about himself, filing away every slight and looking forward to the day he could repay in kind. Disowned by Castlight, he busied himself on a project he was sure Netflix would eat up—some kind of futuristic uprising involving dilapidated freight ships used as prisons.

The scene outside the court was insane. As Strickland and I approached, we were met by a scrum of reporters and photographers. Thankfully, a couple of cops stepped in front and ushered us through. We cleared the security check and made our way to courtroom number 5.

Suddenly, with the outside clamor behind us, I got a kick of adrenaline—the first day of a trial. It had finally arrived. This was my World Series, the kind of trial I'd dreamed of at law school. Me taking on the world to defend the innocent. Not many fantasies of youth turn out just the way you imagined them, but this one held that kind of promise. This is why I loved the job.

Yes, I had game-day nerves, but I channeled them into positive energy. That rubbed off on Strickland a little, but not enough to erase the grim uncertainty that possessed him. He was anxious as hell.

As we took our seats, I glanced over at Lawrence Lewis. Ever officious, he spent several minutes arranging his belongings. I knew his schtick by heart: align and open laptop, lay papers to the left, exactly parallel to the desk edge, open bottle of Perrier then screw the cap back on without taking a sip (it was reserved for the moment before he first got to his feet), take out gold pen, click out the ballpoint and jot down the case name, date and a few bullet points. Then, and only then, would he afford a glance my way, giving me a taut smile and a nod. *En garde.*

Perhaps I should have felt more nervous. Just having to contend with Lewis was a feat in itself, but looking at it all impartially, I felt he was in a better position than me. I knew there were weaknesses in his case but nothing the sharp eloquence of one of the best prosecutors in California couldn't diminish. We had different stories to offer—both based on fact—and Lawrence had the easier version to sell. If that made me the underdog, so be it.

The gallery filled quickly, and soon the courtroom was humming with chatter. The noise died down when a side door opened and in walked Judge Meredith Gleeson. She was a large, matronly black woman who had a big heart that was, in the courtroom at least, impervious to sentimentality. She held a strict allegiance to the law, but when the opportunity presented itself, she used discretion freely. I was glad she was at the helm: you could not hope for a more fair-minded arbiter. With a rap of Gleeson's gavel, the courtroom fell silent and Lewis rose to make his opening address.

It was his usual artful display. Some people think it's all theater, but a strong conviction lies behind Lewis's carefully crafted addresses. Neither of us are so vain as to forget we are servants of justice—whether that justice is putting Strickland behind bars or allowing him to walk free. I watched the faces of the jury as Lewis spoke. You could see the dutiful intent in their eyes, the first-day

163

faith that they would always remain alert, that they would never lose sight of the grave stakes involved. Beginning day two, the attention would not be so rigid, the mindset not so steadfast. It takes its toll, being a juror. But right now, they were gripped by Lewis's oratory.

After listening to him, it would almost seem fair to simply dispense with all this formality, find Strickland guilty and hand him over to the judge for sentencing. I bet some of the jurors had to stop themselves from clapping once Lewis was done. A few in the gallery couldn't help themselves and had to be hushed by Gleeson, who added she would throw out the next person who could not contain themselves.

I had a good feeling about this jury. During the selection process, I'd had to weed out a few but ended up with a dozen citizens I'd be happy to turn my own fate over to.

In my opening statement, I pointed out how imprecise Lewis's case was. While there was no doubt Strickland was present at the murder scene at some point, the fact was, the exact time of death was unknown. Strickland had walked into Landry's apartment with a grievance he wanted resolved, and he left fearing for his own safety. He got into the car, phoned his wife, went home, and then was driven to LAX. His grievance was not a motive for murder. The very fact that he had so much riding on *Sister Planet* meant he could not afford a scandal, let alone risk taking part in a murder. Certainly, a public spat with Landry over false abuse charges would not have been welcomed, so he did his best to engage Landry to prevent that outcome. But these claims of Landry's were, sadly, the product of a deranged mind. Strickland flew to Europe not thinking he had removed his threat—he had addressed the problem manfully with diplomacy and reason.

This was the story of a hard-working, highly successful man doing the right thing, not the tale of a man who chose to protect himself by committing murder. One thing the jury needed to commit to memory for this entire trial was that Strickland loved Landry. He had made mistakes in the relationship in the past, but they were not the acts of a monster—they were common errors made by too-distant fathers. He just wasn't there enough to protect Landry from Hollywood's predators. He dearly wanted to help Landry get back on his feet, not destroy him.

I wouldn't say I outpointed Lewis, but I was marginally less behind the eight ball than when we started. So that, I figured, was a step forward.

Detective Wolfe took the stand in a mood to delete any such gain. The jury warmed to him immediately. It thrilled them to be close to a ruggedly handsome, no-nonsense cop whose daily diet of violence, tragedy and evil would have turned their stomachs. He had a tough integrity about him, a sense that he shouldered a load the rest of us shirked and that he was more than okay with that. He understood not everyone was cut out for his chosen line of work, and he wore his dangerous responsibility like a t-shirt and jeans.

Lewis began a line of questioning to establish Wolfe's credentials. A decorated cop. A gifted detective who'd broken cold cases and highly complex ones. Solving the Landry murder was a walk in the park compared to most cases. The evidence overwhelmingly led to one conclusion. And that's how I expected Lewis to play his testimony out: building Wolfe's nuggets of unfiltered logic one by one into a sledgehammer of persuasion.

But his first question caught me off guard.

"What did your thorough investigation of the crime scene and related leads tell you?"

"That Mr. Landry was murdered by Patrick Strickland."

Lewis wanted Wolfe to say this straight off the bat and it had the desired effect: everyone in the court sat in riveted silence, barely daring to breathe.

"You can place Patrick Strickland at the crime scene at the time of the murder?"

"Yes. We have several witnesses who saw Mr. Strickland's car outside Mr. Landry's apartment, who saw him walk up the flight of stairs to the apartment and who saw his car leave the scene via the back alley."

"Why was Mr. Strickland there?"

"Just before he arrived, Mr. Strickland sent Mr. Landry threatening text messages."

"How do you know this?"

"Phone records. Standard procedure."

As Wolfe said this, Lewis took a sheet of paper from his desk and raised it so everyone could see. He took it to Wolfe and placed it in front of him.

"These are the messages you're referring to, are they not?"

"Yes."

"Can you please read them for the court, Detective Wolfe?"

"'Stop this madness or I will destroy you' and 'Keep this up and you're dead.'"

The gallery broke into a murmur. Gleeson didn't have to reach for the gavel—silence resumed as soon as Lewis began to speak again. No one wanted to miss a word.

"So to be clear, Detective Wolfe, Patrick Strickland made an unequivocal threat to kill Buddy Landry moments before he was murdered."

"Objection!" I called out, springing to my feet. "The time of death cannot be precisely determined, Your Honor. The prosecution is misleading the jury into making a direct link between the text message and the murder."

"Sustained," said Judge Gleeson before ordering the jury to disregard Lewis's last statement.

Lewis kept his head bowed to shield his rueful smile. He'd planted the seed. Gleeson could order the jury to disregard something any time she liked, but she couldn't erase the notions fed into their minds. Lewis then had Wolfe walk the jury through the crime scene before focusing on key evidence.

"Detective Wolfe, as you know, there have been many theories about what happened in Buddy Landry's apartment the day he was killed. Can I ask you, are you convinced this was a case of premeditated murder?"

"Yes."

"Not, say, some other misfortune, such as an interrupted break-in?"

"No. There were no signs of a break-in."

"So Landry knew his killer?"

"That would be the logical conclusion."

"But maybe this was something like a drug deal gone wrong?"

"Well, that's possible but unlikely."

"Why?"

"Because we found a few hundred dollars in Landry's wallet, and there was a bag of cocaine left on the coffee table."

"Anything else?"

"Well, if someone wanted to kill Landry to steal his drugs or punish him for not paying a debt, all they had to do was shoot him and take whatever they could find as recompense. They would not have had to look very hard."

"Now, the fatal wounds delivered to Landry's head were made with the butt of a handgun, is that right?"

"Yes."

"So the killer used his gun as a club. Why didn't the killer just shoot him?"

"Who knows? Probably because of the noise factor."

"By that you mean the killer feared the sound of a gunshot would raise the alarm of neighbors?"

"That's my belief, yes."

"Detective Wolfe, have you retrieved the murder weapon?"

"No."

"But you discovered Mr. Strickland possessed a gun which, if the handle was used as a club, would match the wounds on Mr. Landry's body?"

"That's correct."

"And did Mr. Strickland make his weapon available for your inspection."

"He said his gun had gone missing in the days before the murder."

"Did he offer an explanation as to how it came to be missing?"

"Mr. Strickland said he'd thrown a big party a few days earlier and someone must have taken it then."

Lewis let out a skeptical hum. Everyone knew the message he was conveying. He may as well have come straight out and said it: "So, he gave you the 'dog ate my homework' story?"

"No further questions, Your Honor."

Lewis took his seat, no doubt feeling excellently placed. As I stood to begin my cross-examination of Detective Wolfe, I knew I had my work cut out for me. I stayed at the table to punch a few keys of my laptop and a video clip appeared on the courtroom monitor.

"Detective Wolfe, please watch the monitor. I want to show you two pieces of video footage."

I pressed play.

"This is security footage from Mr. Strickland's residence. Please note the time code of the footage."

"Here we see Mr. Strickland leave the house at 1:47pm. This is him setting off to visit Landry. This next one shows him arriving home at 4:09pm. He leaves again a short time later to catch his 6:40pm flight from LAX to Paris. So would you agree, Detective Wolfe, that it takes about 30 minutes to drive from the Strickland residence to Landry's?"

"Yes, that was our estimate."

"And if Mr. Strickland went straight there and straight home, as he claims, he would have been with Landry from about a quarter past two until about twenty to four. Would you agree?"

"Yes."

I stepped out from behind my desk and approached Wolfe with a sheet of paper.

"Detective Wolfe, these are Mr. Landry's phone records from May 19, the day he was killed. Can you please read out the time of the last entry? It's a text message."

Wolfe squinted a little at the page before reading.

"It says 3:39pm."

"Right, so on our estimation, that's almost exactly the time Mr. Strickland would have had to leave in order for him to be home by 4:09, is that right?"

"Give or take a few minutes."

"So if Landry attacked Mr. Strickland, they struggled, Mr. Strickland beat Mr. Landry to death with the butt of his gun, and Mr. Strickland fled, then this would had to have all occurred in a minute or so. Does that strike you as realistic?"

"It only takes a second to kill someone."

I delivered another piece of paper to Wolfe.

"Detective Wolfe, this is the medical examiner's report giving the estimated time of Mr. Landry's death. Would you be so kind as to read it out loud?"

"The precise time is unknown, but testing indicates Mr. Landry died some time between four-thirty and seven-thirty pm."

"Between four-thirty and seven-thirty."

"But there is a significant margin for error, the earliest of which overlaps with the time Mr. Strickland was there."

"Yes, I'm aware of that. But can you please read the next line of the medical officer's report?"

"It reads, 'Our results suggest the time of death was closer to the end of this time frame.'"

I walked out to the center of the courtroom floor.

"So, Detective Wolfe, do you concede that it's possible Strickland had already left the apartment when Landry sent that last text?"

Wolfe didn't flinch.

"Like I said, you can kill someone in the blink of an eye."

"But it is possible Landry sent that message after Strickland had left the apartment, isn't it?"

Wolfe's jaw tightened.

"Yes, it's possible."

"And so there is a chance that Landry was alive when Strickland left?"

He tilted his head and fired hate eyes at me.

"You can play with the figures to come up with any number of theories. The facts are that Landry was murdered with the type of gun your client owns and that your client went there immediately after sending him a death threat."

"But it's possible. Yes or no?"

"It's highly unlikely, given the evidence."

"Yes or no."

"Yes."

I nodded and allowed enough of a pause to let that fact sink into the jury's collective mind. There we had it—our first vital element of doubt. I stepped slowly towards Wolfe.

"Detective, you interviewed Mr. Strickland about his visit. What did he say happened?"

"He said he and Landry patched things up before Landry turned on him."

"And you don't believe that?"

"It's not what the evidence tells me."

"When you questioned Mr. Strickland, was he ever evasive?"

"No, he was not."

"When you asked if he owned a gun, did he hesitate to tell you the truth?"

"No, he did not."

"Was he at all vague about the visit he paid to Mr. Landry the day he died?"

"No."

"So he incriminated himself in just about every aspect of the case you built against him?"

"As it turned out, yes."

"He told you that at one point he had a constructive conversation with Mr. Landry, did he not?"

"That's correct."

"Did you at any time think Mr. Strickland was being a little too cooperative for someone who had committed murder?"

"I don't know about that. I spoke to him days after the event. He had plenty of time to think through whatever he might want to say."

"You don't think his apparent openness was genuine?"

"Mr. Madison, I've met many liars in my time and many killers. I've met many innocent men who are so uptight about being interviewed by me that you'd swear they were lying when they're telling the God-honest truth. You're right—Mr. Strickland did not appear to be flustered or fearful when we spoke, but the substance of what he said only corroborated what the evidence was telling me."

"Nothing further, Your Honor."

***

The court next heard from a few witnesses testifying they saw Strickland or his car at Landry's. One of them—a woman in her fifties named Fay Lambert, a recovered drug addict—took the stand only to confess her memory was shaky at best.

Lewis reminded her that she'd told police she'd seen a car like Strickland's behind Landry's place at about 2:30pm. But on the stand, she refused to confirm that, saying it might have been later. She apologized for the confusion. Lewis suggested her head might have been clearer when she spoke to the cops than it was today. She didn't like that and stuck to her guns. Lewis dropped her like a stone, but I swooped in.

On cross-examination, she said she was sure it was later—just about dark, about 6:00pm—but wasn't sure the car was Strickland's. But in any case, Strickland would have been at the airport by then.

After a break, Lewis called Julian Dobson to the stand. As he took his seat, Dobson smiled at me and nodded like we knew each other. He looked super confident and clearly wanted me to know it. I found his manner odd to say the least. But cross-examining him could be more interesting than I expected.

Abby had come through with the JPEG of Landry and Tom Hanson, and I'd passed it on to Lewis. To begin, Lewis served up some get-to-know-you questions. Dobson was a few years older than

Landry, but they became firm friends way back when they were both teen actors. Dobson's success plateaued, but he and Landry continued to hang out together, went to lots of parties, double dated. They enjoyed lives every adolescent in the Western world dreamed of. Over the next few years, they got whatever they wanted, had chicks hanging off them and partied harder. They had the world at their feet. Then it all came crashing down for Buddy.

"Mr. Dobson, you say you witnessed Buddy go downhill. Do you mean career wise?"

"That certainly was a factor. Buddy was the hottest talent in Hollywood. Everyone wanted to make a movie for him, with him. It was insane. Then, almost overnight, they dropped him like a stone. He was devastated."

"But that wasn't the only personal challenge he was dealing with, was it?"

"No, sir."

"Can you please elaborate?"

Dobson shifted uncomfortably in the chair and gave the jury a meek 'do I have to?' look.

"This was a hard time for both of us. It was when we found we'd both been abused."

"Mr. Dobson, I know this is difficult, but do you mean physically abused or sexually abused?"

"Sexually. Both of us. It was something we didn't talk to anyone about, but one day Buddy came out with it. And I told him my stories."

"Can you please tell the court what Buddy told you?"

Dobson paused a while and took a deep breath.

"Buddy told me he had been abused by several men a few years earlier."

"And he struggled deeply with that?"

"Of course. So did I. But as far as Buddy went, people thought him going off the rails was because of his career problems, but that was only half the story. He could barely live with himself. And the drugs and alcohol were his coping mechanism."

"Did Mr. Landry have an issue or grievance with Patrick Strickland?"

"Yes, he did."

"What was the nature of that grievance, as far as you are aware?"

"Strickland betrayed him. In the worst possible way."

"What do you mean?"

Dobson's chest started to rise and fall sharply.

"Buddy turned to Mr. Strickland for help. He'd been abused by a man he now hated and he asked to move into Strickland's home."

"And then what happened?"

"He moved into Strickland's house. There was a smaller house out back. And that's where he lived."

"And his parents agreed to this?"

"They obviously trusted and listened to Mr. Strickland. Like everyone did—I mean, you don't get much bigger than Patrick Strickland in the movie business."

"That seems like a kind thing for Mr. Strickland to do. Why do you say he betrayed him?"

Dobson's expression turned to loathing.

"Because he abused Buddy and pimped him out to other men."

Gasps filled in the courtroom.

"Are you sure of this?"

"I'm certain."

"How do you know?"

"Because Buddy confided in me. He said Strickland would tell him, oh, so-and-so, some big name, would love to meet you. Or some other big actor would love to work with you. He has a project in mind and wants to meet you to talk about it. But when Buddy would go along, it turned out these men only wanted to, you know, get into his pants."

"And you believed him?"

Dobson glared at Strickland.

"What he told me—the deep pain, the confusion, the helplessness, the suicidal thoughts—he was describing the way I felt. I'd been abused too, and he was describing the exact same hell I was going through."

"You said Mr. Strickland pimped Buddy out?"

"Yeah, he showed me this photo of him and his abusers."

"Members of the jury, I would like you to see this photo. For legal reasons, we have had to obscure the identity of one individual."

Up on the monitor appeared the photo of Buddy, Strickland, Hanson and Dobson with Hanson's face pixelated out. It was the photo that Dobson gave to Abby and I'd supplied to Lewis.

"What did Buddy tell you happened here?"

"He said Mr. Strickland had brought Buddy to a movie set to meet with... a famous male actor. This actor invited Buddy into his trailer on the pretense of talking about this movie project he had in mind for them. I mean, Buddy was desperate for work anyway, but he idolized this guy. And he offered Buddy a cool new watch."

"And what did Buddy tell you happened in that trailer?"

"The man talked about this movie and about the role he had in mind for Buddy. And Buddy was super excited, obviously. He really thought this could happen. Then the man got up close to Buddy and performed oral sex on him."

"That's what he told you?"

"Yes. See that watch Buddy is wearing there? The actor gave it to him as a present. Buddy said before handing it over, the man made him promise not to tell anybody or he would not get the role. So he walked out of the trailer, and Strickland was there waiting for him."

"Who took this photo?"

"Our friend Emilio Peralta."

"And did Buddy say Mr. Strickland knew about what went on in that trailer?"

"Well, yes. And it wasn't just that one time. That's what got him killed. He finally found the courage to confront Strickland about this stuff. And then the next thing he's dead."

Dobson was in tears now. Lewis turned towards his table.

"Your witness," he said.

I stood up and buttoned my coat. I don't really know why I do this. It's just automatic. I guess it makes me feel a little more intact.

"Mr. Dobson, I'll give you a moment to gather yourself. This must be very upsetting, reliving these events concerning your friend."

He nodded and lifted his chin up.

"No, I'm good. What do you want to know?"

"Would you say you were a close friend of Mr. Landry's?"

"Of course."

"Yes, I know you were once quite close, back when you were both starting out. But I'm talking about now, at least in the recent years before Mr. Landry's death."

"Yes, we've always been good friends."

"Really? I thought you were first and foremost his coke dealer. Is that not right?"

Dobson wasn't expecting that, and it showed.

"That's bullshit."

I returned to my desk.

"Members of the jury, remember these? Mr. Lewis showed them to Detective Wolfe. They are the phone records of Buddy Landry. But they don't just reveal numbers and tell us who Mr. Landry was communicating with. They also reveal the exchange of text messages. Now, Mr. Dobson, in the past three years, you and Mr. Landry have had many exchanges, but none of them are the sort good friends might have. There's not one example of banter, not one clear message to get together, to go out, to meet somewhere. And do you know what the most common word used between the two of you is?"

"The most common word? I don't know—how about 'Hi'?"

"No, it's this."

I showed Dobson the page with my finger pointing to an emoji.

"Can you please describe what this is?"

Dobson was subdued.

"It's a pool ball."

"Ah yes, but what kind of pool ball?"

"The black. The eight-ball."

"That's right. It's an eight-ball. Almost every time you and Mr. Landry exchanged texts, it's Mr. Landry sending you an eight-ball emoji followed by a question mark. And almost every time the only reply you send is a measure of time. Say, an hour or 45 or 3, which might be for three o'clock. And as it happens, this was exactly what Mr. Landry sent you in the last text he ever sent, to which there was no response. Why didn't you reply?"

"I don't know. When was this?"

"3:39pm, May 19. The day Mr. Landry was murdered."

"I was busy. I was on location at Santa Monica getting set for a night shoot. I pulled a sixteen-hour shift from midday till dawn. I've

177

got about twenty witnesses to back my alibi, if that's where you're going with this."

Damn it. That's exactly where I was headed. Now it was clear I was going to hit a wall if I wanted to cast Dobson as a genuine suspect. I had to change tack. I turned my back on Dobson and approached the jury.

"But let's be clear now. These eight-ball messages—the two of you aren't talking about playing pool, are you?"

"What else would we…"

Dobson broke off, not sure exactly what to say or whether he should just keep his mouth shut.

"I think you know exactly what else, Mr. Dobson. You are talking about drugs. In drug lingo, an eight-ball is an eighth of an ounce of cocaine. So what we have is Mr. Landry asking you for drugs and you telling him when you'll deliver them to him. And by the evidence of these phone records, that is pretty much the extent of your relationship with Mr. Landry. You were his coke dealer, weren't you, Mr. Dobson?"

Dobson opened his mouth, but no words came out. He pursed his lips and tried to appear offended, but the result just looked fake. His shoulders sank eventually.

"Look, we both liked to party. That's what we did."

"No doubt, but I'm putting it to you that you did not care too deeply for Mr. Landry. In fact, I put it to you that you were using him."

"I don't know what you mean."

I walked over to the monitor and pointed at the photo.

"Mr. Dobson. Where did Buddy get this photo?"

"How should I know?"

"Because I believe you were the one who gave it to him. Isn't that true?"

"No, that's flat-out wrong."

"I see. What did you and Buddy like to talk about when you got together?"

Dobson was confused at this benign question.

"Just the usual stuff. We'd talk about the good ol' days, about the parties, the chicks. We shared some pretty amazing times."

"And you talked a good deal about Patrick Strickland, didn't you?"

"No, not really."

"Not really? Mr. Dobson, as you might be aware Mr. Landry kept a journal of sorts. Much of it is quite hard to follow but the name 'Jules', meaning you, is featured in there quite a lot. And every time your name is mentioned, there is a corresponding text exchange between you two. Also, every time you are mentioned in the journal, Mr. Landry proceeds to write a lot about Mr. Strickland and how much he hates him. Much of it is hard to follow and reflects a very troubled mind, but there is a lot of anger there."

Lewis sighed and called out. "Is there a point to this, Your Honor?"

I looked up at Judge Gleeson. "There is, Your Honor."

"Well get to it, counselor."

"Yes, Your Honor. Mr. Dobson, would you say in the six months before he died that Buddy Landry was mentally unstable?"

"No, I would not."

"But you of all people knew he was having serious problems with drugs, didn't you?"

"Not particularly. He was a bit high strung at times, but then again, he was doing a lot of coke."

"Supplied by you, right?"

"There were plenty of places Buddy could score besides me."

179

"But you supplied him just about every week. Did he ever seem mentally unsound?"

"I'm not a shrink."

"No, but you say you're his friend. Did you have any concern for his mental health?"

"He was having a tough time. He wanted to get his acting career back on track, so he was uptight."

"Mr. Dobson, you run a successful production company. Did you offer to help him out with work?"

"There were a couple of Netflix projects we talked about, but he had his eye on making a grand entrance—he wanted a blockbuster role."

"I see. Mr. Dobson, being such a good friend of Buddy's and all, did you ask Danny Shapiro to give him a role?"

"What's that?"

"Danny Shapiro—you know him, don't you?"

"Everyone knows Danny Shapiro, at least they know his name."

"But you are a lot more familiar with Mr. Shapiro than most people, aren't you Mr. Dobson?"

"How's that?"

"I'm surprised I have to ask. Have you forgotten that Mr. Shapiro bankrolls your company? You work for him, don't you?"

"No, I don't."

"You are under oath, Mr. Dobson."

I could see from his face that his insides were knotting up. He didn't know what to say. I took a sheet of paper from my desk.

"Members of the jury, I won't bore you with every detail, but these documents show that a company called Inbox Productions, registered in the Bahamas, does an awful lot of work for Mr.

Shapiro. You have to really drill down into it to discover the company is a one-man-show run by none other than Mr. Dobson here. Mr. Dobson, you receive more than $100,000 a year from Mr. Shapiro. So it would be fair to assume you know him quite well, wouldn't it?"

"We're not really friends."

"I'm not asking if you go camping together—but if you were trying to help Mr. Landry land a role in a major release, Danny would have been a logical person for you to approach, isn't that right?"

"No. That's what an agent's for."

"I see. But don't you work as Danny Shapiro's agent?"

"I don't know what you mean."

"Mr. Dobson, do you know Jared Cohen, the reporter at the entertainment news agency *Counterspin*?"

Dobson looked short of air. He dug a finger into his collar.

"No, I do not."

Even he didn't sound convinced he was telling the truth.

"Really? Remember, you are under oath, Mr. Dobson."

"I'm perfectly aware of that."

"I'm glad, Mr. Dobson. But I'll ask you again. Do you know the *Counterspin* journalist Jared Cohen?"

"No, well I may have met him at a party or something. The name's vaguely familiar."

"Vaguely familiar? Let me see if I can jog your memory."

I went to my laptop and pulled a photo up onto the monitor. It was a shot Jack took of Jared Cohen offering Dobson an envelope. Dobson tightened up so hard he couldn't help but let out a small guttural sound.

"Mr. Dobson, this is you, in your car, talking with Jared Cohen outside the offices of *Counterspin*. Isn't that, right?"

Dobson's blood was boiling. His mouth was open but no sound was coming out. I flipped through a series of photos.

"You and Mr. Cohen are obviously well acquainted, Mr. Dobson. Why did you lie to the court? Why did you say you did not know him?"

I stayed at my desk and addressed the jury as I brought up a *Counterspin* article on the screen.

"Members of the jury, the photos you just saw were taken the morning after this article appeared. In the article, Mr. Cohen cites a source who casts dispersions on the character of my client, Patrick Strickland. Mr. Dobson, what was in the envelope Mr. Cohen gave you?"

"I don't recall."

"Was it money?"

"No."

"Mr. Dobson, you do understand that perjury is a serious offense and by committing perjury you can be sent to jail?"

"Yes."

"I'll ask again: was there money in that envelope?"

"Yes. I got paid for what I knew."

"I see. Mr. Dobson, I put it to you that you are working for Danny Shapiro with the explicit aim of discrediting my client."

"That's not true."

"So you didn't seek to turn public opinion against Patrick Strickland by spreading lies?"

"No."

"And you didn't use Buddy Landry for the same purpose?"

"No."

I returned to my desk and picked up a pile of papers.

"Members of the jury, I hold in my hand the photocopied notes of Buddy Landry's diary. When checked against the phone records, a pattern emerges. Every time Mr. Dobson visited Mr. Landry with a fresh supply of drugs, Mr. Landry made a reference to the visit, and every time he proceeds to rant about all the horrible things my client supposedly did to him.

"Mr. Dobson, I put it to you that you preyed on the unstable mind of Buddy Landry to convince him that lies were the truth. You convinced him that Patrick Strickland was a predator and a killer. You plied him with drugs and fed this delusion. Isn't that the truth?"

"That's a lie."

"Did you suggest to Buddy that he should try to blackmail my client?"

"Objection, Your Honor!"

"Overruled."

The court fell silent, and Dobson was left feeling he had to fill the void.

"No. Why would I?"

"Because you work for the man who has the most to gain from my client's demise—Danny Shapiro."

"Patrick Strickland is a murderer and a predator—Buddy didn't need me to tell him that."

"Oh, I think he did. I think that is precisely what happened. I think Buddy Landry was in no position to tell what was real and what was make believe. He was not your friend, Mr. Dobson. He was your tool. You used him. You manipulated him. And you betrayed him."

"That's a lie."

"Really, Mr. Dobson?"

I returned to pick up Landry's diary notes. I found the page I wanted and grabbed a highlighter and marked some lines.

"It says here in Mr. Landry's diary notes that you brought him that photo featuring Mr. Strickland and the actor we cannot name. And the very next day, Mr. Landry commenced his blackmail campaign against Mr. Strickland. I'll ask you again: was it your idea for Landry to blackmail my client?"

"That's insane."

"Do you really expect these good folks to believe you after the lies you have told here today, after the contempt you have shown this court? Your word is clearly meaningless."

Dobson opened his mouth. I shut him off.

"Nothing further, Your Honor."

I turned my back on him and went and sat down. The judge called a break. I ignored Dobson as he approached on his way out. But he stopped next to me and bent down and snarled into my ear: "I should have finished you off when I had the chance."

I was jolted by a powerful flashback: *"You scumbag piece of shit. Keep defending that murdering fucking child molester and you're dead."*

The mugger outside Abby's. It was Dobson! I was torn between retaliation and what this revelation meant for the case.

Dobson moved on, but my mind was racing. His attempt to scare me off the case must have been to sabotage Strickland's chances of being cleared. And he pretended he was a pedophile hater in order to hide his true motive. Suddenly the case was becoming crystal clear. Strickland was the victim of an elaborate scam to destroy his reputation and frame him for murder. And it had Danny Shapiro's fingerprints all over it.

"What's the matter?"

It was Strickland. I'd almost forgotten he was sitting next to me.

"Nothing's the matter, Pat. It's been a good day. Let's get out of here."

When we got back to the office, Megan stood up cupping the phone.

"Mr. Madison, you've got a collect call."

"A collect call? Who is it?" She hesitated a little before speaking.

"He says it's Emilio Peralta."

CHAPTER 16

At first, I thought it was a hoax call. Then I told the caller I had Patrick Strickland with me and was going to put him on the line to question him. The caller agreed. Strickland took the phone nervously—the thought it was actually Emilio gave him a giddy rush of hope, but that was overridden by the ominous fear that this had to be a cruel prank.

I watched Strickland's face as he talked. He asked a few questions about the intervention, about him taking Emilio to the bus station, and as he did, tears streamed down his face. He then began saying, "Thank you" over and over before handing back the phone.

Peralta was very much alive. Since that day Strickland dropped him off, he had decided to disappear. He hated his parents for what they did to him, he hated everything about Hollywood except for Abby and Buddy, and he decided he would start his life over. He had loved the book *Into the Wild*, the story about a young man who traveled the country on a dime and ended up dying in the Alaskan wilderness, and he decided to embark on his own adventure. It was a test of his spirit, enterprise and endurance. He'd also ended up in Alaska, only with a happier ending. He'd fallen in love and was raising two kids on the outskirts of Juneau on a decent income he made from fishing.

Peralta said he had been following the case and had long wanted to help Strickland out, but did not want to return to LA to testify. He'd contacted Abby first by email, then she gave him my number and insisted he call me. It was nice to know she'd changed her mind about helping me.

I told Peralta there were other ways we could get his testimony without him having to appear in court. But I said his surprise appearance in the trial would be sensational news and that he could not expect to avoid scrutiny from the authorities and the media. He said he was ready for that, but they'd have to come to Juneau to find him. I then raised the matter of his parents. I said he had to contact them before we ran his testimony in court.

"No matter how much you resent them for what they did to you, they deserve to hear from you first. I can't imagine what they've gone through all these years."

"I've given that a lot of thought too, and you're right. But it's going to be a hell of a tough call to make."

"Everyone will be the better for it. You included."

"You don't know my parents. But I'll do it."

I had to warn him about the press.

"You know you're going to get hit by a tsunami of media attention. They're going to descend on Juneau like a swarm of wasps."

"Yes, I figured that. But I'm ready to talk. And I figure they'll be bringing their checkbooks."

"So let the bidding war begin, hey?"

"Exactly."

It gave me no small amount of pleasure to know that there was one area in the media where *Counterspin* could not compete—when it came to checkbook journalism, broadcasters like ABC and NBC ruled. Jared Cohen and his colleagues had no chance of getting the Emilio Peralta scoop.

I would have to notify Lewis and Judge Gleeson about my new witness but not just yet. I needed to hold off until after Shapiro had taken the stand. I told Peralta what I wanted him to do and hung up. I now had the perfect plan to take Shapiro down and set Strickland free.

***

Danny Shapiro approached the stand slowly and relaxed, buttoning his jacket and taking it all in—the jury, the judge, the courtroom decor. He slid his hand along the wooden rail of the stand and tilted his head to inspect the grain before looking back at the gallery as he took his seat. It was like he could buy the courtroom and everyone in it with spare change.

He was short, hefty, bald and bearded—the sort of male archetype nobody would look twice at. But his presence was magnetic. All eyes were riveted on him as he sat there in his Armani suit and open neck shirt with a gold chain nestling in his chest hair and eighty grand's worth of Patek Philippe on his wrist. To him it seemed the stand was another ego cockpit for him to play pilot in. We, Judge Gleeson included, were all just passengers. It lifted me to think about bringing him crashing down.

As someone who knew both Strickland and Landry, Shapiro was going to dig up a lot of the past. Lewis stood up and started with the basics, establishing that Shapiro and Strickland went way back. They were friends until ambition for the same goals pitted them against one another. The stats of the movie business—box office sales, Oscars won—became their scoreboard.

"Mr. Shapiro, were you close to Buddy Landry?"

"Well, I don't think Buddy got close to too many people. But I always had time for him. We'd catch up every now and then."

"Did you speak with him in the weeks before he died?"

"Yes, I did."

"Did Mr. Strickland come up in your conversations?"

"Sometimes he did."

"In what sense?"

Shapiro looked at Strickland.

"Look, I didn't really understand their relationship, but I thought Patrick could have supported Buddy more. The kid began to lose his way a long time ago, and a little more care back then might have made all the difference."

"In those last conversations, what did Buddy tell you about Mr. Strickland?"

"He was very upset with Patrick. He kept saying he was not going to let him get away with it."

"Get away with what?"

"Murder, for one."

"Buddy thought Patrick had killed someone?"

"Yes."

"Who?"

"Emilio Peralta. He said he was going to expose Patrick and that he wanted to see him punished for what he had done."

"Did he mention anything about a video?"

"Yes he did. He said he had a video that showed Patrick taking Emilio away, after which no one saw him again."

"Have you seen this video?"

"No, I have not."

Lewis played the video taken at Newman's. The jury looked on as Patrick walks a near naked Peralta through the house.

"Do you recognize the man and the boy here?"

"That's Patrick and Emilio."

"Did Buddy ever tell you why Emilio might have had reason to fear Mr. Strickland?"

"Yes."

"Objection!" I got to my feet. "This is pure hearsay."

Judge Gleeson overruled. Lewis raised upturned hands in the air as if to ask me if it was okay for him to continue.

"Can you please tell us why Emilio might fear Mr. Strickland?"

"He said Patrick had threatened to kill him."

"Why would he do that?"

"I don't know. Buddy clammed up about that. He never told me why Mr. Strickland would make such a threat. Buddy believed Patrick wanted to shut Emilio up about something, and the next thing he knew Emilio was gone."

Lewis was happy to leave it there.

"Your witness."

I stood up and walked straight at Shapiro.

"Mr. Shapiro, you say Buddy Landry confided in you."

"Like I said, I wasn't his best friend, but we spoke occasionally. And I didn't shut him out like some people. After Patrick kicked him out, his life went out of control."

"But who's to say Buddy's life was not already out of control. Were you close enough to Buddy all those years ago to be concerned enough to help him?"

"If I had known, I—"

"But you did know, didn't you, Mr. Shapiro? You knew a lot more than you have let on."

"What are you talking about?"

I went to the desk.

"Members of the jury, I bring your attention back to this video that is supposedly so damaging to my client."

The first frame appeared.

"Now Mr. Shapiro, you can tell me where this party was, can't you?"

"It's Jerry Newman's house."

"Jerry Newman's house, exactly. And you would know that because not only are you good friends with Jerry Newman, but you were actually at this party, weren't you?"

"I was there for a very short time."

"Why a short time?"

"I don't recall. I guess I had more important stuff to do."

"Of course. Now I would like the court to see some more footage that was shot that night."

I played the clip featuring Newman and the drugs. I watched the faces of the jury as the penny dropped as to what was going on.

"Mr. Shapiro, what kind of party was this?"

"It was just a regular Hollywood party, but like I said I wasn't there for long."

"Yes, you've said that already. This appears to be a party for older men to exploit young, impressionable boys. To ply them with alcohol and drugs until they were sexually compliant or too wasted to defend themselves. Are you telling us you had no idea that this was going on?"

"I didn't see anything of the sort. I'd never have stood for it."

"Mr. Shapiro. Do you know who shot the video showing Mr. Strickland leading Emilio Peralta through the house?"

"No, I do not."

"It was another boy at the party who was helping Emilio. Do you know why they were doing this filming?"

"No, I do not." Shapiro tilted his head like he was getting bored.

"And do you know why they were so fearful of being caught that they kept their cameras hidden?"

"No."

"Buddy Landry and Emilio Peralta say they were sexually abused by a certain group of men over a period of two to three years."

"That's very disturbing if it's true."

"Yes, it is very disturbing if, as you say, it's true. But it would be very hard to prove because both Mr. Landry and Mr. Peralta are dead. Would you say they were honest young men, Mr. Shapiro?"

"Objection!"

"Your Honor, the point will be clear very soon."

"Overruled. Answer the question please, Mr. Shapiro."

"Yeah, I suppose I'd say they were honest. They were good kids."

"Have you ever heard of the Titan Club, Mr. Shapiro?"

If I'd caught him off guard, it didn't show.

"Yes, I have. And I've heard of the Lone Ranger and Santa Claus. The Titan Club is a myth, a Hollywood ghost story."

"Interesting. Now, Mr. Shapiro, you have cast dispersions on my client quite freely. It's a serious thing to say you believe my client is capable of murder, which is an odd conclusion to draw about someone. Why would Patrick Strickland want to kill Emilio Peralta?"

"I don't know."

"There is a theory that my client killed Emilio Peralta because he was making a nuisance of himself. And maybe it had something to do with these videos. And maybe my client was a member of the Titan Club and was into young boys. That he just couldn't help himself."

Watching the discomfort seep into Shapiro's expression was priceless. He didn't like where this was going at all.

"Well, that sounds a little out there, but in this town you hear all kinds of crazy stories."

"Actually, Mr. Shapiro, the point I'm making is more relevant to you."

"What do you mean?"

"You have told the court the nature of your conversations with Buddy Landry were amicable. But that's not true, is it?"

He didn't answer.

"He was not calling you for a chat. He was blackmailing you."

"That's absurd. Where did you get this crap?"

"Before Buddy Landry began targeting my client with wild delusions about abuse and abandonment, he was trying to get money or work or both from you, isn't that correct?"

"No, that is a figment of your imagination, I'm afraid."

"You know Mr. Landry kept a diary and there are notes about you. And at the same time he was blackmailing you, Mr. Dobson reappears into Mr. Landry's life. It was your lackey Dobson who gave Landry the video. It was Dobson who fanned the idea that Strickland was a monster. And he did so purely to serve your interests."

"That's quite a conspiracy theory," said Shapiro unfazed.

Lewis was on his feet. "Objection, Your Honor. Counsel is testifying."

"I agree. Counselor, cut it out and resume questioning. Or are you done?"

In Judge Gleeson's tone of voice was the clear intimation that she'd bite my ass if I continued to test her patience.

"No more questions, Your Honor."

I sat down. As Shapiro shuffled his way out, I could hear him breathing hard like he'd climbed ten flights of stairs. I could see dark rings on his shirt extending from his armpits. It gave me a warm, fuzzy feeling to know I'd made that bastard sweat.

✳✳✳

After Judge Gleeson called a recess, I stepped out of the courtroom to check my phone. The email I'd been waiting for had arrived. I contacted Gleeson and arranged to meet her in her chambers along with Lewis.

In the attached video I played for them, Emilio Peralta introduced himself and proceeded to explain what happened after Strickland dropped him off. He apologized for the trouble he put everyone through but said he could not stand by and allow Strickland to be blamed for his abuse, disappearance or murder. He praised Strickland as a decent man who intervened to rescue him from the clutches of other men who did in fact abuse him. He said he feared for his life, as these men still hold powerful positions in Hollywood and might seek to silence him. By the time the video ended, both Gleeson and Lewis were furious.

"This is moving, tragic and very illuminating, Mr. Madison, but why did you not bring this to the court's attention earlier?" demanded Gleeson. "You spent half your cross-examination grilling Mr. Shapiro about Emilio Peralta."

"He purposely withheld this evidence so he could portray Mr. Shapiro as a scheming, deceitful villain."

Lewis was doing his best to look hurt. So was I.

"That's not true, Your Honor. This video was sent to me unsolicited. I called you as soon as it arrived. Look at the time stamp."

I'd told Emilio to send it at eleven in the morning when I knew we would be in court.

"How convenient, Mr. Madison," Judge Gleeson said. "And it just found its way into your inbox unsolicited."

"Peralta must have been following the case and got my email off my website."

"This is not admissible, Your Honor," urged Lewis.

"Your Honor, Buddy Landry's mindset was disturbed by what he was told my client did to Emilio Peralta. That lie was used to manipulate him into blackmailing my client. This is a vital deposition of an unavailable witness, Your Honor. The jury needs to see this."

"They do not, Your Honor. Mr. Madison is playing us."

"As much as I am inclined to agree with you, Mr. Lewis, that is something we cannot prove. I will allow the jury to see this video. They need to expunge any idea that Mr. Strickland was in some way involved in the abuse and murder of Mr. Peralta. It has been used by you, Mr. Lawrence, to taint his character and it is only fair that that injustice be corrected at the earliest opportunity. Once the jury has seen the video and digested what it means, I don't want to hear anything more about Mr. Peralta. Let's move on."

"Yes, Your Honor." Lewis and I spoke at once.

It was a significant victory, but it sparked a near riot in the gallery when it was shown to the jury back in court. Every reporter hit their phones to text their chiefs of staff the news. While we resumed business in Los Angeles, a fresh battalion of the press corps trained its focus on Alaska.

CHAPTER 17

In light of the Peralta video, Lewis had to adjust his strategy. I noticed as soon as we got back into the courtroom that Jerry Newman's name had been scratched from the witness list. Shame. I was looking forward to dismantling that reprobate in public. And although I'd neutralized Shapiro, I knew deep down it was a temporary reprieve. I still didn't have an alternative suspect.

I had a plan to strengthen Strickland's standing in the eyes of the jury. Peralta's testimony was a good start, but it didn't relate specifically to Strickland's relationship with Landry. I had asked Wilfred Landry to take the stand to vouch for Buddy's affection for Strickland. He agreed. I'd also asked Vivien. It was a risk to waive spousal privilege, but she was the only person to see and speak with Strickland after his visit to Landry the day of his death, and what she had told me in our dry runs in preparation was very solid. The jury was going to be left convinced Strickland was not only a trusted friend of Landry's, but that his behavior was not that of a man who'd just been in a fight and had bludgeoned another man to death.

Enter poor Wilfred Landry. I have many regrets in my life, but my decision, no, my insistence on getting him to take the stand will knife me in the heart till my dying days. My intentions were, if not good, professionally sound, and my reasoning was solid. But in truth I was coldly pragmatic, putting my devotion to the case above all else, even a grieving man's soul.

To go a little easier on myself, Mr. Landry was more than willing. In his wonderfully honest and decent manner, he wanted to do all he could to help Strickland. I warned him about what to expect from Lawrence Lewis, that he would try to expose him as a bad father who pimped out his adopted son. We rehearsed it. I hit him below the belt, questioning his love for Buddy, his struggling finances that his boy's earnings had reversed, his scarce visits to his son and then finally the indignity of being sued by his own child. Even in rehearsal this kind of grilling would have crushed most men, but Wilfred Landry was a Sherman tank inside that wiry dungaree-draped frame. He impressed me as a guy who, if he walked out his door to find his farm in ruins, his sheds destroyed and his livestock dead, would just roll up his sleeves and get to work on the first of a million things that needed doing and not stop until he'd got everything back to how it was. By deed and character, he personified that humble steel of rural America.

If Wilfred was the slightest bit intimidated by the packed city courtroom and its grand formality, it didn't show. I was confident this LA jury would be moved by his story and lifted by his dignity. He opened by telling the court Buddy was a happy boy. Breaking the news to him that he was adopted was very hard, but even though he nursed some sorrow that he would never meet his birth parents, the boy flourished under the love of the Landrys.

"He was our pride and joy," said Wilfred. "He was the best thing that ever happened to us. And we thanked God every day for giving us this opportunity to make up as best we could for this poor boy's misfortune."

"But at the age of twelve everything changed. Isn't that right, Mr. Landry?"

"Well, yes. Our world was turned upside down. One day we were running a pig farm with our beautiful little boy, and the next day he was a movie star. Mr. Strickland contacted us out of the blue, and he came to Fairmont to see us. To say this was a dream come true for Buddy does not come close to the excitement he felt. Mr. Strickland told us then and there he had a movie project that he wanted Buddy to star in, but he said the boy would have to go to LA for screen tests and whatnot. Initially, we saw no harm in it. We didn't think it would amount to much, but we didn't want to deny Buddy. We figured it would just give him a taste of something he might pursue later in life."

Wilfred said Layla traveled to LA twice to accompany Buddy. After *One For The Road* was made, they thought Buddy would just return to school and have something exciting to tell his friends. But suddenly they were hit by an avalanche of attention. Almost overnight their boy became a world-famous movie star.

The media zoned in, the offers started flowing and their lives were turned upside down. During this hectic time there was one person who helped them navigate the giddying turbulence—Patrick Strickland.

"We came to trust Mr. Strickland implicitly," said Wilfred. "He had plans to do more movies. He helped us with the money side of things—in the space of a few months, the college fund we'd set up and had spent years adding dollars and cents to was full to overflowing. Buddy seemed to take it all in his stride—he was humble, charming, thoughtful and grateful—just the young man we hoped he would be. But there came a time when he pretty much had to live in LA, so we sought Mr. Strickland's advice. And even when things went bad, we still believed Mr. Strickland had Buddy's best interests at heart."

"Mr. Landry, do you think Patrick Strickland could have murdered your son?"

"No. Never. I just cannot conceive of that happening. He cared a lot for our boy, and I believe that with all my heart. Mr. Strickland may be a powerful man, and an intimidating man in some respects, but we know there's a softer side to him. I know he and Buddy fell out, and Buddy had become so very difficult because of all the drugs, but Mr. Strickland always tried to do the right thing."

"Was their relationship more than just professional?"

"Yes. The way Buddy used to talk about Mr. Strickland on the phone in the early years you could tell he was providing some good guidance and not letting Buddy get too carried away."

"Can you give me an example?"

"Um, well. Yes, I can. Buddy told me he would not have turned another page of a school book if it weren't for Mr. Strickland encouraging him to persevere. At the same time, he made sure Buddy got to know the movie industry, how it works. He introduced him to scriptwriters, directors and cinematographers, and ultimately Buddy just wanted to be a part of that industry—not just as an actor but as a writer or director one day. I mean, he'd shown an aptitude for it at school before all this started. Writing, that is."

"When did things start to go wrong?"

"When Buddy was placed under the care and management of Jerry Newman. This was a move suggested by Mr. Strickland. He thought it would be good for Buddy to be living in Mr. Newman's stable, so to speak, of young actors. He said Buddy would be well looked after and would have great company. But it turned out to be the wrong decision, I'm afraid."

"Why do you say that?"

"Because Buddy changed."

"In what way?"

"His whole manner began to change. Sometimes we could never get hold of him, and he would never call. And then when we did get to speak, he was sometimes very rude to us. But it was different from one week to the next. Sometimes he would make any excuse not to come home. Then other times he would be in tears saying he missed us terribly and wanted to come back."

"So he would fly home?"

"Yes, but then he would tire of it quickly. He just plain didn't want to be back in Fairmont living on a pig farm. It was the last place on Earth he wanted to be."

"At what age did he move in with Mr. Strickland?"

"He was fourteen. He had been in LA for the better part of two years by then, living with Mr. Newman."

"Why didn't you just pull him out of Hollywood and bring him on home?"

"We were in over our heads, Mr. Madison. In hindsight we should have never let him go but we... our world changed so dramatically, so completely, we just found it very hard to cope."

"Thank you, Mr. Landry. No further questions, Your Honor."

Lawrence Lewis was in no hurry to rise. He sat there, leaning back in his chair and looking at Wilfred Landry as though he was a lauded artwork whose merit eluded him entirely. He leaned forward slowly and rose heavily, keeping his head bowed, as though making a physical apology in advance for taking a cold scalpel to the word of an elderly, heartbroken farmer.

"Mr. Landry, forgive me, but there are some things, some very important things, I believe, that I don't quite understand."

He was on his feet now, looking straight at Mr. Landry while buttoning his jacket. His brow was dutifully knotted, as though LA's finest, fiercest prosecutor had empathy hurdles to wrestle with. He picked up a sheet of paper.

"Your son, your adopted son, was what... twelve... when you sent him to Hollywood?"

"That's right, sir," said Wilfred. I could see he wanted to provide a fuller explanation, a justification even, but he buttoned his lip. He was doing exactly as I told him: "Keep your answers short; do not be tempted to elaborate". Adding tangential material risked presenting Lewis with a new flank to attack. That's when you'll end up where you don't want to be, I told him—compelled to provide spontaneous answers to uncomfortable questions. And that's where Lewis wants you—as baffled and vulnerable as a calf cut from the herd.

"I'm sorry, but how did that ever seem like a good idea?"

"In hindsight, it wasn't. Layla, my wife, and I have spent many sleepless nights wanting to undo what can't be undone. We thought it would be a one-off experience for Buddy."

"A one-off experience. But you had him signed up to Mr. Newman and living with him a good deal of the time within a few months."

"We trusted Mr. Newman, and we trusted Mr. Strickland."

"Yes, as Buddy trusted you."

"We didn't just dump him there!"

"I never said you did, Mr. Landry."

"Layla always accompanied Buddy. Well at least initially, but then I got sick and she couldn't leave me."

"I understand, Mr. Landry. But the fact is Buddy was defenseless and was ruthlessly exploited by many people who he thought he could trust, who he was told to put his faith in. But there was an upside, wasn't there, Mr. Landry."

"What do you mean?"

"Your son Buddy was earning an extraordinary amount of money. And that meant you and your wife were too."

"We put all of Buddy's earnings into a trust for him to access as an adult."

"All of it?"

"Well, the contract we signed with Castlight Studios—we signed it on Buddy's behalf—well, that contract paid us some money."

"The contract paid you. That's one way to put it. Another way would be that you made sure you got your cut and a very generous cut at that."

"You are making it sound awful."

"Am I? I don't mean to, Mr. Landry. I'm sure the jury can see what a head-spinning opportunity it was to have a twelve-year-old movie star earning millions of dollars that you had to take care of."

"Most of the money ended up in Buddy's trust."

"How much did you earn from your son, Mr. Landry?"

"I'm not sure."

"Well, I can take an accurate guess. From the finance records it's clear you and Mrs. Landry were earning a quarter million dollars a year. You cleared your six-figure debt with Buddy's money. You upgraded and expanded your farm with Buddy's money. And you both treated yourselves to new cars with Buddy's money."

Wilfred was visibly disturbed by the personal onslaught.

"Those cars we bought were not new."

"Did Buddy ever say to you that he just wanted to come home?"

"Yes, sometimes."

"And did you bring him home whenever he said this to you?"

"Whenever it was possible. Sometimes he had commitments he couldn't break, Mr. Newman would say, and then once they were done or something exciting happened, all was forgotten and Buddy was happy to stay."

"But he wasn't happy to stay, as you have already told the court. He wanted out. But he couldn't leave because he was bound by contracts to work. This is a twelve, thirteen-year-old boy we're talking about. I'm sorry, but it does begin to look like child slave labor. Is that not a fair way to put it, Mr. Landry?"

"Objection. He's badgering the witness, Your Honor."

I was on my feet, wanting to run and tear Wilfred away from the stand.

"Overruled," replied Judge Gleeson. Lewis continued.

"Mr. Landry, it could be viewed that you betrayed your son, could it not?"

"I beg your pardon?"

"I think you heard me crystal clear. You didn't just feed Buddy to the wolves, you became wolves yourselves."

"That is so far from the truth. I think you are going out of your way to be hurtful."

Judge Gleeson's voice rang out: "I agree. Watch yourself, counselor."

"Mr. Landry, you suggest Buddy was happy with how you managed his life and affairs. But then why did he sue you to wrest control of his finances?"

"Buddy was desperate and addicted to God knows what by then. It wasn't that he distrusted us; it was that he wanted all his money immediately rather than waiting until he was twenty-one."

"And what did the court say about that?"

"I think you know the answer. The court ruled in his favor."

"So Buddy wants to get his money off you, you resist, it goes to court, and you are ordered to give him his money, isn't that correct?"

"Yes."

"But not only that—he sued you for some of the money you had taken for yourselves. Isn't that right?"

"Yes. Financially, we ended up right back where we started on this terrible journey."

"But what does that tell us about how Buddy felt about you, Mr. Landry? That's what I think the jury needs to understand. You've told us how much you loved Buddy, but the fact is you sold him to Hollywood, you enriched yourselves on his earnings, and you had to be sued by your own son to get you to repay the money you took from him."

"Objection!"

"Your Honor, if the defense cannot tolerate hearing the bare facts, then we have a serious problem."

"Overruled. Mr. Madison."

Lewis resumed the onslaught.

"Mr. Landry, you say you trusted Mr. Strickland."

"That is right."

"You trusted him with your son's welfare."

"Yes, we did."

"And you vouch for Mr. Strickland as a good man with a heart of gold."

"We believe he is a good man."

"Mr. Landry, forgive me. But how can we accept such an endorsement when it has become quite painfully obvious that the judgment of you and your wife Layla is seriously flawed?"

"I don't—"

"Would it be true to say that you only want the jury think good of Mr. Strickland because it would help them think better of you? Could there be a greater betrayal of your son than for you to champion the cause of his killer?"

"You son of a bitch!"

"I take it that's a no, Mr. Landry. Nothing further, Your Honor."

What a wretched sight Wilfred made there on the stand. Stunned and disconsolate, he shuffled across the courtroom floor and straight past me without a glance. He went and sat next to his tearful Layla. She threw her arms around him as he doubled over and sobbed.

✳✳✳

Strickland was furious. We had retired to my office. After Wilfred's scalding experience on the stand, he and Layla decided not to stay for the remainder of the trial. They wanted to be on the first flight home or just the first flight out of LA. I had Megan make the bookings. The best she could do was a New York layover with a morning connection to Fairmont. She booked them into a nice hotel on my insistence and my dime. I apologized profusely for putting them through such an ordeal. I felt terrible about the way Lewis had painted them as craven opportunists. It was nothing but a trick, a deception built by the artful rearrangement of facts, but I feared the jury fell for it. The fate of my client had taken another grave hit, and I needed to pull a swift recovery.

Next up was Vivien, and that gave me heart. I believed once the jury got to hear her account of events, they could never believe, beyond a shadow of doubt, that Patrick Strickland was a killer. She and I had run through the order of questioning. I'd start with how long she and Patrick had been together. She would detail what attracted her to him, how she had met him when he was previously married and found him a charming, charismatic man. When he became single, she was surprised, flattered and delighted to get a call from him. She'd heard through a friend he was trying to track her down. He was old-fashioned and wooed her, so to speak. Wined, dined and sublimed her. She quickly fell in love. Within six months he proposed. He said she was the woman he wanted by his side, that in her he'd found the perfect partner—she knew a lot about showbiz (one of her ex-husbands was a studio exec who left her for a younger woman), and she was elegant, sophisticated and not intimidated by fame.

When he bought the Bel Air house and they moved in, she felt her life was complete, and she wanted more than anything to see his ambitions realized. She helped him secure the film rights for *Sister Planet*—the author was an old friend—and the rest, as they say, was history. He was on track to making the biggest movie since the dawn of time, and she was right there by his side.

As far as temperament goes, he was not quick to anger and was never cruel. He was pragmatic about business and sometimes that meant being brutally honest with people. Not everyone liked that. But there was not a violent bone in his body. She'd seen people give him cause to lash out, but he never did so physically. The Patrick Strickland she knew was a powerful, driven man who did not have to resort to threats. He was a man who pursued what he wanted and did not stop until he had it. She was a case in point, though she didn't like to say.

All eyes were on Vivien as she walked to the stand. She was Hollywood glamour personified. From the high heels to the sleek emerald dress to the flame of hair held high over her bejeweled neck, she was the hallmark of Tinseltown beauty. The entire court would have been no more enthralled if Sophia Loren herself was making her way to the witness box.

Having settled in her seat, Vivien sat straight-backed and beautifully composed, looking at me to begin. As we ran through the initial questions, I was surprised to find Vivien somewhat nervous. Her voice was so soft at times I had to ask her to speak louder to be heard.

There was a hint of reluctance in her that forced me to adjust the line of questioning I'd prepared. I'd have to go by feel, and hopefully she'd warm up to the point where she could deliver what we agreed upon with utter confidence. But if I sensed she could not get there, I knew I'd have to take a short cut and get her to repeat a bare bones version of his behavior after returning from Landry's—his unflustered demeanor, his unruffled, spotless clothing, the done-this-a-hundred-times manner in which he prepared for his flight. That is, not the demeanor of a man who had, supposedly, just moments earlier bludgeoned Buddy Landry to death with his own gun.

I approached the stand during these initial exchanges in the hope of providing some reassurance to Vivien.

"Mrs. Strickland, would you say your husband Patrick had a temper?"

"No, I would not."

"Have you ever seen him react violently to any situation of provocation?"

"No, I have not. That is, not until he threatened Buddy."

The courtroom buzzed. I would say I had to do a double take on what she said, but I heard her loud and clear. Confused, I thought her nerves were getting the better of her. I could not understand how such a strong woman could melt under the spotlight, particularly when her husband's life was at stake, when the empire he built had enabled her to live in a rarefied tower of opulence. She was his queen; his kingdom was, by extension, her domain. She had everything to lose if he fell. Yet here she was, a pretty picture of clumsy uncertainty.

"By that you mean the threatening text message your husband sent in the heat of the moment?"

"No, I mean the verbal threats he made over the phone."

Audible gasps came from behind me. The gallery was charged. I did my best to convey my alarm to Vivien with a look. *What on Earth are you doing?!* It was all I could do to keep my reprimand silent. I decided to cut to the chase, to get her first-hand observations of Strickland's behavior that day on the record and end it there.

"Mrs. Strickland, your husband called you on his way home after visiting Buddy that day. How did he sound to you?"

"He sounded stressed."

"Stressed?" Now I was worried. I looked at Strickland, who could barely sit still, rubbing his mouth roughly, looking at his wife and dreading what she would say next.

"Yes. Stressed. He was very agitated. Not himself. He was breathing hard and telling me things had not gone well with Buddy. He said he had not been able to talk sense into him. That it had gone horribly wrong."

Gone was the meekness. Her voice carried across the courtroom loud and clear.

"Mrs. Strickland, I must remind you that you are under oath. You have given me a very different account before this trial. You said your husband told you he and Buddy had appeared to make up before Mr. Landry had another mood swing, forcing your husband to leave."

"I know that's what I told you before, but it's not true."

"So you didn't chide your husband, telling him he was too soft on Mr. Landry?"

Vivien lifted her head slowly and struck me with the reproachful stare of a maligned woman.

"Most certainly not, Mr. Madison. I said nothing of the sort."

"Mrs. Strickland, there seems to be some confusion—"

"There is no confusion from my end, Mr. Madison. It seems you would like me to say anything to defend my husband for what he did to that poor boy. But in all consciousness, I cannot do it."

The prior uncertainty had been shed, and resolute confidence had taken its place. For a moment I froze, my mind scrambling to bypass the shock of Vivien suddenly becoming a hostile witness. I had to change tack while simultaneously trying to figure out why she had turned against her husband.

"Mrs. Strickland, let's set aside the fact that you have gone on the record as saying you perceived no agitation in your husband during that phone call. Let's address what you have also gone on the record to say. You told me that you greeted your husband at home when he returned, that he was wearing the same clothes as he did when he left, that there were no blood stains on his clothes, that there was nothing about his appearance to indicate he'd been in a physical struggle and that, apart from briefly discussing his conversation with Mr. Landry further with you, he routinely set about packing for his trip before getting into the car with Baxter and leaving for the airport. Is this a true account of the events as you saw them?"

"No. He looked disheveled and was in somewhat of a daze, like there was something of grave importance on his mind distracting him," she said.

The gallery stirred excitedly, relishing this sensational turn of events. On the blowback scale, this was nuclear. First Wilfred Landry goes to hell, and now this.

Vivien was clearly out to condemn her husband. I had no idea why, but I had to change strategy. I lit upon an old standard—discredit the witness. But I had to make it quick. The more she opened her mouth, the higher the risk to her husband.

"Mrs. Strickland, I must remind you again that you are under oath. You are telling the court a different version of events to what you have so far professed to be the truth. Is that true? Yes or no."

"Yes, but—"

"I think a simple yes will do. So you either lied, under oath, to me and to your husband, or you are now lying, again under oath, to the court. Which is it?"

"I'm telling you the truth now."

"Were you under any pressure or persuasion when you made your statements to me, in a process that was recorded on video I might add? And no one coached you or advised you on answering my questions relating to the events following your husband's visit to Buddy Landry's residence? Is that true?"

"Yes, that's correct, Mr. Madison. I took it upon myself to lie for my husband."

Again, the courtroom stirred. I had no choice but to withdraw. If I sought out an explanation from her, it would just give her the opportunity to bury Strickland further, which it was now clear she meant to do.

"No further questions, Your Honor."

Lewis's voice rang out: "Oh, but I have a few."

He looked like the cat that got the cream—he'd just been dealt four aces, and he wasn't even going to bother with deploying a poker face. He was practically panting.

"Mrs. Strickland, unlike Mr. Madison, I don't feel the need to remind you that you are in court speaking under oath. Would it be fair to say you have had a crisis of conscience in regard to your defense of your husband?"

"I have. I can't continue to lie for him."

"Mrs. Strickland, the court has already heard your husband threatened to kill Mr. Landry in a text message. Did you hear him make such a threat over the phone?"

Yes."

"When?"

"On the day he went to see Buddy. Maybe an hour or so before he left the house."

"Did your husband know you could hear him while he was on the phone?"

"No, he was in his study. I had come down to speak with him, and I heard him shouting before I got to the door."

"And what did you hear your husband say to Mr. Landry?"

"He said, 'I'm going to blow your stupid brains out.'"

"That's a lie!" Strickland had been like a caged animal, huffing and puffing every time Vivien spoke. Now he was on his feet glaring at his wife.

"Order! Mr. Strickland, please control yourself."

I put my hand on Strickland's arm. He jerked it away and glared at me as though I was party to his wife's betrayal, or at least that I was to blame for this train wreck. Once the court settled down again, Judge Gleeson invited Lewis to continue.

"Mrs. Strickland, do you believe your husband set out that day to kill Buddy Landry?"

"I can't say what he set out to do, but he seemed intent on crushing Mr. Landry into perpetual silence."

"And what of his appearance when he returned? Did it look like he had been in a fight?"

"I didn't get a close look. When he got back we spoke briefly across a large room, before he stormed off to get ready for his flight."

"But you told the court earlier he was somewhat distracted. Can you please elaborate?"

"He looked frantic."

"But you were a long distance from him, as you said. And you could still tell he was highly agitated?"

"Yes. It was the way he was moving as much as his expression. It was like, as I said, he had something extremely worrying on his mind. He could barely think or talk straight. I thought something dreadful must have happened at Buddy's place."

"And when you heard days later about Buddy's death, what did you think?"

"I thought," Vivien paused and looked at Strickland almost sympathetically.

"I thought Patrick must have killed him."

Strickland stared at Vivien in horror, mouthing words of silent protest. He moved in his seat as though strapped to it, straining to prevent himself from making another outburst. He swore under his breath before turning his attention to me—a look of such wrath and scorn there could be no doubt as to who was to blame for this catastrophe. And he was right. His case was a train wreck.

Court was adjourned for the day. We made our way back to my office to lick our wounds and regroup, Jack spearheading a path through the media scrum. My mind was a storm of conflicting thoughts—the case was doomed, I had completely stuffed it up, an innocent man was going to spend the rest of his life behind bars because of my errors.

An innocent man? Was he? Did I really believe Patrick Strickland was innocent? What if Vivien was telling the truth?

I didn't know what to believe.

CHAPTER 18

Patrick Strickland paced around my office like a caged lion. He took the crushing blow of his wife's betrayal like a warrior: the burden of heavy losses only made him fight more furiously against his doom. I did not want to ask this next question, but I had to.

"Patrick, she's lying, isn't she?"

Strickland stopped in his tracks.

"Of course, she is! To the devil with her. I don't know what she's scheming. Maybe she's sold me out to Shapiro. The conniving whore!"

He was hammering the redial button on his phone, but Vivien wasn't answering. He then began leaving an abusive message, but I snatched the phone from his grasp and killed the call.

"You can't afford to give her any more ammo," I said.

I'd tried calling Vivien too but to no avail. I had to get us all on track for productive, strategic thought.

"Patrick, you said that in your phone conversation with Vivien after leaving Landry's she called you soft."

"That's the polite version. She said I was a pussy—that I was always too soft on people and that I was never tough enough on Buddy. She said I should have severed ties with him long ago, that I was stupid to have allowed him into the party that night. She went on and on, saying there would be no end to Buddy's demands, that he would not stop until he had bled us dry. She was mighty pissed."

"So she was the angry one?"

"Not shouting angry—there was just a, you know, a cold boil to her voice."

Suddenly I was struck by a chilling notion.

"Maybe she did it," I said.

There was silence as we all thought the same thing—it seemed entirely plausible. I continued thinking aloud.

"Maybe Vivien took it upon herself to do the job she thought you should have done."

My mind went into overdrive—we had to shift all our focus onto Vivien.

"Jack, we have to check the video files again. The security tapes. We've already pored over them to corroborate Patrick's account of his movements—but what about Vivien's movements? Did she fetch the gun from Patrick's office? We need to know everything she did after Patrick went to the airport."

The three of us gathered around Jack's laptop as he pulled up the clips.

"There are three internal cameras—one in the office, one in the lounge area and one covering the entrance. Then there are four external cameras covering the grounds."

"Start with Patrick's office," I said.

The clip showed Patrick leaving his office, then nothing. Jack fast-forwarded through it.

"There's nothing happening—no one comes in or out. Not for days. I've already checked. The next person to walk into that door is Patrick after he got back from overseas."

"Wait a minute," I said. "Rewind back to when Patrick leaves his office."

Jack did so. On the screen Strickland stood up from his office chair and left the room. Then nothing. But something was not right.

"Play it again," I said. Jack obliged.

"Stop," I said. "I wonder…"

I leaned forward to take control.

"See here, Patrick. You get up, put your pen in the inner pocket of your jacket and leave."

I moved footage forward.

"But here, your pen is still on your desk."

"I took it with me. I always do. It's my lucky Parker. I've had it for almost twenty years."

"The footage has been tampered with," I said. "Whoever's done it has probably copied footage from a previous day."

Jack swung the laptop back under his control and examined the clip again and again.

"Who had access to your security system?" he asked Strickland.

"No one but me. You need a password to access the files stored on the hard drive."

"And only you have that?"

Strickland's face dropped like a grave epiphany came over him.

"No, Vivien knows it too. When I had it installed it was logical for her to have it because I was away so often. She could not have planned this so far in advance, surely? My God, how long has she been deceiving me?"

Strickland sat down, dazed by the weight of the thoughts spinning around his head, one being the question, how long his marriage had been a fraud?

"Who installed the system?" asked Jack.

"Cyclops Security."

Jack tapped away at the keyboard.

"What are you doing?"

"Just a second. There might just be a chance that your computer is not the only place where your video records are stored."

Jack stopped typing and looked up at Strickland from Cyclops Security's website.

"Please tell me you signed up for the premium service," he said.

"I must have. That system cost me thousands to set up plus a hefty monthly fee. I could just about buy another Rolls with what I've paid that company."

Jack spoke while looking at the screen: "Then you should have a year's worth of footage stored on the cloud. Cyclops promotes this as a selling point—'We don't erase. Any crime or attempted crime on your property WILL be recorded and kept on file. Let us be your witness.'"

"You need to call them, now."

Five minutes later we were told the files would be delivered via Dropbox. While we waited, Strickland's anger rose again. This time it was directed at me.

"Why the hell didn't you think of this before?!"

"Because your wife wasn't on trial, Patrick. We did check the security footage, and everything we saw backed your version of events. When you left, when you got back from Landry's, when you left for the airport. We had no reason to be digging any deeper into your home security footage. The police did exactly the same."

Jack raised his hand to shut us both up.

"The files are here," he said. "Let's see. May 19. From about three o'clock onwards. We want the section after... when you leave the office."

He cued the video to the appropriate time code and hit play. The first difference was obvious—the pen was gone. For about 40 minutes into the clip nothing happened. Then a figure appeared and walked into the office: Vivien Strickland. She bent down at the desk, opened a drawer and took out Strickland's gun. She dropped the clip into the palm of her hand then started removing the bullets.

"Looks like she knows how to use that weapon," said Jack. "But why is she taking out all the ammo?"

Vivien dropped the bullets back into the drawer, closed it and walked out of the office.

"Where's she going? Jack, what have we got on the other cameras?"

Jack browsed the files for time codes before selecting the driveway footage. He advanced through the footage at speed. Soon enough, we saw Vivien's Mercedes leaving the premises.

"Drop that onto a thumb drive for me, will you, Jack?"

"Sure thing."

As soon as it had loaded, Jack handed me the stick. I grabbed my jacket and made for the door.

"Jack, I need you to check the sat nav history of Vivien's car. We need to know where she went. Can you get it?"

"You really know how to make a guy feel under-appreciated, you know that?"

"Great then. Text me as soon as you know."

"Where are you headed?" Patrick asked.

"To see Judge Gleeson and Lewis. They need to see this fresh evidence. It's not enough to save you on its own. But it's enough to warrant putting your wife back on the stand."

"You really think she killed Landry?" Strickland asked soberly.

"She's just left your house with what's probably the murder weapon, Patrick. Something tells me she's not off to Pilates."

✳✳✳

I was grateful to have the night to plan a fresh inquisition of Vivien. In considering her the main suspect, I'd had to ditch my theory about Shapiro and Dobson framing Strickland. It could be that Shapiro was merrily going about the business of turning Landry against Strickland when suddenly the murder became a golden opportunity to help complete his rival's ruin. The payoff for Shapiro would be three-fold: Landry would not be threatening him with public accusations about him abusing Peralta, he would see Strickland not only ruined but jailed, and he would take the reins of *Sister Planet.*

Abby had told me this Hollywood game could be ruthless, but this behavior was Shakespearean in its wicked depths. So my strategy was reworked once more to center on Vivien, a woman who seemed to have channeled her own Lady Macbeth.

Judge Gleeson had no objections, and a subpoena was issued. Of course, Lewis objected strongly, but Gleeson said it was only prudent for her to be asked to explain the footage. By the following morning, the word was out that Vivien Strickland was being recalled.

Calls started coming in from reporters, Jared Cohen included, looking for more detail on what more could Mrs. Strickland possibly add to the case. I let them all go through to my message bank. The press had covered Vivien's performance in the court the day before as an act of heroism. They waxed on about how the wife of one Hollywood's most powerful men had placed justice above loyalty to her husband, not to mention the security and fortune that was built like a castle upon their matrimonial bedrock. What would become of her, they wondered, if her husband was convicted of murder and sent to prison the rest of his days? Had she brought about her own financial ruin by betraying him in the name of justice? There was so much more to this woman than they had previously given her credit for. Maybe she wasn't just a candied socialite, a vapidly vain housewife, an empty vessel who was gifted stratospheric wealth yet bore it like something earned from birth. Maybe Vivien Strickland had a depth of character to date unrecognized by the facile gossip

218

media. Maybe in her chest beat a noble heart that could inspire others, women of all stripes, to better themselves. You just knew the glossy mags were already mocking up covers graced by Saint Vivien Strickland—Hollywood's Bravest of the Brave.

Oh, and no small part of the coverage rounded on yours truly and how my case and my career prospects were blowing up in my face. They made quite a sport of detailing just how disastrous my day had been. There was no way back for me, as far as they could see. The next thing they expected to be reporting was that we'd caved in and taken a plea. After Jared called a third time, I answered.

"Make it quick, Cohen."

"Brad, what's going on? Why's she getting back out there on the dance floor?"

"You've just had a field day making me look like a fool, and now I'm supposed to give you a lead?"

"Well, you have to admit it wasn't your best day."

"I've had worse," I lied.

"I don't think so. It'd have to be Titanic worse, and you sure as hell wouldn't have had Patrick Strickland come knocking on your door."

"What do you want, Cohen?"

"Just one thing—is it true you've accepted a plea deal?"

"What?"

"I have it on good authority that—"

"Good authority? Cohen, here's something straight from the source—your authority is a jackass. Good luck with that."

I hung up before he could get another word in.

The courtroom filled quickly again that morning. The air was thick with the static of excited dread. It was the guilty pleasure of expecting to witness someone else's pain, anguish, embarrassment or condemnation. Hell, I'm sure for half of the gallery, guilt didn't come into it. The word had obviously spread that Vivien Strickland was making a return appearance in the witness box. They had no idea why, but going by the previous day's effort, she was unlikely to disappoint. Perhaps they looked forward to seeing if I could dig the hole for my client any deeper.

Once Judge Gleeson took her seat, we were ready to begin. I didn't catch a glimpse of Vivien until she was called. Then, amid the silence, I heard her heels approach from behind.

As she crossed the floor, it was clear her demeanor was different from yesterday's. Instead of gliding demurely to the stand, she marched. From that and her stiff bearing, you didn't have to be a mind reader to know she was here under protest.

On the stand, she raised her right hand and recited the oath with a hint of tedium in her voice, like she was repeating an order she'd made to a dim waiter. She had no idea why she'd been subpoenaed to reappear, but she seemed to be a tad annoyed that anything more could have been asked of her. She fixed her bothered gaze on me and waited.

"Mrs. Strickland, I'm sorry we've had to ask you back here."

"I'm happy to oblige," she said flatly.

"I'd like you to cast your mind back to when your husband returned home from his visit to Buddy Landry's residence."

"Didn't we do this yesterday?" Her tone implied I might be wasting her time. I was a tad surprised she would so willingly let her impertinence slip.

"It's for me to ask the questions, Mrs. Strickland. Not you. Do you understand?"

She adjusted herself slightly, disappointed in herself for handing me an opportunity to put her in her place.

"Of course."

"Now, can you tell the court what you did once your husband Patrick left for the airport?"

Vivien cocked her head as she tried to remember, or at least feigned to.

"Let's see. I'm not sure I did a lot, to be honest. I think I went for my massage and then got ready for a dinner. I went to Providence with some friends."

"I see. And when you went out for your massage which car did you drive?"

Vivien's eyes narrowed, their focus on me sharper. She sensed a trap and felt sure she was not going to fall for it.

"I took mine."

"That would be the red E-class Mercedes coupe."

"If that's a question, then yes."

I walked back to my laptop and pulled up a clip. I hit play and it showed the Mercedes exiting the property.

"Please note the time stamp—6:17pm on May 19—this is you leaving for your massage."

"Yes."

"Where did you get your massage?"

She blinked.

"Well, as it turned out, I changed my mind on the way. I decided I fancied doing a bit of shopping instead."

"Okay, so where did you go to do your shopping."

"Just a few places along Melrose."

"Melrose, you say?"

Her brow was beginning to shine with a faint sweat.

"Yes."

"Mrs. Strickland, can you remember what you did before you got into your car to go get a massage?"

"Nothing comes to mind. I just got a few things and headed out. Nothing out of the ordinary."

"I see. So taking your husband's gun wasn't out of the ordinary?"

I watched her closely as I said this and saw the force she had to apply to remain calm. Her chest rose as she took in a deep breath. She didn't know how to reply, whether to spin a spontaneous lie or try to work with the worst she now saw coming. She chose the latter.

"A girl never knows when she may need a gun. It gives me peace of mind."

"Let me get this straight—you're off for a massage and you think, 'I'd better take Patrick's handgun with me'?"

"It may sound odd to you, but I'm very familiar with guns, Mr. Madison. I like them. I happen to be a darn good shot, if you want to know the truth. I like the Colt 45. It's a fine weapon."

"I don't doubt that you know your guns."

I went back to my desk and brought up the video shot in Strickland's office. Before I hit play, I told the jury they were about to see some original security footage taken in Strickland's office on the day of the murder. I told them the police had not seen this tape because somebody had removed it and replaced it with fake footage.

All eyes were riveted to the monitor as they watched Vivien empty the Colt of its bullets and drop them into the drawer. I kept watching Vivien. She didn't have to see it all to know what it showed. She turned her head back towards me. Her composure softened. I didn't know whether this was surrender or the relaxed state that comes with renewed confidence.

"Why did you take the bullets out of the gun, Mrs. Strickland?"

Vivien just kept looking at me. After a long pause she spoke.

"I didn't want him to get hurt."

The courtroom stirred as those unable to hear Vivien asked the person next to them what she had said.

"I'm sorry. Could you please repeat what you just said?"

"I said, I did not want him to get hurt."

"You did not want who to get hurt?"

"Buddy."

"So you weren't off to get a massage or shopping in Melrose, were you?"

"No."

"You believed your husband had been too soft on Mr. Landry's blackmail attempt, and you decided to take matters into your own hands. You got into your car and went to Mr. Landry's residence. There, a struggle ensued, during which you hit him over the head violently with the butt of the pistol. Is that correct, Mrs. Strickland?"

Momentarily lost for words, Vivien gaped like a landed fish. She grabbed the rail of the witness box and turned to the judge.

"No, that's not what happened," she said.

"But this is you leaving your home armed with your husband's gun."

I picked up a document.

"Please take a look at this, Mrs. Strickland. This is the sat nav record taken from your car that day. Your husband gave us the authority to check since the car is in his name. It shows you did not go shopping. It shows you went to Mr. Landry's place."

There was a look of dread on Vivien's face. She was cornered, and it was time to confess.

"It wasn't me driving the car."

"Do you really expect us to believe that, Mrs. Strickland?"

"It's the truth. I swear."

"Okay, if it wasn't you, who was it?"

Vivien moved about in her seat as she struggled to accept her grim fate, but she knew she was a queen locked in check mate.

"It was Freddie. Freddie Baxter."

The court erupted. Judge Gleeson hammered her gavel.

"Order!"

As the din slowly settled down, I replayed the footage. Unfortunately, the tinted windows obscured the driver the entire time. Even the hands on the steering wheel were never clearly visible—I'd hoped that at least that rock on Vivien's wedding finger might have caught the light, but no. I then wondered whether Vivien had noticed you couldn't make out who was driving and so quickly decided to blame Freddie.

"Mrs. Strickland, you need to explain to the court what happened. The truth this time, because right now it looks like you set out to commit a serious crime. What we are seeing here looks very much like premeditated murder."

She collected herself.

"All right," she said, her voice deeper and quieter than before.

She was doing her best to look genuine, but I could see she was still trying to find an acceptable way to edit what she knew into its least damaging form.

"It's true that I thought Patrick had not done enough to discourage Buddy. I thought he needed to be persuaded more forcefully. Buddy was so desperate and deranged I believed he would only respond to threats. He was threatening my husband, and I thought we should fight fire with fire."

"I see, go on."

"I thought Freddie could pay him a visit and make it clear that he would not be getting a cent from my husband, and that if he so much as contacted Patrick again the consequences would be dire."

"So you sent Freddie around to scare Mr. Landry off?"

"That's why I took the bullets from the gun. I thought Buddy would take Freddie more seriously if he was armed. But I didn't want him to shoot Buddy. That was the idea—to scare him."

"So you sent Freddie around to strong-arm Mr. Landry. What happened next?"

She shook her head in determined denial.

"Nothing happened. I don't know. You have to ask Freddie."

"I'm asking you, Mrs. Strickland. I want you to tell me the truth."

"Nothing happened."

"That's what you might like to tell yourself, Mrs. Strickland. But it does not stand up in a court of law. Tell us the truth!"

"Nothing happened. That's all I know. I swear."

Her voice had softened, as though there was some chance she could be excused on grounds of pity. I kept my voice calm and firm.

"I don't think anyone in this courtroom believes that's all you know."

She turned to the jury, pleading.

"Freddie said everything was fine. He said he'd set Buddy straight and left."

I cut my finger quickly through the air out in front of me and held it pointed at her.

"No! That is not the truth. Is it?"

She didn't answer.

"Tell us what happened!"

Tears flooded her eyes. She looked down to her lap and dabbed them with a handkerchief.

"I didn't know what he'd done."

225

I moved closer.

"You didn't know what he'd done? What are you saying, Mrs. Strickland?"

"I didn't know that he killed Buddy!" she cried. "I didn't know!"

Audible gasps came from the gallery behind me. I turned away and looked at the jury as I spoke.

"But you sent Freddie there to kill Buddy. You told him to do it. You kept the bullets because people would hear the sound of gunfire. But they wouldn't hear Freddie beating a man to death. That was your idea, was it not?"

"No! No! I swear! I didn't want him to kill Buddy! I just wanted Freddie to scare him."

I rounded on Vivien sternly.

"How can you say that? You tampered with the security footage to protect Freddie. You knew what happened. Don't you take this court and this jury for fools! You wanted Mr. Landry dead, didn't you?"

"No. That's not true."

"That's first-degree murder, Mrs. Strickland. That's life in prison—no chance of parole."

"I didn't know. Freddie came back to the house and told me all had gone well. I didn't know Buddy was dead. I didn't know that until I read about it."

"But when you did learn of Buddy's murder, you helped Freddie tamper with your home security footage so the police wouldn't see you take the gun. Is that right?"

Vivien nodded her head slowly.

"Yes." She turned to Strickland. "I'm so sorry, Patrick. I hope you can find it in your heart to forgive me some day."

"That'll be a cold day in hell," replied Strickland. "What a wicked mess you are."

Suddenly, all the fight seemed to leave Vivien. She doubled over, her sobs shuddering her entire body. The courtroom was chaotic, yet over the din of the crowd you could hear agonizing moans rising from deep within her wretched soul.

CHAPTER 19

The days following Patrick Strickland's case being thrown out of court were sheer madness. Presented with a once-in-a-lifetime baitball of celebrity scandal, the press went into a feeding frenzy. They didn't know which way to turn.

The story of the Hollywood wife and her handsome British goon was gold, but it was soon overshadowed by the airing of Emilio Peralta's explosive *60 Minutes* interview. In it, Peralta swore the Titan Club was no urban myth before outing Shapiro, Newman, Dobson, Finlay, Hanson and Webster as abusers and describing how they went about their sordid business. CBS devoted the entire hour to Peralta's story, drawing the biggest ratings in the program's history.

Peralta's courage inspired others to speak out, and with each passing day new victims stepped forward with fresh allegations. They came thick and fast and by every means of public expression: Twitter, Facebook, radio, TV, blogs, you name it. It was a landslide of revelation.

Three days after the program aired, Jerry Newman hung himself. Shapiro and the others all made strident denials and cried "witch-hunt," but they were socially blacklisted and professionally dead. It was only a matter of time before charges followed.

With pedophilia being described as a "Hollywood epidemic," the Buddy Landry and Emilio Peralta stories were heralded as catalysts for profound change. No more turning a blind eye to child exploitation, Hollywood was promising. The exoneration of Patrick Strickland served to enhance his name and standing more than ever. Those who had doubted him now bent over backwards to convey their fondness. The publicity rounds of new films allowed actors and directors to voice their allegiance, since just about every entertainment reporter asked: "Are you happy to see Patrick Strickland exonerated and back in show business?" And they all lied and said how much they loved him. They all said they knew justice would prevail and that they were certain he'd clear his name. He was one of the true geniuses of our time, they said, and they were so glad he could now get back to making movies.

And that's exactly what Strickland was doing. He patched things up with Castlight and was getting back into the wheelhouse to drive *Sister Planet* full steam ahead. His phone had been running hot with all his first-choice principals calling to express their eagerness to sign. The news was already out that Abby Hatfield had gotten the female lead. And I was very happy for her. And she for me, it appeared.

After the trial came to an end, I gave the office a wide berth for a few days. I had a huge night out with Strickland and Jack, and then Strickland put me and Bella on a Learjet to spend a few days on his Colorado ranch. When I finally did drop into the office, I found a three-thousand-dollar bottle of Macallan whisky on my desk. The note read: "You're incredible. And this bottle better be. Enjoy Ax."

I was about to text Abby when Megan came in to tell me Vivien Strickland had arrived unannounced and demanding to see me. As Megan would tell me later, Mrs. Strickland expected to just waltz on through to see me only for Megan to set her straight about office protocol and the need for an appointment. Vivien had stiffened her back, said she was quite prepared to wait, and taken a seat. Megan took her sweet time to come in and let me know I had a visitor. I told her to send Vivien in.

She walked up to me with an outstretched hand—a gesture that suggested she hoped we could put the past behind us and move forward with new business. I kept my hands in my pockets.

"Vivien. This is unexpected, to say the least. I didn't think I'd be seeing you again, to be honest."

"Well, here I am. You look well."

I gestured for her to take a seat. She looked a million bucks, as usual, but there was a telling lack of her usual confidence. She looked like someone who'd dressed for a job interview believing looks might just outweigh experience.

"Why are you here, Vivien?"

"I won't beat around the bush, Bradley. I want you to represent me."

I was able to keep my reaction to a wry smile rather than laugh in her face. She disgusted me, but I understood her desperation. She was out on bail after being charged with involuntary manslaughter. The authorities had caught up with Freddie Baxter in Spain and extradited him to the US, where he was also being charged with manslaughter. He was understandably denied bail on grounds of being a flight risk.

I put my straight face on and leaned back in my chair.

"So after deceiving your husband and me, you expect me to try and keep your ass out of jail. I can tell you now that that's impossible. Given the testimony I got out of you in court, you're looking at four years minimum. And any attorney in LA who says they can get you less is flat out lying."

"You could get me the minimum."

"Maybe. I have my doubts. But let's not get too far ahead of ourselves. Let's say for the moment I'm weighing things up. Now one thing I need to know from the outset when I engage a client is whether I can trust them. Forgive me for saying this, but I couldn't trust you as far as I could—"

"You can trust me, Bradley. I've got no reason to lie to you now."

"Well, you would say that, wouldn't you, Vivien? You're in deep shit, and you think I've got a magic rope to pull you out with."

She looked like she was deciding whether or not to bring on the tears.

"I'll tell you what, Vivien. Why don't we conduct a little exercise in trust?"

She shifted slightly, uncomfortable with where this might head.

"Okay."

"First, I'd like to know why you didn't just throw Baxter under the bus from the outset."

She took a deep breath and eased back into her seat a little.

"After we changed the security footage, he kept a copy of the original. He told me if I ever betrayed him, he'd say I explicitly asked him to kill Landry."

"So you were willing to see your husband go to jail for life to save yourself?"

She shrugged her shoulders and pursed her lips. "I'm a survivor, Bradley."

I moved on.

"Next. Why did you jump into bed, so to speak, with Danny Shapiro?"

"Believe it or not, that was not planned. I had no idea Shapiro was trying to undermine Patrick by using Buddy. If I did know, then why would I have tried to get Buddy to back off? I supported my husband until Freddie gave me his ultimatum. And once I was on that path, I learned Danny was working the back channels to get his hands on *Sister Planet*. So I went and told him I was the one who got Gordon Banks to sign his book over to Patrick just when Danny thought he had it sewn up."

"Shapiro must have been pleased to hear that."

"He's a businessman, Bradley. He knows it's nothing personal."

"So he enlisted you to help him get Banks onside."

"Yes. If I'd wanted Gordon to stick with my husband, I'm sure I could have persuaded him. But my husband was about to lose everything, and Danny offered me a very large finder's fee, for want of a better term."

"Judas fee, more like it. How do you sleep at night? That's a rhetorical question. I don't care what you might be wrestling with in that head of yours."

She got that uppity bored look that implied that she occupied a more real world than me, an environment where every despicable act can be reasoned away. I'd never encountered a more brutal embodiment of the end-justifying-the-means concept.

"Thanks for your honesty, Vivien. But the answer is no. I will not represent you."

I saw the anger rise in her because I'd led her on, but she held out hope that a charm offensive might still work.

"Bradley, if it's money you're worried about, please be reassured that I'm wealthy independent of Patrick."

In the process of investigating Vivien's background for the trial, Jack had told me about an interesting lead he had unearthed that could have been vital in the Strickland trial. The fact that the trial ended before he could get to the bottom of it didn't dull his interest. And just this morning he had presented me with his findings. The news concerned Vivien and was so profound I thought Patrick might be the person to deliver it to her. But now that Vivien had turned up in my office, I felt it may as well be me to tell her.

"Vivien, it's not about the money. It's about you, and the kind of person you are. And it's actually weird that you came here today, because I have something for you that arrived just this morning."

She raised her eyebrows.

"Really? How intriguing. Are you going to just come out with it, or are we going to play twenty questions again?"

"During the case I asked my investigator to dig around into your background."

"Yes, I'm sure you did."

"He spoke to your ex-husbands, your friends and so on until he came across the name of a man out in Phoenix."

"Yes?"

"A man called Jake. Jake Hayes."

She forced a smile of fond reminiscence.

"Ah, good old Jake. How's he doing?"

Her entire body was dead still save for her eyelids blinking hard.

"Not so good, Vivien. Jake died about twenty years ago."

She flinched with something like a pang of grief or remorse.

"And because the mother had run out on Jake and could not be found, his three-year-old son ended up under the care of his uncle and aunt."

Vivien's eyes widened.

"Do you know who that uncle and aunt were, Vivien?"

Her head was absolutely motionless.

"Wilfred and Layla Landry," I said.

She recoiled slightly from an inner blow.

"The kid's real name was Aaron, but they called him Buddy, just like Jake used to. And they followed Jake's wish for the boy to adopt his new guardian's surname. So the person we know as Buddy Landry was actually born Aaron Hayes."

As I said these words, Vivien's head began to turn very slowly from side to side in desperate denial of the truth. Tears began streaming down her cheeks. She gripped the chair as though she was aboard a wave-tossed boat.

No matter how despicable I found this woman, it was extremely hard for me to press on.

"Vivien. Buddy was your son."

THE END

NOTE FROM THE AUTHOR

Thank you so much for reading *Force of Justice*. I really hope you enjoyed the ride. Please make sure to leave a review on Amazon. Positive reviews on Amazon mean an awful lot to a small-fry writer like myself.

Just as helpful is for you to recommend my book to your friends.

There are two more Brad Madison books available right now: *Divine Justice* and *Game of Justice*.

There will be more Brad Madison to come, but I've also started a second series that centers on a young defense attorney in D.C. named Cadence Elliott. The first book *I Swear to Tell* is available now.

One last thing: please sign up for my newsletter to receive news and details about upcoming books. You can find it at my website: jjmillerbooks.com.

All the best

J.J.

PREVIEW

DIVINE

JUSTICE

(Brad Madison Legal Thriller, Book 2)

J.J. MILLER

CHAPTER 1

The sounds were loud, sharp and unmistakable.

I didn't need six years in the Marines and two tours in Afghanistan to tell me they were gunshots. Two of them; half a second apart.

A dreadful high-pitched din erupted from within the adjacent theater. Screaming, hundreds of young kids screaming. Within seconds, a flood of frantic bodies came spilling out. They ran for their lives, tears streaming down terrified, baffled faces, heads swiveling desperately in search of the quickest way out.

"He's shooting at us!" one boy cried.

"There's a gunman! Run!" shouted another.

Everyone around us was doing exactly that—bolting for the exits.

I pulled my seven-year-old daughter Bella close. Then I lifted her up. Her face was pale with fear. Her arms tightened around my neck.

"What's happening, Daddy? I'm scared."

And just like that, our world changed.

Just a few moments earlier, I'd been enjoying my first moments of ease in what had been a morning filled with drama, tears and fury... all on account of a monumental stuff-up by yours truly.

Weeks ago, I'd surprised Bella with two tickets to VidCon, something I'd never heard of until she'd breathlessly mentioned it to me months back. A three-day love-in for the world's most popular YouTubers and their fans. I'd have thought the local McDonald's would have been a big enough venue for such an event. But here we were at the Anaheim Convention Center—sold out and swarming with kids.

It wasn't just the prospect of going to VidCon that had rocked Bella's world. I'd managed to get us into a limited-access performance and meet and greet with Cicily Pines, a young singer Bella had been raving about. When I'd delivered this news by phone Bella's squeal of delight almost burst my eardrum.

But come the day, I'd steered the good ship *Awesome Dad* straight onto the rocks.

I only got Bella every second weekend, and yet over the past few months I'd managed to sabotage our time together regularly. Usually, the excuse was work—a criminal defense attorney's job can't always be shoehorned into a Monday to Friday work week, and I'd had to leave Bella waiting while attending to some client's predicament that couldn't hold until Monday.

Other times, there was no one to blame but me. I'd been cutting loose a bit lately, and more than once I'd woken up late with a blank memory and a strange woman, only to realize I'd broken yet another promise to Bella. Today, I hate to admit, was one of those days. I'd spent the night with a young paralegal—getting slam drunk in some bar before winding up in my bed. Both of us slept through my alarm. Only the persistent calls from my ex-wife Claire managed to rouse us.

When I'd picked Bella up it was clear we were going to miss the start of the meet and greet. Claire said we'd be lucky to make it before it ended. And she was right. In the car, after Bella had cried and scolded me, she'd fallen into a silent funk. Then she ordered me to turn around and take her back home. I tried reassuring her, telling her we'd make the show, but she knew I didn't really believe what I was saying. And in the past few months, she'd learned better than to take me at my word.

The Cicily Pines gig was scheduled to run for thirty minutes. It had already been going for twenty by the time we got our wristbands.

A dead weight tugged at my arm as I pushed through the crowd of teenagers crossing one expo hall after another. Holding my hand was not just fifty pounds of seven-year-old daughter but about two hundred pounds of resentment.

When I finally caught sight of the venue we wanted there was, to my immense relief, a queue forty yards long parked outside. The show had been delayed. Though I didn't deserve it, the gods had smiled upon me.

Bella bounced up onto her toes, her spirit soaring. As soon as we joined the queue it began to move. Relieved, I made some stupid dad jokes. Bella laughed and bumped against me as we shuffled forward. I almost felt like a decent father.

We'll cherish this day for the rest of our lives, I thought.

A thought that was obliterated by gunfire.

Run! That's what everyone's survival instinct was telling them.

But amid that sudden chaos and frantic evacuation, I knew I couldn't run. It had been almost ten years since I'd served, but that Marine instinct flipped on like a switch.

Like most Americans, I'd wondered many times what I'd do if I was ever caught in a public shooting. Even though my daughter was with me, that didn't give me pause—I had to neutralize the shooter.

I looked around and saw a nearby stall. Between us and it, though, was a stampede, a boiling river of chaos. People were sprinting, tripping over each other, pushing, screaming, crying. We had to get through. I tightened my hold on Bella and stepped steadily through the turmoil, buffeted by the frenetic torrent of bodies. When we reached the stall, I swung Bella down and knelt beside her.

Seeing her terrified face did make me stop and think twice. For a brief second, I landed in mental quicksand.

Do I get Bella out or go for the gunman?

How could I live with myself if I get us out safely while defenseless kids are slaughtered?

My mind was made up.

"Daddy, what are you doing? We need to get out of here!" Bella pleaded; her face sheet white. I didn't know how to explain my actions to her. It was part instinct—I was hard-wired to engage the enemy—and part duty. I just couldn't let another Columbine go unopposed.

"Bella. You'll be safe here."

"What do you mean? What are you doing, Daddy?"

"Sweetheart, I need to stop this man," I said breathlessly as I lowered her down and moved some large plastic storage containers out of the way. "I can't let him go on shooting innocent people. I need you to stay here. You understand? Don't move. Please. And don't make a sound."

"Don't leave me here, Daddy! What if you get shot?"

It was the obvious question for which I had no answer.

"Darling, I'm going to come back for you real soon. You hear me?"

The noise all around us was unearthly terror. Sadly, it was something I'd heard several times before when we'd stormed villages in Afghanistan. But here, it felt surreal, and I struggled against the fatherly instinct to save my daughter's life above all else.

Under my guiding hands Bella obliged. She lay down, her expression still bewildered yet trusting.

"Please come back, Daddy. Please come back for me."

"I promise," I said, as I quickly piled up the containers around her to conceal her presence. "Now not a sound, under any circumstances. Is that clear?"

She nodded. It killed me to see her so afraid, but I snapped myself out of it and got to my feet. I leapt back into the tide of hysterical kids and pushed my way upstream until I reached the entrance of the theater.

I'd heard no more gunshots, but that didn't mean the killing was done.

CHAPTER 2

I slid in through the doors and crouched low in the middle aisle to scope out the scene. I fished my phone out from my pocket and flicked the airplane mode on. I was going after a shooter unarmed. I didn't want an incoming call ruining the element of surprise.

At first, I couldn't see anyone in the dimly lit room. Further up, towards the stage, I could make out rows and rows of empty seats. Past them was a dance floor area just in front of the stage. As I panned to the right, I saw him. A man standing dead still. I had no idea if he was the shooter, whether he was solo or whether there were others at large. But there was an eerie silence and no shouting, so I figured no one else was being hunted down.

I stayed low and crept up the aisle toward the stage. As I did, I noticed people hiding behind the seats. I didn't know whether they felt too petrified to move or thought it was a good place to hide, but they all noticed me. Some looked up from lit phone screens. Probably texting their parents. This triggered the realization that word of the shooting would be spreading like electricity down a wire. In a distant corner of the room, I heard a phone. It rang twice before the owner snuffed it out.

I paused next to a young man, about sixteen, who was breathing hard. Relief came over his face at the sight of me. I was a grown-up, so I must be the cavalry.

"Did you see the shooter?" I whispered.

"I think so. Up there. The black guy in the blue hoodie."

I nodded. That fit the description of the figure I'd seen standing to the right of the stage. At least the blue hoodie part.

A few seconds later, I was at the front row. I stuck my head out for a peek. It had been about ninety seconds since the shots were fired. I couldn't see his left hand, but there was no weapon in his right. I didn't know why he was standing there, but I couldn't waste any more time. I had to act. I shuffled to get around the end seat, put my hands to the ground like a sprinter and prepared to launch. It was about twenty yards between me and the shooter. If I was quiet and quick enough, I could tackle him before he heard me and swung his weapon round. I'd drop my shoulder and hit him hard in the ribs, then pin his arms to his sides as we crashed to the floor.

Just as I was about to spring, two figures rushed the shooter, doing exactly what I'd planned to do. But after tackling him to the ground, they struggled to contain him. He broke free, rolled away and got to his feet. Now it was my turn. The guy swiveled around and saw me. He was a young black man in his late teens. I launched at him. Seeing me come at him, he turned and ran. I was barely two few yards into the pursuit when a voice boomed down from the stage.

"Freeze, asshole, or I'll shoot!"

I knew better than to assume that whoever called out knew I wasn't the bad guy, so I stopped in my tracks, raised my arms, and looked up at the stage. A security guard had his arms straight out and his weapon pointed at the shooter.

"Don't you move an eyelid, you son of a bitch!"

This was another voice, coming from behind me. I turned slowly around to see another guard walking forward steadily, his weapon firmly trained on the shooter, ready to unload if the target so much as scratched an itch.

"We've got this, sir. Thank you," the second guard said, tapping my shoulder as he walked by.

I watched as they closed in on the suspect and ordered him to the ground. He was just a kid—eighteen or thereabouts—but he was physically imposing; tall and solidly built. For a moment, I thought I recognized him. There was something vaguely familiar about his appearance that I couldn't quite put my finger on.

"I didn't do it," he kept telling the guards. "It wasn't me."

Of course, he didn't do it. What else was he going to say?

Guilty or not, he was going to need a lawyer, and a damned good one at that.

The suspect lowered himself onto his knees. One of the guards stepped forward and kicked him in the back to flatten him. Then they both jumped on and cuffed him.

"I didn't do it!" the suspect cried out again. This took a great deal of effort as he now had an overweight guard sitting on his back.

My eyes fell to the dead body on the ground a couple of yards from my feet. From the clothing, it appeared to be a young man. Next to him lay a Glock 17 pistol.

"Shut your mouth!" shouted the guard before smashing the suspect's face into the ground.

I figured the kid was lucky in one respect: he'd probably avoid being lumped with a judge-assigned public defender who couldn't give a shit. A sensational crime like this involving hundreds of teenage kids? His case was sure to be a media circus, and that meant every publicity-starved defense attorney in L.A. would come sniffing. I half felt compelled to step in. But I had to go.

I turned and ran to fetch Bella.

"Bella!" I called as I rounded the stall where I'd left her and began pulling away the storage containers.

"Bella, darling. It's Daddy. I'm back, sweetheart. Everything's okay."

But my words fell away as I removed the last box. My blood went cold with a dreaded revelation.

Bella was gone.

CHAPTER 3

Now I was the one running through the Anaheim Convention Center in a state of panic. An internal monologue helped me keep a lid on my worry, saying Bella wouldn't have moved unless it had made absolute sense for her to do so. She wouldn't have just disobeyed me and fled. But no one would have just taken her... surely.

I shouted out her name as I ran, stopping to check a few obvious hiding places where I thought she may have taken new refuge. I swept back through the vast, now empty expo halls, through the ticketing area and then out to the large foyer. Everywhere was empty. I called and called but got no response.

Outside, hundreds of people stood huddled together in groups. Many looked at me, having emerged late, as though I'd have some answers for them. But all I had were desperate questions.

"I'm looking for a young girl. My daughter. She's seven. Long light-brown hair. Have you seen her?"

Their blank but sympathetic faces made it clear how idiotic my quest was. As if, while running for their lives, they'd have noticed a young girl by herself and thought it odd enough to recall.

"Sorry mister, but I haven't seen her," one teenage boy said. "But a lot of people went that way."

He pointed down Convention Way, a broad promenade leading away from the venue.

I thanked him and ran on. People were milled around the fountains and statues, many embracing one another. Others were on their phones, calling loved ones to let them know they were okay.

My phone!

I'd wondered why Bella hadn't called me. Then I remembered I'd switched it to airplane mode. As soon as I reconnected, the phone began ringing.

With a flash of alarm, I saw it was Claire. Unable to say where Bella was, I didn't want to answer, but I had to.

"Hello."

"Brad!" Claire was breathless. "Where have you been? I heard there's been a shooting. Are you okay? Is Bella okay?"

"Yes, we're safe. It's over. They've got the guy."

"Oh, thank God. How's Bella? Can you put her on, please?"

"I can't right now. I've got to do something."

"What do you mean? I just want to speak to her quickly."

I wasn't about to tell Claire that that wasn't possible.

"I'll call you back," I said and hung up.

I resumed searching for Bella but there were so many people it was impossible.

I was flicking through my phone to find a photo of Bella to show people when it rang again. It was Claire.

Somewhat defeated, I answered.

"Claire, I'm just..."

"I cannot believe you. You left her?!"

"What? What are you talking about?"

"I just got a call from a lady who's with Bella. She says you left her by herself and ran off!"

"Claire, that's not what happened. I hid her. She was safe."

"What do you mean she was safe?!"

"I had to do something Claire. I wasn't going stand by and let a bunch of kids get shot while I ran to save my own life."

"Your job was to keep our daughter safe."

There was nowhere else for this conversation to go.

"Where is she?" I asked.

"How insane is it that *you* have to ask *me* where your daughter is?! My God. She's in Starbucks, waiting for you."

"Thanks. I'll bring her home straight away."

I walked to the coffee shop feeling yet again like I'd let my daughter down. Now, my idea of playing the hero seemed like just an egotistical glory dash, an extravagance performed for dubious reasons.

Within a few seconds, I had Bella in sight. Our eyes met, and she ran towards me as I walked through the doorway. I lifted her up and held her tight, never so relieved and thankful to have her in my arms. The dread of not knowing where she was or whether she was safe had spun me into a place I never wanted to be again.

Her own relief came in a flood of tears. Amid her sobs, I felt her rest her head on my shoulder.

"Daddy. Why did you leave me?" she said.

I realized it was going to be a huge job to convince Bella that abandoning her at a time of mortal danger had somehow been the right thing to do. She wasn't versed in America's history of mass shootings. Both Claire and I had done a good job of shielding her from the worst of the news.

"Darling, I didn't want to leave you. But I made sure you were safe, and then I had to do something to make other people safe too."

"What did you do?"

Suddenly I was stumped. *What had I actually done?*

"I tried to make sure no one else was hurt, honey. I wanted to make sure everyone else would get back to their families again. I thought..."

A steely female voice from behind interrupted me.

"I thought it best to get her properly out of harm's way."

I turned to see a rather stern looking woman aged in her late-thirties. She wore a gray skirt suit and very little make-up. Her blond hair was pulled back with a black band and her sole piece of jewelry was a string of pearls. She regarded me with an expression that was at once pleasant and disapproving.

I extended my hand.

"Thank you,..." I said, searching for something to add in place of a name. Neither "miss" nor "ma'am" seemed appropriate, because I took an immediate dislike to her. Maybe it was self-defense: after all, she clearly didn't wish to hide her judgment of me.

"I'm Francine. Francine Holmes."

We shook hands quickly and coldly.

"I'm ex-services," I tried to explain. "I had to see if I could help nullify the threat."

Francine smiled and looked down at Bella, patting her on the head.

"Quite the hero, your daddy."

"Thank you for helping Bella," I said. "I'm sure you meant well."

She sensed, rightly, that I was having a hard time conceding that I didn't have everything, my daughter's safety included, under control.

"Well, I think it turned out for the best. What a delightful young woman she is."

Bella piped up with some news.

"Francine says she can arrange for me to meet Cicily Pines," she said.

"Really?" I said. "Wouldn't that be something? How could you do that?"

Francine's bearing softened, as though she was prepared to entertain the possibility that I wasn't entirely a deadbeat dad.

"I'm part of the Halo Group," she said. "We run UpliftInc, a promotions company for YouTubers, and we put on the event for Cicily today."

"I don't understand. You're her manager?"

"Not quite. We're her primary patron. We love what she does and want to help her flourish, that's all. Her and others like her."

"So you're like the Motown Records of YouTube?"

Francine practically shuddered.

"No, we support a select number of young people who we think are the flowers among the weeds."

I figured Halo must be behind the stable of Christian stars I'd read about. I'd done my homework on Cicily Pines and watched just about every post on her channel. The clips were all similar—just her, an acoustic guitar and a voice from heaven. She was sweet without being guileless. She seemed humble and genuine. There was a hint of religion about her but nothing overt. She occasionally expressed her gratitude to God, but that was about it. A few minutes on Google revealed she was aligned with a Christian network of social media "influencers." I was okay with that. Wholesome is just fine when it comes to a seven-year-old girl's role model. I didn't expect Bella to grow up a saint, but I wasn't going to complain if her influencers were people who encouraged her to like herself and not strive to please others—boys, namely—in order to feel validated in life.

But there was something about the company's name that rang a bell in a dim corner of my brain.

"The Halo Group. That sounds familiar to me."

"We have been around for ten years. We used to be the Halo Council; a non-profit group founded by Victor Lund. We ran security and development projects in war-torn countries. But these days, we are purely US-focused. Everyone in our YouTube stable is American as apple pie."

My mind was ticking. I was sure I'd heard the name Victor Lund before, and the Halo Council too. Then suddenly, the grim realization clicked. It was the name of a place I wanted to keep well behind me: Bati Kot, a dusty village in Nangarhar province, east Afghanistan. My unit had gotten into a firefight there, one that resulted in several civilian casualties, including the death of a foreign aid worker. In response, Lund had launched a vociferous public slur campaign against my men in the media. A few years later, as I recalled, the Halo Council had been expelled from Afghanistan by President Karzai, apparently under intense pressure from the US ambassador in Kabul.

"The Halo Council. You were in Afghanistan, for a while," I said flatly.

Francine's eyes narrowed.

"Yes, we were."

"So was I. Am I right in thinking Halo was kicked out for some reason?"

"It would take too much time to answer that question now. I will leave you two alone. When things calm down, we will organize another event." She rested a hand on Bella's shoulder. "And when we do, young lady, you will be the first to know. You will be welcome as our VIP guest. By then, this dreadful experience should be well behind us."

"That would be wonderful. It's very kind of you," I said. "Here, I'll give you my card."

I fetched one from my wallet and handed it to her.

"So you're a lawyer?" Francine said as she read the print. "A man of many talents." It seemed like she wanted to tack "except for fatherhood" onto the end of that statement. "Well then, Bella, I will certainly be in touch, and we will arrange for you to come and meet Cicily another day. How does that sound?"

"That sounds great. Thank you," Bella said, all smiles.

I put my arm around my daughter.

"I'd best be getting her home."

"Yes," said Francine. "What a dreadful ordeal. She will want a big mommy hug, I imagine."

We'd only just begun walking back along Convention Way when a teenage girl walked straight up to Bella with an excited smile.

"Excuse me. You're Bella Madison, aren't you?"

Bella nodded silently with a half-smile.

The girl was looking her up and down with admiration. It was clear she was taking stock of Bella's "look". Until now I'd barely given Bella's outfit a moment's thought. Normally I'd complement her but this morning my admiration got lost in the rush. She did have a striking talent for putting clothes together, something that was evident even before she was out of diapers.

"Oh my gosh, I follow you on Instagram," the girl said. "Can I get a photo with you?"

Bella looked flattered. As I watched her chat with the girl and join her for a selfie, I felt proud of the humble, graceful way in which Bella conducted herself. I never liked the idea of her having an Instagram account. According to the platform's terms of service, users had to be older than thirteen. I'd argued with Claire about it a couple of times, saying she was too young to be making images of herself public. But Claire insisted I was overreacting and that Bella enjoyed having a dynamic outlet for her love of fashion. She assured me she had total control of the account and that she'd had the social media version of the "birds and the bees" talk with Bella. When I raised the subject of creeps who followed kids online, Claire said she scanned Bella's account daily, blocking and reporting anything inappropriate. I remained dead against it but eventually gave up arguing.

The girl worked her phone and asked Bella to choose the filter she preferred.

"I like that one," Bella said, pointing at the screen.

"So do I," said the girl who then tapped away again. "Done. Posted. I'll tag you. You'll be sure to like it, won't you? That would be so awesome."

"Okay, no worries," said Bella. She pulled her phone out of her small handbag and tapped away the screen. "There you are. Done."

The girl swooned at what she saw.

"You're following me! You're amazing. Thank you so much."

A minute later, as we continued to the car, my phone buzzed. I took it out to see five desperate text messages and several missed calls from Bella. All the frantic calls being made around the convention center must have jammed the networks.

"Your messages just arrived," I said.

"Well, they're no use now, are they? That's just not good enough, is it Dad?" She'd applied a remonstrative tone to her voice. I knew she wasn't directing the comment at me. I did that myself. *A bit like your daddy*, I thought regretfully.

"No, it's not, sweetheart."

Bella and I barely spoke as we drove back to Claire's house at Venice Beach. I asked her a few times how she was feeling, and it was clear she was still in shock and struggling to process things.

But I had to ask why she moved from where I'd left her.

"Francine found me and told me it would be safer outside."

"She found you?"

"She said she saw us go behind the booth."

"What else did she say?"

There was a long pause before Bella answered.

"She said she couldn't believe you'd run off and left me like that."

I did not like this woman at all. I just kept my mouth shut.

"It's okay, Dad," she said before everything went quiet again. Eventually she resumed talking. There was a train of thought she wanted to share. "You know, it was weird. I was so scared. And there was all that screaming. And I knew you were there. But…"

"But what?"

"Well, you were there. Just not for me."

That winded me. She said it like it was a lesson learned, something for her to store away as a coping mechanism for future disappointment.

"Bella, I'm always going to be there for you. That's a promise."

I said the words knowing she believed them to be, on current evidence, hollow. From my end, I meant every word—I never wanted her to feel like this ever again.

But that's just the sort of thing a father says. Right?

END OF PREVIEW

Made in the USA
Las Vegas, NV
30 June 2023

74094047R00152